· 1986 ·

I'VE JUST TURNED six when Olof Palme is shot. It's the first of March and very cold outside. My dad and I are sitting in the kitchen, we're eating crusty rolls for breakfast and I'm drawing. We hear it on the radio. My dad turns up the volume. The woman on the radio sounds as if it's important. Big news. I chase a poppy seed across the table with my fingernail. Then my dad tells me to get dressed. I can't find my socks. My dad bends down and sticks my bare feet into my wellies.

WE WALK DOWN the street. My dad holds me by the arm. He's looking straight ahead. Dragging me along. I've become luggage. A suitcase on small wheels. I tell him that it hurts, that I can't keep up, but the wind blows away my words.

There are always lots of people out and about on a Saturday. Cars going in and out of carports, elderly women with grocery bags doing last-minute shopping before everything shuts. But not today, today we have the road to ourselves.

It's not a big town and we soon reach the main street.

My dad looks straight ahead; his mouth is just a line across his face. I think he has forgotten he's holding my arm.

My dad has shoulder-length blond hair with the same reddish tint as his beard. He shaves once a week and lets it grow in between. He cuts his hair with a pair of scissors in the kitchen. The cigarette is an extension of his hand, an extra joint on his finger. He wears only a T-shirt under his coat which is always open, but he's never cold. It's rare for him to feel the cold. I'm almost always cold. I look like him, I think. When I grow up, I won't shave, either.

He says I look more like my mum. But that it's a good thing. She was beautiful.

I tell him that when I grow up I'll only shave once a week like him, but again the wind takes my words, tears at the branches and shakes the trees, whistles down the drainpipes.

We reach the town's only television shop. The TV sets in the window all show the same picture, some in color, others in black and white. We've already walked through the door, but my dad doesn't let go of me until we stand in front of a wall of screens. Big and small ones, price tags with long numbers. When the lady in one television turns her head or glances down at her papers, the ladies in all the other televisions copy her movements. It reminds me of a game we played in nursery school in another town.

The shop assistant is standing next to us. He wears a striped shirt with a name tag and he's staring at one of the TV sets, his mouth hanging slightly open. An elderly woman has put down her shopping bags and hasn't noticed that four apples have rolled away. My dad looks around as if he's searching for something; he finds it hard to make up his mind. Finally he opts for a huge color television in the center. The sound is already loud, but he turns it up even more. Then my dad stands very still too. I'm convinced that the first person to move has lost the game.

The television shows images of a dark street, road signs and snow. Stockholm. A sidewalk has been cordoned off with red and white plastic tape, people have gathered behind it. They, too, are standing very still. Some are clasping their mouths. The woman in the television speaks very slowly, as if she has just woken up. She says that Olof Palme came out of a cinema not far from there. That he was with his wife, that they had been to see the film *The Mozart Brothers* and were on their way home.

On the gray pavement are dark stains that look like paint. The camera zooms in on them.

"It's blood," my dad says, never once taking his eyes off the screen.

WE'RE BACK IN the street. We walk quickly as if rushing away from the images on the television.

I think we're heading home until we turn right by the closed-down butcher's. Towards the harbor, down a narrow, cobbled street.

My dad sits down on an iron girder; I sit down beside him, as close to him as I can get. The water in front of us is black. A couple of fishing boats are sailing into the harbor; there's a huge crane to our right, its hook hangs just above the surface of the water. The sky is gray.

My dad hides his face in his coat sleeve. I hear loud sobs through the thick fabric. He squeezes my hand so hard that it hurts.

"They got him," he says. "The bastards finally got him."

I don't remember ever seeing my dad cry. I ask him if Palme was someone he knew, but he makes no reply. He holds me tight. My feet are freezing in the wellies.

"They got him," he says again.

The wind whips the sea into foam.

"I think we're going to have to move again."

· 1987 ·

WE'RE SITTING IN the car my dad has borrowed from a farmer with mean, filthy dogs in his yard.

Everything we own is on the backseat or in the trunk.

"It's about time we returned to Copenhagen," my dad says. "You were born in Copenhagen, did you know that?"

He rolls down the window. As he turns the handle, the white station wagon rattles and creaks as if it's about to fall apart. Then he finds a hand-rolled cigarette in the breast pocket of his denim jacket.

He drums his fingers on the steering wheel, blows smoke out of the corner of his mouth, and removes a piece of tobacco from his lower lip.

He's always happy when we move and he laughs a lot.

We drive past tall concrete buildings. There are cars all around us. The motorway ends and the houses get lower. We could be anywhere. It looks like many of the places where we've lived before, places with supermarkets and hairdressers.

I CLOSE MY eyes and nearly fall asleep; we've been driving since the morning. At first I see white rings, then flashing lights on the inside of my eyelids. I'm gone a moment, perhaps longer.

My dad's voice brings me back to the car. "We're here," he says, and I open my eyes.

We've stopped for a red light. My dad revs the engine, which hisses and splutters. He explained to me earlier that he does it to stop it from stalling.

I look out of the car's dirty windows and I see the city. It's different from anything I've ever seen before.

I hold on to my seat belt. It stretches tightly across my chest; I press my thumb against the edge of the seat belt until it hurts. Outside the car the city is teeming with people, all moving in different directions. So many sounds, so much noise. Cars beep and brakes squeal when a bus comes to a halt next to us.

When my dad drives across the intersection, I hold my breath.

I can't understand how we don't knock down a cyclist or crash into any of the other cars.

I put my hand against the cool window and feel the city growl and snarl like an angry dog.

I roll down the window, open my mouth, and stick out my tongue. The city tastes of exhaust fumes and rotting apples.

MY DAD PARKS the car and we walk under an archway and into a courtyard. We walk on smashed paving stones past a wooden shed with some of its planks missing and a roof that's about to cave in. The tenement block is a redbrick building. My dad walks down the steps to a basement door and knocks.

"I hope this is it," he says, and smiles at me. We wait, my dad is about to knock again when the door opens. The man is big and quite a bit older than my dad. He has small tufts of gray hair on an otherwise shiny head. A brown coat above dirty work trousers. Small blood vessels run like blue and red rivers across his cheeks towards the root of his nose and inside one nostril. I want to tell my dad that the man looks like a map, but I'm too scared to open my mouth.

"About time, too," the man says, and wipes his hands on his coat, leaving dark traces of oil.

WE FOLLOW THE caretaker across the courtyard. The bunch of keys dangling from his belt is the biggest I've ever seen. It jingles so loudly that we could follow him with our eyes closed. We walk past rusty bicycles and several wooden sheds.

On the way up the stairs the man fills the entire space; I wouldn't be able to get past him if I tried. The stairwell smells of mouse droppings and meatballs. He stops in front of a wooden door with peeling green paint and knocks on it.

"The bathroom," he says. "You'll be sharing it with the man below you, old Nielsen. He's all right, nothing wrong with him." We continue up the stairs. "If you still want the apartment, that is."

He finds the key and unlocks the door.

The apartment looks like something that has been cut away, something that wasn't needed.

My dad beams as though he has been dreaming of a place like this his whole life. The small kitchen with windows facing the courtyard has just enough room for a narrow table, two chairs, and a wooden foldout bed against the wall. When we eat our breakfast, we'll be able to see into the apartments opposite us. My dad reads my mind and waves at the dark windows across the courtyard.

"The bedroom is in here," the caretaker says, pulling in his stomach so he can squeeze past the small table. He opens the door to the only other room in the apartment, the room my dad has promised me will be mine. My very own. The room is tiny and has a single window so high up that I can't look out of it. Once, when this apartment was a part of something bigger, a forgotten part, it must have been a broom cupboard. Shelves lined with yellowing paper. Tall glasses with preserved plums or apples. Now there's a bed where I'll be sleeping tonight. The smell is dirty in a dry, dusty way.

The caretaker's voice is no longer quite so confident when he says, "Eh, I thought the apartment was bigger than this. I've got another one if you want to . . ."

"It's excellent," my dad says. "I'm sure we'll be very happy here."

WE FOLLOW THE caretaker back to his workshop. There are oil stains on the floor and tools on the wide worktop under the window. Keys hang on one wall. Lots of keys, there must be one for each apartment. At night when people are asleep, he lets himself in and nibbles cold leftovers in their fridges. He takes a bit of chicken here and some meatloaf there. That's why he has grown so fat.

"You're paying cash?" he asks.

My dad nods.

They shake hands. This always makes me proud because I know that my dad has a good, firm handshake. I've heard people say so.

MY DAD AND I lug all our stuff from the car. My dad takes the bigger items, old suitcases close to bursting with his books. I fetch the carrier bags with our bed linen and towels. Finally, my dad picks up the wooden crate with his records; he holds it with great care and puts it down on the kitchen table. I can't see the record player. I don't ask where it is.

WE HAVE BACON and eggs for supper. Bought from the farmer who lent us the car.

"This is going to be great, I just know it is," my dad says, while the bacon sizzles in the frying pan.

I can tell from his eyes that he isn't just talking about the food.

"This is going to be great," he says again.

THE DOOR TO my new room refuses to shut properly. Every time we try, it squeaks and springs open. The building must have shifted since it was built; it has stretched and twisted, yawned and coughed. I can see my dad from my room, see his feet stick out over the wooden foldout bed, see the toe that he stubbed against a door last week and which has now turned blue.

I listen to his heavy breathing. I've always fallen asleep to sounds. Often to the sound of cars. A car on the gravel road not far from my window. Cars on the motorway, from an apartment high above the ground. I've fallen asleep to the rustling of the wind in the tall trees outside. Whenever there was a storm, I would close my eyes and imagine the trees bowing down before straightening up again.

When we lived near the sea, the waves would lull me to sleep. They would roll further and further across the beach and over the coarse yellow grass before they would come through the bushes, into my room, and carry me off.

I'm in my new bed and the city has its own sounds.

MY DAD IS sitting in the car now.

A moment ago I heard his footsteps on the stairs. His leather shoes tapped against the old boards. I heard the front door open. I saw him cross the courtyard, pass the low wooden bin shed. Walk across the paving stones and past the bicycle with the flat front tire.

My dad puts the key in the ignition. The car refuses to start. It wouldn't start when we picked it up yesterday, either. Not after the first or third go.

I'm in the kitchen. My dad has tidied away the bed linen and stowed it in the drawer under the foldout bed which he has covered with cushions. "Our sofa," he said, and smiled.

Today I'm going to be home alone.

"Is that okay?" he asked, pointing to the food on the dining table. Bread left over from breakfast, a small packet of butter, and three bruised apples with gravel stuck to their skin. I nodded. I'd promised myself not to cry. I'm seven years old, so I don't cry.

I'd have liked to go with him, though the rattling of the car and the smell of gasoline made me carsick yesterday. We had to pull over a couple of times so that I could throw up. Even so, I'd have liked another day of sitting next to my dad, listening to his stories.

"It's too far," he said. "All I'm doing is returning the car. I'll be back tonight. Late. I might wake you when I get back. Don't wait up."

He put a set of keys on the table.

I asked if I was allowed to go down to the courtyard. "Of course," he replied, and said that he wasn't going to tell me what to do. But I had to be careful and look after myself. Then he kissed my forehead and was out the door.

This time the car starts. The engine hums, backfires, and splutters. He drives down the street in the big city, surrounded by other cars. Everything moves quickly. I hope he's careful.

What if I never see him again? I think. What if he just disappears?

But I know that he'd never leave me.

I TAKE THE keys from the table. There is an owl on the key ring. It blinks with one eye as if it knows something I don't.

I open the door and walk down the back stairs.

My dad has told me that old maps of Africa and South America always had dark areas. Places whose secrets nobody knew. There might be vast treasures, gold and precious stones. There might be animals no one had ever seen, butterflies the size of seagulls. But there might also be monsters and cannibals. Things so dreadful you couldn't even imagine them. Every now and then an explorer would venture out to map some of the dark areas. Many explorers never returned.

I walk slowly down the stairs. Today I take every step with caution. I don't think there are any traps, but I don't want to risk it.

The courtyard has grown overnight. Last night when we followed the caretaker it was big; today it's enormous. We've lived in towns that could easily fit in between its walls. Slowly, I move forward, one step at a time, and I pass two apple trees that have become entwined. I walk across the broken paving stones and along the small bushes that grow by the wall. My eyes are a camera and every time I blink, I take a picture. When I'm back in the apartment, I'll get out my pencils; I'll take the pictures from my head and put them down on the sketchbook my dad gave me a couple of weeks ago.

As I walk I keep thinking about how I arrived at this particular spot. How I turned right, how I turned left. I'd have made a good explorer. I clutch the little owl on the key ring in my pocket. I press its plastic beak into my thumb.

A CAT SITS in the sunshine, licking its paws. Its fur is gray with white specks. I approach it slowly, trying not to scare it. I squat down close to it. Suddenly it looks up and disappears between the bushes. I hear the sound of keys; the caretaker is standing behind me.

"What the hell are you doing here?"

I don't answer him.

"You've got no business being here."

Yesterday he was just a big man with keys and filthy trousers. Now I know that I don't like him and that I'll try to avoid him in future. I don't think that'll be difficult, all I have to do is listen for his keys; there must be lots of places to hide in the courtyard, places where he won't be able to get in.

I run back towards our stairwell. He has frightened me and I run home, that's how I want it to look. And perhaps I really am scared of the caretaker, but an explorer never runs away. Just before I reach the door, I turn right and race past the bike sheds. I stop and listen. I can hear cars in the street and a bird chirping in one of the trees in the courtyard, but no keys.

I stay there for a while just to be sure; I count inside my head, one Mississippi, two Mississippi, but still no keys. I'm about to move. I plan to sneak along the wall when I suddenly feel a sharp pain in my neck like I'm being stung by a wasp. My eyes well up, mostly because it's taken me by surprise. I raise my hand to touch the spot where it hurts. Then I hear someone laugh; quietly, at first, as if he's trying to suppress it. The laughter grows louder, the bushes rustle, and a boy appears among the branches. He's a few years older than me; he has dark, shoulder-length hair and wears a denim jacket with fringes. In his hand he holds a white plastic peashooter wrapped in red and blue tape; it's the longest peashooter I've ever seen.

"Sorry," he says, but he doesn't stop laughing.

"That hurt," I tell him.

"You speak funny, what's your name?"

This is a question you should always respond to quickly, that much I've learned.

"Peter." I think it's a good name. I could easily be a Peter.

"Have you met the caretaker?"

"Yes."

"He eats little children. Smaller than you, I mean. He makes soup with them. He waits outside the hospital and when a baby is stillborn—do you know what that means?"

"Yes."

"Never mind. Where do you go to school?"

I don't want to tell him. I want to get away now, back to the apartment.

"I asked you where."

"We've just moved here."

"Which school did you use to go to?"

"I don't go to school," I say, and regret it instantly.

"How old are you?"

"Seven."

"Then you have to go to school—unless you're a retard. Then you go to a special school where they teach you to make clothes pegs. Are you a retard?"

I shake my head. I'm almost certain I'm not a retard.

"So which school do you go to?"

I make no reply.

"We're going to be friends," he says. "You and me."

I walk back towards the apartment. I walk as slowly as I can, I don't want to run. When I reach for the handle, I hear something hit the door right by my head.

When I lie in my bed that night, I miss the sound of my dad's voice. I miss his fairy tales. My eyes are half-closed when he comes home. I don't let my eyelids close fully until he has lit a cigarette and opened a beer.

MY DAD SAYS that most people don't see the world. We're on the bus, sitting at the back. His voice is hushed. I'm glad he's speaking only to me. I'm the only one who gets to hear his words.

He says: "Most people only see what they want to see. They're afraid to see the world as it really is. Are you afraid?"

I gulp, then I shake my head. I can tell from the sound of his voice that this is important.

"Of course you're not," he says, and hugs me so tightly I can feel the metal buttons on his denim jacket. "Most people stumble blindly through the world. Do you remember what I told you about electricity? That we use it when we make toast and turn on the light?"

"Yes."

Last night my dad let me flick the light switch until the bulb blew and we had to eat our dinner by candle-light. He wasn't cross because I'd learned something.

"Have you ever seen electricity?"

I shake my head.

"We know it's in the wires, but we can't see it. And yet people believe it exists. Their television sets would die without electricity. Imagine them just sitting there staring."

He laughs and I laugh with him.

"Just because something's hard to see doesn't mean it's not there."

Slowly, the bus fills with passengers. My dad looks out the window. At first I think he has finished talking, but then he leans close to me, his breath tickling my neck.

"It's not because people can't see. They've always been able to see. Books and fairy tales tell such stories. But people got scared. They lost their courage. Now they pretend they never see anything. If they walk down the stairs to the basement late one night and hear a strange sound, they just laugh it off. They laugh at themselves because there couldn't possibly be anything there. They've made up their minds that there can't be."

My dad looks at me, squeezes my shoulder.

"I'm telling you this because you're a big boy now."

"I'm seven."

"Yes, you're a big boy."

I look out the window. I try very hard to see the world the way my dad wants me to, but I'm not sure what I'm meant to be looking for.

"Shouldn't I be in school, Dad?"

"Would you like to be? You already know how to read."

I nod. I've been able to read for as long as I can remember.

"Yes, but there might be other things."

"Such as?"

"Math. Things you learn at school."

"Yes, but you know it's too late to start school this year, don't you?"

I nod. It's April. April is the cruelest month, my dad always says.

He looks at me for a long time. Scrutinizes me. As if he's amused by something and might have shared it with me if I'd been older. I can't wait to be older.

Outside, the city glides past. It's so big that I never see the same people twice.

My dad ruffles my hair.

"If you want to go to school, you'll go to school."

LITTLE BY LITTLE I get to know the city. It's out there. Right outside the courtyard. Through the archway. Slowly, one street at a time. Less than that. From here to the corner, thirty-one steps. From the corner to the newsstand, fifty-two steps.

Always holding my dad's hand. Sometimes we just go for a walk, other times he stops to buy tobacco and cigarette paper. We buy a big sack of potatoes from the grocers and the two of us lug it all the way home.

Slowly the apartment becomes "home"—as in "Do you want to go *home*?" or "Where's your teddy? It's *at home*."

EVERY MORNING MY dad gets up early and we eat breakfast together. From the window I watch him cross the courtyard and disappear through the archway. I wash our plates, get dressed, and go downstairs.

I'm still an explorer, but now I keep to the bushes and I always listen for the jingle of keys.

I discover new nooks and crannies in the courtyard. I find a plant growing between two paving stones, it has purple leaves and tiny white dots on its stem.

When the sun is at its highest, I go back to the apartment. I know the courtyard is no longer mine then. The boy with the dark hair is the first to arrive, then women on bicycles with shopping bags and crying babies.

I sit in the kitchen, where I draw and wait for my dad.

When he finally walks through the door, he doesn't say anything. He shuffles over to the table and flops down on the chair opposite me. I know exactly where he has been. All day he has been walking around the city asking "Any jobs going?" and been told no, hundreds of times. He smokes half a cigarette before reaching for my drawings.

I'M LYING IN bed; my dad has moved a chair from the kitchen into my bedroom. I can hear a television from one of the other apartments and a toilet being flushed. I can smell tobacco on his clothes.

"Where were we?" he asks me.

"They had just escaped the White Men."

"Yes, so they had."

Every night my dad tells me a little more of the same fairy tale.

The story of the King and the Prince who no longer have a home.

The King and Prince have gone out into the world to find the White Queen and kill her. With an arrow or a knife, a single stab through her heart will lift the curse.

They're the only ones who can do it because the King and the Prince are the last people who can see the world as it truly is. Only they haven't been blinded by the Queen's witchcraft.

"Is she really called the White Queen?" I ask my dad.

"No, of course not. She has a name, everyone has a name. But when she was little, she looked so much like her sister that one of them dressed in white and the other in black so you could tell them apart. And the name stuck."

TWO WEEKS LATER my dad gets a job.

He comes home one Friday with an advance of his pay and we eat Wiener schnitzel with potatoes and melted butter for dinner. My dad drinks beer and laughs, and I drink so much soda I need to go to the bathroom all the time. My dad comes with me down to the bathroom, I'm too scared to go there on my own after dark.

MONDAY MORNING MY dad gets up early and goes to work. He doesn't come home until late in the afternoon, then his clothes are soaked with sweat and he smells of wood. His hands are covered with splinters. I grow the fingernails on my right hand so I can tease out the tiny wooden splinters that stick out of his skin.

Every other week my dad gets paid and we celebrate. And every other week we go down to the caretaker to pay the rent.

"When it's cash, there's nothing to stop people from taking off," the caretaker says, and grins.

When I'm with my dad, I'm not scared of him. Then he looks like a small whale in overalls.

"Though I know you'd never do anything like that." He grins again.

I'M SITTING ON the back stairs with my legs crossed. The old man who lives below always spends a long time in the bathroom, hours sometimes. He uses old-fashioned expressions as he wails. I've met him once. His face was contorted. He pointed at his fly in the gray fabric and said that everything down there was ruined. Everything was rotten. Then he apologized.

Sometimes I pee in the kitchen sink. I have to stand on a chair in order to reach. But the sink is often blocked and I don't want the whole apartment to stink of pee when my dad comes home.

The tears well up in my eyes. I haven't wet my pants for over four years and I've no intention of starting now. Slowly I walk down the stairs, hoping all the time that the door to the bathroom will open.

IT'S THE AFTERNOON and the courtyard should be full of children playing. I don't know if it's the caretaker who keeps them away or if they're scared of the boy with the dark hair. Every now and then I hear children's voices out of one of the open windows. But only very briefly, as if they've reminded one another to be quiet. I find a corner between a bush and a wooden shed. I manage to undo my trousers just in time. I hold my breath and paint the tree with the stream. While I pee, I listen for the jingle of the caretaker's keys, but all I can hear is a bird tweeting and cars driving in the distance. I carry on peeing. There's a rustle in the bushes behind me. The voice is high-pitched and a little hurt.

"I thought you were my friend?"

It's the boy with the dark hair.

"You haven't been down here, I haven't seen you," he says.

I quickly zip up my trousers.

He scrapes the soil with the toe of his shoe as if he's drawing a picture.

"I thought we were friends, but you've been avoiding me, haven't you?"

"No."

He pushes the dark hair behind his ears in a way I've only ever seen girls do.

"Please would you be my friend?" He tilts his head slightly.

"Yes."

"And you won't do a runner, will you?"

"No."

"Right then, we're friends," he says, and takes a tennis ball from his jacket pocket.

"Let's play Hit the Monkey, do you know it?"

"Yes."

"You're lying!"

"No."

"Yes, you are. I know you are because I invented Hit the Monkey. It's a really good game. Do you want to be the monkey?"

I shake my head.

"Are you sure? Are you quite sure . . . ?"

When I don't reply, he shrugs his shoulders.

"Then I'll have to be the monkey. Too bad for you!"

I follow him to a corner where there's a small patch of worn tarmac. He stands with his back against the wall.

"Can you count?"

"Yes."

"Walk backwards while you count to ten."

When he's satisfied with my position, he rolls the ball to me.

"If it's a bit slippery and gross it's because a dog chewed it once."

He stretches out his arms and legs.

"Now you have to hit the monkey."

I throw the ball and hit his chest. I'm convinced that he'll try to dodge the ball, but he doesn't move.

"You throw like a girl," he says. "The game's no fun then."

He picks up the ball.

"Remember that if you miss, then you're the monkey. Remember that." He rolls the ball back to me.

I throw it again, a little harder now. He doesn't move this time, either, just stands there smiling as the ball hits his shoulder.

"Not bad, but I'm sure you can throw harder."

I hit his stomach. It must leave a red bruise under his T-shirt.

"You're getting good at hitting the monkey. But you need to throw even harder."

Each time I throw the ball harder. I hit his stomach, his chest, and his arm. I clip his ear.

"Hit the monkey," he shouts. "Hit the damn monkey!"

The ball leaves a large red mark right under his left eye. He blinks away the tears.

"Good throw," he says. "I'm so glad you're my friend. Now hit the damn monkey."

I throw the ball again; it flies past his right ear and hits the wall. I clearly missed.

The boy smiles as the ball bounces lazily across the tarmac.

"You didn't hit the monkey, now that's not good."

He rubs his cheek, massages the red bump that's merging with his swollen lips.

"It's my fault. The monkey moved and it's not allowed."

He rotates the ball in his hands. "And it's filled with dog spittle, too." Then he rolls it back to me.

"It's a foul ball. Hit the monkey."

I'M DRAWING WHEN my dad comes home.

"I want you to see the city," he says.

We go out in the early evening.

There is a big greengrocer's a few streets from our apartment.

The man in the shop cuts off a piece of cheese floating in a cloudy liquid. He talks funny and smiles at us as he passes it across the counter. I don't like it, it's too salty, but I keep smiling at the man and I force myself to swallow it. My dad gets a small bag of olives and he doesn't have to pay for it. We walk on.

I ask my dad where he comes from, the greengrocer. He had dark hair and didn't look like the Chinese man in the chip shop.

"A place completely different from our city. Or maybe not so different after all."

I notice that my dad now thinks of this as our city and though the city scares me, I hope that we'll be staying here a little longer.

We carry on walking. Down streets, around corners, past benches and bars where people talk loudly and yellow light spills out through the windows. I'm convinced that the city must end soon. Surely it can't go on forever? The fields must begin around the next corner. Or there will be low concrete buildings, main roads, or motorways. My dad eats olives from the bag and spits out the stones. If we get lost, we can use them to retrace our steps.

We reach a large open square.

"They once sold hay here," my dad says.

We pass girls in short dresses. Their heels click as they take tiny steps on the spot.

I ask my dad what they're doing.

"Making a living," he replies. "Everybody has to make a living."

I nod. We've lived in other places where the girls sold the same thing, though my dad didn't know that I knew.

He spits out an olive stone and it hits a trash can.

WE RIDE THROUGH the city early in the morning. I'm sitting at the front in the bicycle's large basket; it's an old, black butcher's bike my dad has borrowed from the man he works for. The chill of the night still lingers in the air. The sun is rising, but it's not warm yet and my dad has wrapped me in a blanket. My nose is running and my eyes water, but I'm smiling so much that my lips hurt and my teeth dry out, and I have to moisten them with my tongue. I lie back and look up at the sky. I see gulls high above us. I see clouds big and white as milk.

My dad stands up on the pedals; I can see his head above me.

"What, then, extraordinary stranger, do you love?" he says, looking down at me.

I know what to reply. "I love the clouds—the clouds that pass—yonder—the marvelous clouds."

WE RIDE UNDER an archway and into a yard. I jump out of the basket.

"If the boss turns up, you should probably make yourself scarce. He doesn't like children."

My dad unlocks the door to a small, dark workshop. Many of the windows have been smashed and are boarded up.

At the back of the workshop there's a door with a huge padlock. I ask my dad what's behind it. He says it doesn't matter.

I help him carry tools out into the yard: an electric drill with a very fine bit, a screwdriver, and a file. A jam jar of coffee grounds and a bottle of acetic acid. Paint brushes and a roll of sandpaper.

The last thing my dad does is lug two old armchairs outside.

I'M SITTING IN the corner on a rusty metal box that used to contain nails. It doesn't open, I've tried.

I'm well aware that I won't be allowed to come here again if I'm a nuisance, so I don't move. I love watching my dad work. He looks as though he has never done anything in his entire life but this exact task; his movements are fluid and he never stops or scratches his hair. The cigarette dangles from the corner of his mouth; the ash grows and drops off by itself. He's oblivious to everything around him, me included. He uses the sandpaper, the screwdriver, the drill. He dips his fingers in the coffee grounds.

I'll never be as good as my dad. Not at anything, I know that. I get bored far too quickly. Or I forget what I was meant to be doing; I take down the garbage and don't remember why I suddenly find myself in the courtyard.

"But what about when you're drawing?" my dad asks.

He's right, I can draw for hours. It's like blinking and finding that the sun has gone down.

MY DAD TAKES a few steps back; the armchairs are finished. He finds another cigarette in his shirt pocket and smokes it while he examines his work. He gestures for me to come over so I can have a look as well. The wood is darker. The varnish on the armrests is peeling now, I saw him use sandpaper and a file on them.

The holes he's drilled into the legs of the armchairs are so tiny that I have to kneel in order to make them out.

"Woodworm," he says. "Real nuisance, those woodworms."

I look at him, but I don't understand. My dad smiles.

"People like new things. They also like really old things. They throw out everything that isn't one or the other. I make things look older."

AFTER WE'VE EATEN our packed lunches, my dad starts taking a grandfather clock apart. He tells me to watch the sky, to look out for the first signs of rain and warn him. He hates working indoors.

My dad carefully places the clock face on some newspaper and dips a brush in a tin of nitric acid.

"When I've finished with this clock, it'll be more than a hundred years old. And English."

A MAN ENTERS the yard. I nearly burst out laughing because he looks like a tumbler toy. One of those ones you can knock down, but which keep standing up again. He has short legs and a broad lower body, but his confident stride makes me think he must be the boss.

He comes over to the armchairs, bends down and slowly runs his index finger over them.

"Not bad," he says.

"Thank you." My dad carefully puts the hands back on the clock; he holds the tiny screws in the corner of his mouth. The boss looks up and glances around the yard as if he can sense that something's wrong. He spots me in the corner even though I've been sitting as still as I can.

"Who the hell is that?" he says, pointing at me.

"My son."

"This isn't a bloody kindergarten, you know."

My dad places the glass over the clock face.

"I don't want him here."

I sit very still on the metal box, wishing I could be invisible.

"Get him out of here." The boss's voice is trembling slightly.

My dad straightens up; he's a head taller than the boss, but weighs less than half.

"We don't mind leaving, if that's what you want."

The boss turns around and marches into the workshop. I hear the sound of tools being thrown on the floor. Even though nobody's looking at me now, I continue to sit very still on my box. When my dad has wiped down the clock with a cloth, he comes over and strokes my hair.

"I won't get fired. Not today and not because you're here." He tugs my ear playfully. "He can't afford to fire me. He can't find anyone else who'll do the work for so little money. And—it just so happens that I'm rather good at this."

On the way home I ride in the basket of the bicycle again. It starts to rain, warm summer rain. My dad laughs. I open my mouth and feel the drops hit my tongue.

THE NOISE THAT wakes me up sounds like an animal that has crawled into our kitchen to die. I recognize it and I know that it'll continue. Sometimes for ten minutes, sometimes until sunrise.

My dad is curled up on the couch. His T-shirt is drenched in sweat. He twists the blanket in his hands; sometimes I've seen him tear sheets apart.

I stroke his hair; long sweaty wisps stick to his skin. I fetch a clean tea towel and wipe his brow and his neck.

Every time we move I hope that the nightmares won't follow us.

Though I no longer dare to believe it.

We move into a new place and, for a while, we're free of them. A week or several months. It changes every time.

I lie down beside him. The foldout bed is narrow and I'm perched on the edge; I can feel the hard wood digging into my side. I put my arm around his neck, I stroke his forehead, my fingers catch in his hair and yet he doesn't wake up. He never wakes up. I could scream right into his face and his eyes would still stay closed.

My dad sobs in his sleep, too. But less now; he can feel he isn't alone.

"We'll be all right," I whisper to him. It's what he says to me when things are tough. We'll be all right, you and me.

WHEN WE'VE FINISHED our breakfast, my dad wipes the table with a damp cloth. He takes great care to catch every little poppy seed and crumb. Today I'm going to school for the first time. When the table has dried, he puts an exercise book in front of me. Then he finds a pencil. A brand-new red pencil with a gold stripe down the side. He presses the point against his thumb, nods contentedly, and places it beside the exercise book. The eraser follows next. When we were in the shop, he held it up and asked, "Are you thinking of making any mistakes? No?" Then he laughed. I also got a book about dinosaurs which I'd spent ages looking at, a lunchbox with a picture of a smiling tractor, and a water bottle with no pictures on it.

We bought all the items last Saturday in a big bookshop in the city center. We bought them, but my dad never took his wallet out of his pocket. He has already explained this to me: how it might look as if we're stealing, but that there's nothing wrong with taking what you need. And that way, you never have to line up.

Before we went home, we went to a small cinema. My dad told me to wait while he spoke to the girl at the box office. I couldn't hear what they said, but I could see him pointing at me. The girl smiled and I smiled back. We got the tickets and again he didn't take his wallet out of his pocket.

I was hoping it would be the robot film. I've seen posters all over town, a picture of a robot and a boy my age. They look like they're friends. But the film turned out to be in black and white and there was no sound. When they were about to burn the girl, I started crying.

MY DAD SITS down at the table opposite me. He lights a roll-up, drinks coffee, and looks at me.

"What would you like to learn?"

"Numbers," I say.

My dad teaches me one number a day. I can count to ten easily, to one hundred, even, but he says that's not enough. We start with the number one.

"The smallest number," my dad says. "And possibly the greatest. In the old days that number was associated with God. One God. A holy number. Today people have forgotten its original meaning. That's why you don't go to school with all the other children. Because they've forgotten what everything means. They see an apple. A bicycle. And nothing's that important anymore."

SOMETHING'S KNOCKING ON the door. A small bird eating seeds, tap, tap, tap. The tapping gets louder, like a landlord wanting his rent. I must never open the door if I don't know who is outside.

"Why isn't your name on the door?" I recognize the boy's voice, the boy with the dark hair. "Everyone's got a sign with their name, why don't you?"

The stairwell falls silent again. I hope he has left, but I haven't heard his footsteps going down the stairs. I hold my breath, then I hear a strange sound coming from the other side, a scraping as if he's dragging his fingernails down the door.

"I think I'll have to talk to someone about it, maybe ask my parents. Ask them why there's no sign on your door."

I crawl out from under the table, unlock the door, and follow him down the stairs. He holds my hand while we cross the courtyard and go out through the archway.

THE BOY DIPS a stick in dog poo. Something that looks like a sweet corn kernel sticks to the end. We're outside the neighboring block.

"I don't know what the boys' surnames are," he says, smearing poo on the buttons for the building's intercom. "But they give me strange looks at school and they call me names."

The boy daubs poo over the button next to "I and H Madsen."

"So we'll just have to smear shit on all the buttons."

We move on to the next stairwell. The boy smears poo on the intercom. Carries on until all the buttons are pale brown.

We fail to find more dog poo when we walk around the corner; we look, but there's none in sight. The boy pulls down his trousers and squats in an archway.

While he strains and groans, he says: "We can't give up now. What if we haven't got the right buttons covered in shit yet? Think about all the poor people who'll get shit on their fingers for no reason. That wouldn't be fair, now would it?"

EVERY DAY THE boy waits for me in the courtyard. "I can count on you," he says, when I come downstairs. I don't like that so I start to dawdle; I draw and I look at the clock.

And yet he's always there when I come down.

We play Squeeze the Rabbit, a game where I jump up in the air and he has to try to remove his hands before I land on them. Other days we play Bear with No Eyes, where I put a plastic bag over his head.

MY DAD HOLDS up a carton of milk to me; we're in the dairy section of the supermarket.

"Möchtest du Milch?" he asks, and I know that if I want to drink milk in the next few days, I'd better get it right.

"Möchtest du Milch?"

Find the right words, find the right answer.

He cups a hand behind his ears: *"Entschuldigen, ich habe dich nicht gehört."*

When we've paid at the till, he says *"Danke schön"* to the cashier.

At night he kisses me on the forehead, tucks me up.

"Schlaf gut, Liebchen."

MY DAD'S WAITING for me at the breakfast table. He has been to the baker's for croissants.

"Bonjour, mon fils," he says. He pours a little coffee into my cup and tops it up with milk.

My dad says you learn best when you're standing up. Even better when you're running. And best of all, if someone's after you. Then he laughs.

We visit museums.

"It's easy to sneak in," my dad says. "There are lots of ways you can do it: you can join a group of visitors, you can look for a discarded ticket on the sidewalk outside. But it's always better not to."

My dad goes up to the attendant at the entrance; if it's a woman, he'll stand there for a little longer with her hand in his. If it's a man, the handshake is short and firm. My dad's voice gets louder when he talks to men; when they laugh together, it's even louder. Sometimes he'll touch their shoulder. Then we get in. Always without paying.

We walk down a white corridor leading to the first floor, where the paintings are.

"I know it looks as if they're doing us a favor," my dad says. "The nice people who let us in. No matter where we go, people help us."

I nod to show him that I'm listening. We're standing in front of a painting of a fisherman beside a boat that has been dragged ashore; the sky behind him is gray.

"But we're also doing them a favor. Take that man . . ." My dad nods back in the direction of the attendant who has just let us in, an elderly man with gray hair and a full beard, his uniform a little creased. "He has been standing there all day, he tears tickets, he tells tourists that they can't bring ice cream inside, that photography isn't allowed."

My dad always looks at me in this way right before he tells me the important part. The part I must remember.

"That man rarely gets the chance to do something for others. Do something without getting paid, just because he can and because he wants to."

In my head I try to repeat what my dad has just said.

He points to the picture of the fisherman in front of us. "Good, isn't it?"

I nod.

We walk on; I can barely make out the small boat in between the big waves in the next painting.

My dad says, "When that man goes home tonight and has his dinner, he'll remember us and know that he was the one who gave us the chance to see these paintings. His dinner will taste better."

I'M TOLD TO look closely at each painting. Then my dad says, "What can you see?"

At first I just answer him. I tell him I can see a man on a seawall. A man on a horse.

"No," my dad says. "Look properly."

I'm about to open my mouth to speak.

"No," he says. "Keep looking at it."

We stand there for a long time. When I open my mouth but no words come out, my dad gives me a really big hug.

"That's right," he says.

FRIENDS VISIT EACH other," says the boy in the courtyard. "Today I'm going to show you where I live."

He takes my hand and I follow him.

We walk up the back stairs; my hand sweats inside his. He has the key on a leather string around his neck and he doesn't let go of me until he has to unlock the door.

The kitchen we enter is big; our apartment could fit inside it several times. The cupboard doors shine, everything looks as if it has a place of its own. And yet there's a slightly sour smell, as if the residents have gone on holiday and forgotten something in the fridge.

The apartment is quiet, we're alone. The boy drags me through a passage and into a room that's pale blue and smells of perfume. On one wall is a big mirror with photos of teenagers wedged into the frame.

The boy goes over to the dresser; he pulls out bras and panties and throws them on the floor. Eventually he finds a newspaper cutting at the bottom of the drawer. He unfolds it and puts it on the bed so I can see it.

Summer girl, reads the caption underneath the picture of a naked girl who's smiling at the camera. She holds a beach ball over her head and looks as if she's just about to throw it.

"That's my sister," the boy says. "She has lots of hairs on her pussy. It's so you don't see her crack."

The boy grabs my hand and drags me into the living room.

The carpet is dark red and so thick my feet sink into it. A big leather sofa is pushed up against the wall; a porcelain vase with Chinese characters and golden dragons stands at each end of it. The television is huge, black, and shiny.

He pushes it and it wobbles on its wheels.

"How about we smash it up? You decide. Wanna smash it up?"

When I make no reply, he grabs my sleeve and drags me back out into the kitchen again.

He climbs up on the kitchen table. There's a small padlock on one of the cupboard doors.

He tells me to get a knife from a drawer; I hand him a butter knife. He sticks it in between the cupboard door and the cupboard, wiggles it back and forth. To begin with the door gives only a little: it creaks and a wooden splinter flies off and lands on the kitchen table.

The boy pushes his hair behind his ears and applies greater force. The door gives off a loud bang and flies open; a piece of wood is still attached to the padlock.

I jump to avoid being hit by bags of fruit gums and licorice. The boy stands on tiptoes and sweeps the shelves with the knife. Sweets rain down on us, boxes and bars of chocolate, fruit gums, hard candy, and toffees.

We sit on the kitchen floor surrounded by sweets. The boy tears open the bags. Multicolored, sugar-coated licorice balls roll across the floor.

"Eat!" he orders me.

I do as I'm told. I carry on eating until my tongue hurts and swells up in my mouth, sour, salty, sweet, my teeth are made of wood.

"You look like a darkie," the boy calls out and points to my chocolate-smeared fingers.

"Won't your parents get mad?" I ask him, my mouth stuffed full of gummy bears.

"Of course they will, eat up!" He tosses a piece of licorice into the air and catches it between his teeth.

On my way down the stairs I have to lean against the wall for support. When we cross the courtyard, I throw up in different colors. When my dad gets home, I'm lying on my bed, clutching my stomach. I turn my back to the door and pretend to be asleep.

THERE'S A POSTER on the wall of a teddy bear holding a big toothbrush between its paws; other posters show teeth eaten up by cola. We're sitting in the dentist's waiting room. There are building blocks on a small table and a pile of comics. Goldfish swim around in an aquarium, nibbling fish food that floats in the water.

My dad holds my hand; I'm trying not to cry. A toothache kept me awake last night. I told my dad about the boy in the courtyard, about the games, about Squeeze the Rabbit and Bear with No Eyes. I told him about all the sweets we'd eaten. My dad smiled and said that you don't get cavities that quickly, that it's good that I've made a friend. Even a bad friend. Often they're the ones who teach you the most. And yet it feels like a punishment. I vow never to see the boy again. Never ever. He can wait for me in the courtyard all he wants; I'm not going down there.

I pick up a Donald Duck comic from the table, but I can't read the words. I've got tears in my eyes and I don't care if Uncle Scrooge loses all his money.

"The dentist will have a look at it," my dad says. "I'm sure it'll be all right."

I want to believe him, but we haven't spoken to anyone since we arrived. We just sat down on the last empty chairs in the corner. I don't understand how the dentist will know when it's our turn.

My dad takes my hand and says: "*Virtute et armis.*"

I reply: "With bravery and weapons."

He says: "*Iacta est alea.*"

"The die is cast."

"And who said that?"

"Caesar."

"And he was?"

Slowly the waiting room empties while we go through the *ads*, such as *ad infinitum, ad libitum, ad notam.*

We've reached *ad vitam aeternam.* I say: "Towards eternal life."

We're now the only two people left. My dad gets up and takes my hand; I follow him past the door to the secretary and into the surgery. We stop in the doorway; we see the dentist, busy putting out tools on a metal table. He looks my dad's age, possibly a little younger. He has dark hair and high temples. A cigarette is smoking itself in an ashtray on the windowsill; he glances up at us.

"You need to make an appointment with my secretary. We're closed for today."

My dad crosses the threshold, and says: "I'd like you to examine my boy."

His voice is almost pleading.

The dentist looks up again, rather surprised that we're still there. He takes a drag of his cigarette and stubs it out in the ashtray.

"I can't help you if you haven't got an appointment."

"My boy's in pain."

"I'm sorry . . ."

We enter the room, my dad at the front, me right behind him.

"You can see that he's in pain."

"I'm sorry, but . . ."

"I don't have a health insurance card and I haven't got any money so I can't pay you. But I know that you'll want to help us."

The tone of my dad's voice has changed; it's now a friendly demand. The dentist is about to say something, but my dad starts speaking again. "All those years of study just so that you can tick boxes and live in a nice house . . . ?"

The dentist looks a little confused; he opens his mouth, but he doesn't say anything. My dad holds his hand a few centimeters from his arm, so close that he can almost touch the white fabric of the dentist's coat.

"You want to help us."

My dad could say anything now and I would believe him.

"We need your help. I know that you'll want to help us."

The dentist stands there, he has stopped moving, then he lets his arms fall down by his sides.

"You can go to the dental school, that's free," he says.

"No," my dad says. "We can't."

The dentist nods and puts a couple of steel tools on the tray next to the dentist's chair, then he leans out of the doorway.

"Karina, I'll just see one more patient."

I sit down in the dentist's chair and a white piece of paper is clipped under my chin.

The secretary appears in the doorway; she's blonde, she has a dark brown coat over her arm and her eyes are tired.

"I didn't see any more appointments in the diary . . ."

"I'll deal with this last patient, you can go now. I'll manage."

She hesitates, then she shrugs and leaves. The door slams shut after her.

The dentist has a small mirror at the end of a metal stick; he sticks it into my mouth. The steel is cold. He nods to himself, finds a syringe. My dad holds my hand while the dentist injects my gum.

"That was the worst part," he says, and tells my dad to wash his hands. While he rummages around my mouth, he points to the different steel tools my dad needs to pass to him. I can smell cigarettes on the dentist's hands. Then I hear the sound of the drill. My jaw buzzes; it's like having a bee inside my mouth, but it doesn't hurt, not like before.

When the dentist has finished, one side of my mouth feels slack. I wipe off spit with my sleeve. We're about to put on our coats when my dad goes back and gives the dentist a big hug.

MY DAD IS sitting at the table. In front of him lies every single newspaper he could get hold of.

The newspapers don't have to be today's as long as they're proper newspapers. That means the ones without colors and pictures of naked ladies.

He sits there for hours holding a newspaper in front of him. I can't see him; I can only hear the pages turning.

He doesn't put down the newspaper when he wants to smoke; he simply reaches his hand out. He always finds the cigarette packet on the first attempt. I see smoke rise up behind the pages, and soon afterwards his hand reappears, he taps the cigarette lightly, twice, and the ash falls into the ashtray underneath. I've yet to see him miss.

I TIPTOE UP to him very quietly. It's Sunday and he's reading one of the thick newspapers. I avoid any floorboards that creak.

Very carefully, I move the ashtray slightly to the right; I manage to do it almost without making a noise.

My dad reads on, he smokes and turns the pages. His hand reaches out; he finds a fresh cigarette in the packet, lights it, continues reading, moves on to the next cigarette.

My dad folds the newspaper and is about to reach for the next paper in the pile when he looks down at the table. His mouth opens in surprise: in front of him lies a small mountain of ash and cigarette butts.

He looks at me; I'd thought that he'd notice me much sooner.

I'm scared that he'll shout at me like he did when that car came very close and nearly ran me over.

My dad blinks a couple of times, then he starts to laugh. He keeps on laughing until he has tears in his eyes. He sweeps ash and cigarette butts into the ashtray with the side of his hand. Not even the sight of burns on the table makes him stop laughing.

"Do you still have your white shirt?" he asks me, and I know that he has seen something in the paper, perhaps in one of the small ads at the back. I shake my head; that shirt disappeared a couple of moves ago.

MY DAD PULLS my woolly cap over my ears. It's a cold autumn day and he whistles as we walk down the street. I know that he loves spring and autumn: beginnings and endings, as he calls them. Everything else is just filling the gaps.

My dad holds the heavy door open for me and I follow him through a lobby with dark wooden panels and a staircase. We pass young people who hug books to their chests and we reach another door. Behind it I can hear voices speaking on top of one another. My dad takes off my cap and smooths my hair. He puts his hand on the door handle and hesitates for a second before he opens the door to a room filled with people. We're the only ones not dressed up for a party.

I hold my dad's hand tightly, scared that I'll get lost. He leads me past people drinking wine from tall glasses, talking, and laughing out loud. I'm constantly about to bump into someone.

We stand in front of a table with food on it and my dad lets go of my hand.

"Eat as much as you like," he says. "I'll be back in a moment."

He disappears between trouser legs and backs.

The food is set out on large silver platters and is skewered with toothpicks.

Tentatively, I pick one up, convinced that someone will call out "Hey, what the hell are you doing here?" But nobody looks in my direction; in fact no one's looking below chest height. I start from one end of the table. Most of it tastes disgusting: those bits I chuck under the table where my dog is sitting. If people weren't talking so loudly, they could hear it slobber.

I avoid the strong-smelling cheese, but I eat a lot of grapes. I end up next to a platter with egg salad on tiny pieces of toast.

I start from the edge and eat my way towards the center.

"My, haven't you grown," I hear someone say close to my ear, and my stomach starts to rumble.

I turn and look straight into a pair of dark brown eyes: a woman has knelt down beside me.

"If you've finished eating all that egg salad, I think we should go find your father."

She takes my hand and I go with her.

"Our old professor is retiring today, but I'm sure your father has already told you that," the woman says over her shoulder. She leads me through the labyrinth of legs and backs.

My dad stands between two men. One has white hair and a beard that reaches all the way down to the knot on his tie. I'm almost certain that he must be the professor.

"You've met Nana," my dad says, and smiles.

The professor takes my hand in his. It feels like baking paper.

"The last time I saw you, you weren't much taller than a pint of milk," he says to me, and carries on talking to my dad. The woman called Nana offers to get some wine; she asks me if I like lemonade. I nod.

The professor and my dad use words I've never heard before, but it's clear that the professor isn't asking him to fix a radiator or paint a fence. My dad's happy, really happy, which makes me happy, too. Even dressed in his denim jacket he fits in much better here than anywhere else I've ever seen him.

Nana has neither wine nor lemonade when she returns. She leans in towards my dad so it looks like she wants to blow on his neck. I catch only a single word, one that hides itself behind the hundreds of others being spoken in the room at the same time. That word is police. She has stopped smiling. My dad empties his glass and puts it down.

"Come with me," the professor says. "Come with me now."

I can't see my dad, only his arm dragging me along. I bump into people; they turn around, but we've already moved on. Nana holds the door open; she blows my father a kiss before she closes it behind us.

We follow the professor down a long corridor. The afternoon sun pours in through the windows and I can see every single bit of dust that hangs in the air.

The professor struggles to walk and speak at the same time; he forces the words out.

"I don't know what happened," he says. "People would rather gossip than do research. Drink coffee and gossip. I don't know what happened and I don't care, either."

The sound of people disappears behind us. The professor opens a door and we enter a small office. Every wall is lined with bookcases; below a high window, an old desk is completely covered with papers and books. The professor pulls out a brown leather office chair that's worn through in many places. He pats the back of the chair.

"You should've been sitting here," he says. "You should've been sitting here now."

My dad makes no reply and the professor starts rifling through the papers on the desk. He moves books and puts them down on the seat of the chair. A bunch of keys appears and the professor hands them to my dad.

"I won't be needing these after today."

We follow the professor out of the office and down several other corridors. Then he stops. He leans against the wall and wheezes.

"I can't go on. You know the way."

My dad pulls him into an embrace. The professor's eyes are wet and he kisses my dad's cheek.

Then I'm dragged along again. Several times I'm close to stumbling; the toes of my shoes scrape across the floor.

On our way down the stairs my dad picks me up and throws me over his shoulder like a sack of potatoes.

We walk through a small room filled with books and dust, through a large room with a blackboard and lots of benches, through a big closet with brooms, and a kitchen with tiles and steel sinks. My dad uses every single key. We emerge into a courtyard.

My dad glances up at the small windows that look like eyes. Then he pulls the cap over my ears and we walk out through the archway. We walk as fast as we can without running. My dad keeps looking over his shoulder.

"You must always keep an eye out for the White Men," he says.

WHEN I LIE in my bed that night, I ask my dad how I'll know the White Men.

He has told me about them before; I know that they're the Queen's helpers, and the King and the Prince are always in danger of being captured by them.

"It's difficult," he says. "There are lots of little things you need to look out for. The expression in their eyes. Most of the time they look like ordinary people. They seldom transform themselves, and only when they think they're alone with their victim. Then their heads become those of eagles, lions, or wolves. That's when they'll bite and tear you apart."

I ask my dad if the White Men are evil; I'm almost sure he'll say yes. But he shakes his head.

"They're only doing what the White Queen tells them to. They don't know the difference between right and wrong."

I lie awake thinking about the White Men that night. I hope I'll be able to recognize them.

I'M DRAWING A dragon. I practice in the sketchbook before copying it out on a piece of cardboard. The dragon has snake eyes, its brows point downwards like a V, it's angry. Its tongue is forked and its teeth are very sharp.

I color in the neck. I use greens and blues. The dragon should look as if it lives in a lake or a bog, perhaps. It has just poked its head out of the water because it can smell people or animals it can eat.

I've been drawing the dragon since I got up. I don't hear the sounds from the courtyard or the ticking of the clock. My only thought is to make the dragon as scary as possible. Right now it's harmless. Its head is bigger than its body. Its claws look small and ridiculous. The sun is high in the sky and I know that the boy's waiting for me downstairs. I've decided I don't want to see him again. I color in the tail of the dragon. I wonder if the boy is busy feeding cheese to the rats in the courtyard. I pick up the dark green coloring pencil in order to draw the scales on the dragon's body. My pencil stops drawing.

THE BOY IS grinning as I step out of the main door. He looks as if he knew all along that I would come.

"You're the lookout today," he says. "Just like when we smeared shit on the doorbells."

He starts walking, knowing that I'll follow him.

"What are you doing?" I say to his back.

"We. What are we . . ." he replies, without turning around. I'm almost certain that he's smiling. "I could tell you, of course, but then it wouldn't be a surprise."

We pass the outhouses; we pass the stand with the rusting bicycles.

"Surprises are always nice," he says.

I nod, he's probably right. When I'm with him, I think more slowly.

"You're my friend," he says.

By now we're standing in front of the door leading down to the caretaker's workshop. The boy points to a paving stone.

"Stand there and keep a lookout. If you hear the caretaker's keys then run down and knock three times."

The boy quickly sneaks inside. I stand on the paving stone. I want to run away, but I stay where I am. I can hear the wind rustle the leaves in the trees; I can hear my own breathing, but no keys.

Then the door is flung open. The boy waves a key over his head like a prize he has just won in a competition. He grabs hold of my arm and drags me along.

"Just you wait until you see this," he says.

We cross the courtyard, pass a bird bath, and arrive at a different basement door. The boy quickly pulls me down the steps. He inserts the key into the lock and opens it. The darkness inside is total.

"Hurry up," he says. "Don't just stand there."

The door closes behind us.

We walk down a short passage. There's a sharp smell: glue, possibly, but I'm not sure. I hear the boy fumble with something. The light in the ceiling flickers a couple of times before it comes on. We're surrounded by cats smoking pipes, by redheaded girls with bushy tails peeking out from under their dresses.

Along the walls there are worktables and piles of fabric in different colors and patterns. "Surprises are always nice," says the boy again. We're in a doll workshop.

I know I ought to leave, but I can't take my eyes off an anteater with a top hat and a monkey with a walking stick and red shoes. I follow the worktables: more dolls, and giraffes with long ties that reach all the way down their necks. On a bulletin board is a photo of an old woman bent over a sewing machine. She's stitching ears onto a rabbit and sewing paws on a dog. In other photographs she sits surrounded by children who hold the dolls on their laps. The children are laughing and she smiles proudly at the photographer. In the last few pictures there's a little girl with no hair in a hospital bed. She's hugging a crocodile with glasses.

I hear a growl behind me like a dog with a bone. The boy is standing with a full-size male doll. At first it looks as if he's embracing it, then I see that he has sunk his teeth into its neck. The boy rips off half the head and yellow stuffing spills out. Our eyes meet and he throws down the doll. The boy takes a pair of scissors from one of the worktables and ignores me while he cuts the arms and legs off the dolls. I walk backwards out of the room. The boy cuts the ears off a zebra and the trunk off an elephant. I walk down the passage and emerge outside.

I stand on the basement steps while my eyes get used to the light. Then I hear a jingling. A large bunch of keys getting closer and closer.

I throw myself behind the bushes along the wall. Below the leaves I can make out the caretaker's trousers. He stops right outside the bush I'm lying behind. I press my eyes shut and hope that he can't see me.

He lingers for a while before he continues down the steps and opens the door to the doll workshop.

I'M IN MY bed, I still can't sleep. My dad comes home from work late. He sits in the kitchen eating a rye bread sandwich he has just made.

I hear the sound of the bottle top when he opens a beer.

I hear my dad rinse his plate in the sink. Then he stands in the doorway; he asks me if he should continue with our fairy tale. The last couple of days the King and the Prince have been traveling through an enchanted forest. They're walking down a narrow path with carnivorous flowers on both sides. I ask my dad if we can wait with the fairy tale until tomorrow. Or will the flowers eat them? Of course we can wait, he says. The King and Prince will be all right. My dad kisses my forehead and leaves the door ajar. I hear the crackling of the thin paper when he rolls himself a cigarette; "rolling smokes," as he calls it.

He flicks through a book and I hear the metallic squeak from the lamp when he adjusts it to get a better reading light.

I don't know if I did the right thing today. You shouldn't tell tales. But technically I didn't tell on anyone. My dad says bad choices are rare. The most important thing is to make a choice and stand by it. I turn my face to the wall.

WHEN FATHER CHRISTMAS stirs the porridge, he opens his mouth and closes his eyes. He looks as if he's laughing, but no sounds come out. His beard is white, his suit is red. My dad says there's a motor somewhere under his jacket. I stand in front of the shop window for a long time, looking at him.

At first I thought he was funny; now he just looks creepy.

We're the only people not laden down with shopping bags, the only ones not in a hurry. I've gorged myself on the small spiced Christmas biscuits which are set out in bowls in practically every shop. The mulled wine leaves a red stain on my dad's teeth. The snow in the city is only white when it has just fallen. Then it turns gray, before going black.

YOU CAN COME with me to work today," my dad says, as he sprinkles soft brown sugar on his porridge. "The boss has gone to Jutland."

He takes a big mouthful, as much as he can pile on the spoon, and opens his mouth to let out the steam.

"He's clearing out a house after someone died."

The boss is angry: I imagine him stomping through the front door of a small, yellow brick house. He heaves a cupboard outside while an old man sits on the sofa. Very still and very cold. The tip of his tongue sticks out of the corner of his mouth. The boss lifts the old man's feet to pull the rug free.

AS SOON AS my dad has let us in, I go to the door at the back of the workshop. The one that always has a padlock on it. The boss is bound to forget the padlock one day.

"Do you really not know what's behind it?" I ask my dad again as I pull at the padlock.

"It's none of our business," he says as he gets out the tools.

"Don't you want to know?"

He shakes his head. "Everyone's entitled to their secrets."

Today I'm allowed to help my dad varnish a table. He shows me how to make an even brush stroke, how you have to be careful not to leave edges.

"Wet on wet," he says. "Always paint wet on wet."

I want to show my dad that I can do it. The sound of cars in the street disappears. Even brush strokes. I keep my eyes on the wood all the time in case a single hair from the brush has come loose.

A COUPLE OF days later we scrub the varnish with a steel brush.

"You're getting the hang of it," my dad says. "I think you might be ready for something more difficult."

He lifts me up on the table in the workshop so I can get a better look at the color photographs on the wall: pictures of furniture with water damage or mold. Old English furniture with tea stains. French furniture with scratches from the tiny, tiny claws of noble ladies' lapdogs. You make those with a metal coat hanger, my dad explains.

Before I drill my first woodworm hole, I spend a long time studying the photographs. The distance between the holes must be just right. The drill needs to go in perfectly the first time or the edges will fray.

My palms are sweaty as I press the drill against the wood and it almost slips out of my hand. When I've retracted it, I test with my finger. The hole hasn't frayed. It's quite small, and you have to bend down in order to spot it halfway down the chair leg. A proper woodworm hole. I'm proud, but I say nothing, I don't shout for joy. I don't want to get ahead of myself. With my fingers I measure the distance, just over half the length of the nail on my index finger. I make a mark with the pencil. That's where the next hole needs to be. I'd prefer to measure it with a ruler to get the perfect distance between each hole, but my dad says it doesn't work. That the holes become too regular. Woodworms don't use rulers, do they?

IT'S CHRISTMAS EVE and the streets are almost deserted. A few people are still driving around, some of them very fast; my dad says they're probably running late. Others slow right down and rub condensation off the windshield as they scout for house numbers.

"We're going to have duck," my dad says. "The best duck in town. But first you're going to school."

"To school?"

"Religious Studies."

The church is squashed in between two other buildings. It looks as if they've built them as close to it as they could without knocking anything down. Warm, yellow light floods out the open door.

Inside people are smiling, making room for one another, speaking in whispered voices. The men have coats over their arms. The women wear shoes or boots with high heels.

We sit down on one of the wooden pews, which fill up quickly. I should've gone to the bathroom before we left home. My dad whispers to me that we should've brought popcorn.

I look around the church, trying to draw all of it inside my head in case my dad decides to test me later. I draw the large candlesticks with the wax candles and the pulpit with the wooden carvings. I draw Jesus on the cross. He hangs at the back of the church, thin and with nails through his hands and feet. He's bleeding, but his expression is serene.

Then the vicar appears and people fall silent. Everybody stands up, the vicar smiles; he seems pleased to see us. He lowers his hands and we're allowed to sit down again.

The organ plays and my dad points to a board on the wall that lists the numbers of the hymns. By the time I find the right place in the hymn book, everyone has already started singing. I try to join in by opening and closing my mouth at the same time as everyone else.

My dad looks up at the vicar while he sings; my dad's eyes are shining.

When the final notes from the organ have died out, the vicar mounts the pulpit. I see a flash of dark blue fabric and I'm almost certain that he's wearing jeans under his cassock. He looks down at his papers, straightening them a little. Then he looks out at us as if he'd like to make eye contact with everyone before he starts. He wipes his lips with his index finger and thumb.

"We've all done too much shopping," he says. "Far too much."

Again he looks around the church. "Does anyone here disagree with me?"

When there's no reply he nods, but continues to smile; he's still very pleased to see us.

"I'm no better myself, even vicars aren't holy. Not any more. And thank God for that."

I hear scattered laughter. I didn't know people were allowed to laugh in a church; I'd have liked to join in myself, but the moment has passed.

The vicar's tone grows more serious: now he's talking about the poor.

"Those who have nothing," he says. "We've all forgotten what the word 'poor' means. People who are truly poor. Those you don't think about when you're looking for the last duck in the supermarket freezer."

My dad leans close to me, whispers into my ear. "Take a look around, just look at them all. Tradition and faith are two completely separate things."

The vicar reads from the Gospel according to Matthew. He talks about bread and fishes, about sharing.

"People confuse God with Jesus," my dad says into my ear. "They like Jesus because Jesus cries."

An elderly man in the pew in front of us turns around and holds a finger to his lips.

"They worship the son as if there was nothing else," my dad says. He's talking more loudly now. "They forget that the father is a vengeful God. A cruel and jealous God. They forget what happened to Job's daughters and to all the people who didn't get to go on the ark."

More people turn around and look in our direction.

"They really shouldn't step inside a church without a life jacket," my dad says. His laughter sounds very loud in the church.

The vicar pauses in his sermon and looks around to discover who keeps interrupting him. I'm scared that he'll shout at us. Throw us out, possibly. My dad catches his eye and, for a brief moment, it looks as if the vicar recognizes him, but then he busies himself with his papers. The vicar is still smiling, but his voice is less certain when he talks about how seven loaves can feed a thousand people.

My dad leans back in the pew. He folds his hands across his stomach and lets the vicar finish his sermon without further interruption. People around us seemed relieved; they're no longer staring at us.

The vicar gathers up his papers. The organ plays as he steps down from the pulpit. He stands in the middle of the floor.

"Let us pray," he says, and folds his hands.

"We're leaving," my dad says. "God's not here."

People have to stand up so we can get past; an old lady asks if the sermon is finished already. While we walk down the center aisle, the vicar tries to continue; the last words I hear him say are "deliver us from evil." Then the door slams shut behind us.

OUTSIDE IT HAS grown colder. The sidewalk is slippery and I have to watch my step. I liked the people in the church. They wore nice clothes and they smiled.

They held hands and they smiled at me, too, even though I didn't know them. I liked the warm glow from the candles. I don't tell my dad this; he's marching on ahead and I try to keep up with him. I jump over snowdrifts and puddles of slush and I leap aside to avoid getting sprayed when cars pass. The wind makes my eyes water.

"So we don't have to believe in him?" I ask my dad.

"Who?"

"God."

"Oh, right. Him."

"Don't we have to believe in him?"

My dad rummages around his pocket for a cigarette.

"Maybe that's not the question." He holds out his jacket as a screen against the wind while he lights the cigarette, then he takes my hand.

"Let's go get ourselves some duck," he says.

We walk past restaurants. Through the windows I can see people sitting around white tablecloths.

"Are we going to eat in there?" I ask.

"No. We're going to get the best duck this city has to offer."

We carry on walking. Past more restaurants, down many streets, many more snowdrifts. We reach the street with the girls in high heels; today they wear short quilted jackets that fall just above their hips. We walk past the old warehouses and places that could be small factories. A couple of the streetlights have gone out, others blink.

"Here we are," my dad says. "Best place in town."

Across the street lies a small, square wooden house with red and yellow signs on its roof. Two taxis are parked outside the entrance. I kick the snow off my shoes before we go inside.

People are sitting alone, one to each little table. They look down at their food. Two climbing elves have been stuck to the window with tape; golden glitter from them has scattered down onto the windowsill.

My dad finds a table for two in the corner. He goes up to the counter and returns with two plates of duck and gravy. One plate of roast pork. The fluorescent tubes above us are so bright they make the food shine.

"You prefer breast, don't you?" My dad swaps with a thigh on my plate.

The jukebox in the corner makes a loud ping.

"I remember a Christmas with Mum," I say. "It was in a house. Have we ever lived in a house?"

"We have. And your mum roasted the duck and I made the gravy. She cooked a great duck."

"Better than this one?"

"Yes. But only slightly."

He breaks off a piece of pork crackling, pops it into his mouth.

"I'm glad you remember. You look like her. More and more with each day."

A MAN AT one of the other tables gets up and stubs out his cigarette on his plate; he drains his coffee cup and leaves. Shortly afterwards the headlights on one of the taxis come on. I follow the red rear lights with my eyes as the car drives off.

"Why is everyone sitting alone?"

My dad puts a couple of slices of roast pork on my plate and a spoonful of red currant jelly.

"Not everyone has someone to celebrate Christmas with," he says.

"Like us?"

He looks up from his food.

"No, not at all like us. We've got each other. There's a very big difference."

For dessert we have cold rice pudding with vanilla, almonds, and a warm cherry sauce. My dad drinks coffee. When we leave, I'm so full that my tummy hurts.

YOU HAVEN'T ASKED about your present yet," my dad says as we walk up the stairs.

I wait in the kitchen while he goes to the basement to fetch it. He struggles to get the present through the narrow kitchen door; it's enormous and wrapped in red paper.

At first I try to unwrap it slowly, but then I can't bear it any longer and I tear off the paper. Pale wood appears.

"An easel," my dad says. "For painting."

I know what it is. I've seen easels in shops where my dad buys paints and coloring pencils for me without spending any money. But this one is different. Every edge has been sanded down and the wood is varnished. It looks more like a musical instrument than something you would splatter paint all over. He must have made it in the workshop, spent hours on it on the days when I didn't come along.

THE SUN IS setting outside the windows of the train. Quickly, as if it has somewhere to go.

The gaps between the houses grow bigger.

"Where are we going, Dad?"

"You'll see."

At first I'm scared that we're about to move, but we haven't brought any of our things.

"Where are we going?"

"Do you intend to keep on asking questions?"

"Yes."

He laughs.

"Of course you should."

"So where are we going?"

"You're going to school; we'll continue where we left off."

"Religious Studies?"

"Not quite."

We walk from the railway station past big houses with warm light coming from the windows and cars in the driveways. We keep walking until we reach a large red gate. We pass people heading in the opposite direction; they walk closely together with their hands buried deep in their pockets and their collars turned up. Soon we're alone on the path.

"People from Copenhagen have visited the Dyrehaven for hundreds of years," my dad says. The sandy soil under our feet glows against the dark grass and the trees. "They wanted a kind of nature that wasn't dangerous. One that didn't ruin their shoes. The paths here are straight and the deer are culled to control their numbers. But when the sun goes down, the park no longer belongs to humans."

Behind us the red gate grows smaller and smaller until I have to narrow my eyes in order to still be able to see its outline in the twilight. My dad takes my hand and helps me across a ditch as we leave the path. We walk through coarse grass, rotten branches snapping underneath our feet.

"We've forgotten the things we used to be able to do," my dad says, as he helps me across a fallen tree trunk. "We've forgotten that we could do all the things that animals can."

We reach some trees; it's difficult to see more than a few meters ahead.

"Animals always know exactly what to do. Have you ever seen a fox looking confused?" My dad chuckles in the darkness. "We've invented television, sent people to the moon. We can make gunpowder and bullets. But we've completely forgotten the things we used to be able to do. The things animals can do. I know you've seen birds fly in formation, several hundreds of them forming a large V in the sky. How do you think they do that? Do you think they sit on the ground and decide who'll fly where? Issue numbers?"

We keep walking until we reach a clearing. My dad stops; I bump my nose into his back and it hurts. He points: there's a stag on the far side of the clearing. It turns its head and stands completely still while it looks at us, then it disappears between the trees.

We carry on walking; the ground beneath us is uneven.

"Fishermen who've sailed for many years, the ones with the small boats who truly know the sea, they can look across the water and feel a storm coming even though the wind is calm. If you ask them how they do it, they can't tell you."

My shoe sinks into a little hollow in the grass, a puddle. I struggle to pull up my foot, my shoe and sock are soaked.

My dad has already moved on ahead of me, and I hurry to catch up with him.

We continue through the trees on the other side of the clearing. I put my hands together and blow hot air into them. I can sense the outline of my dad's back somewhere in front of me. I follow the sound of his voice.

"At some point we started believing in things we didn't understand. It happened when people moved to the cities. The little hairs at the back of their necks fell out."

The branches grow denser, they scratch my face, grab my clothes. I dare not stop, scared that I will lose my dad.

"In the city they learned new ways to survive. You could trick people. You could con them and take their money. It was no longer necessary to get your hands dirty. That's why we're so clever today. Because some of us have learned to cheat. And everyone else spends their time trying not to get cheated."

We head deeper and deeper into the forest. I can hear the sounds of small animals, see their eyes shine before they disappear again. I cover my mouth with my sleeve. I don't want the animals to hear me cry.

Then we walk around a tree stump through some low bushes and suddenly we're back on the path. I can see the red gate we came in through and the streetlights along the road outside.

My dad picks me up, he carries me and he doesn't put me down until we reach the vending machine at the small railway station. He puts money in the machine so I can have some hot chocolate. He smokes two cigarettes while I sip my drink. The train arrives.

MY EYES ARE right up close to the wood. The fifth woodworm hole must be perfect, it must be better than the woodworms themselves could make it. I was unhappy with the fourth one. I find the pencil dot with my drill. Suddenly the light disappears and I sense something behind me. Something big and dark like the monsters in the fairy tales my dad tells me before I go to sleep. So big that it can gobble up an entire town and clean its teeth with the church spire. So ugly that you can't look at it without going blind.

"What the hell is this?"

The boss's voice thunders.

"I can't believe you're letting him drill holes. Have you gone completely . . ."

The boss's fists are clenched.

My dad comes over to us; he doesn't stop stirring the coffee grounds in the jam jar.

"Just take a look at it," my dad says.

"You're going to pay for the damage that little shit has done."

"Just take a look at it."

The boss takes a deep breath and finds his reading glasses. He leans over the chair. I just manage to get out of the way before I'm squashed.

The boss traces the holes with his finger, he growls under his breath.

"Not bad," he mutters and straightens up, taking off his reading glasses. He scrutinizes me as if he can't quite believe that I did that. He goes inside the workshop without saying another word.

My dad smiles. "Back to work," he says. "These woodworm holes won't drill themselves."

My hands shake when I put the drill to the wood again.

THE NEXT COUPLE of days the boss visits. Every time he stops and looks over my shoulder. I try to carry on as if I haven't noticed. The boss then grunts a little before moving on.

At the end of the week the boss buys us lunch. Again he doesn't say anything; he just puts a small parcel in front of me, greaseproof paper with an elastic band around it. I don't dare unwrap it before the boss and my dad have started eating. The mayonnaise on top of my potato sandwich is too yellow; the meatball is a little burnt. I'm full after the first sandwich, but force myself to eat up.

THROUGHOUT THE DAY my dad has said: "Sleep. Go to sleep. What are you doing up? Go to your room and sleep. It's going to be a late night."

We eat beef burgers with soft onions. Once the plates are in the sink, my dad reads a book and I paint on my easel. I try to paint a horse, but I can't get the legs right; they hang under its belly and look like boiled spaghetti.

My dad looks up at the wall clock and says it's time to go. But first I need to put on my clothes. All of them.

"All of them?"

"Yes, all of them."

I put on sweatshirts on top of T-shirts on top of other T-shirts. Three pairs of socks.

"Where are we going?" I ask.

My dad just smiles and pulls the woolly cap over my ears. His bag makes a metallic sound when he picks it up.

The women in the street wear high heels and dresses that stick out under their winter coats. The men wear shirts and ties or bow ties. Some look like they're in a hurry; others are laughing, drinking, and shouting. I waddle down the street with my arms sticking out from my body. I wish I could lie down so my dad could roll me.

After a few streets we stop. I follow my dad's gaze to a redbrick building across the street.

"Jump on the spot so you don't get cold."

A man and a woman are standing in a first-floor window, drinking wine. I can hear music coming from the building, and through the ground-floor windows I can see a man with a party hat on his head jumping up and down. The cold creeps through my woolly mittens; I curl up my toes in my shoes and count the cigarettes my dad smokes. He finishes his fourth one and flicks the cigarette butt away; it lands in a snowdrift.

He fumbles in his pocket for his next cigarette when the front door opens. My dad grabs my hand and we cross the street.

"Take off your cap and pretend you're going to a party," he says.

A man comes out of the door. He stumbles and slumps across a parked car. Another man follows him, he has a bottle in his hand. They grin at each other. My dad is just in time to catch the door before it slams shut. We walk up the stairs. I can hear music and loud voices through the doors in the stairwell. I can smell the food they've eaten. On the third floor a man is asleep on a doormat. We step across him and carry on walking up.

At the top of the stairs is a single door. My dad takes a screwdriver from his bag and then a hammer. A couple of floors below us a door opens; we hear footsteps, but they're going down, not up. My dad slips the screwdriver in between the door and the door frame and holds the hammer ready in his other hand. He looks at his watch.

"Five, four, three, two, one."

It gets more noisy. People shout, stamp their feet, blow their horns.

"Happy New Year," my dad says, and whacks the screwdriver with the hammer. It digs into the wood. He hits it again; the sound is drowned out by a thousand others.

My dad forces open the door and we walk down a narrow passage with wooden doors on both sides. A small ladder at the end of the passage leads to a hatch in the ceiling. It's locked with a padlock, which also receives a couple of blows from the hammer.

We climb up on the roof and come out next to the chimney. The roof slopes to both sides, but there's a flat area in the middle, three to four meters wide. My dad takes a blanket from his bag and spreads it on the ground; then he takes out more blankets and wraps us up in them. Finally he produces a Thermos of hot chocolate from his bag. We lie on our backs next to each other as we watch the fireworks. The city explodes in light; I cover my ears while I laugh. Around us rockets fall into the gutters.

· 1988 ·

THE FROG STARES at them. It's enormous; its skin is green and knobbly.

"So you want to get across?" it asks, and grins.

Its echoing laughter stinks of rotten water; its jaw is so big it could easily swallow a car. The King and the Prince look at the lake. The far shore has disappeared in the thick fog.

"I won't eat you," the frog says. "I promise."

The King and the Prince look at each other. Should they do it, should they trust the frog, run the risk?

I lie on my bed, holding my breath. The toilet being flushed downstairs becomes a huge pike splashing about in the murky water. Next door's television becomes birdsong in the trees behind us.

"Couldn't they just have walked around the lake?" I ask my dad.

"It would've taken them years. The Prince would've grown just as old as the King is now. And the King would've turned into a very old man who couldn't see or hear anything. They'd never have found the White Queen. They'd never have managed to kill her and lift the curse."

"Weren't they scared? Really scared?"

"Yes, of course. But it's a great deal easier to be brave when you don't have a choice."

The King climbs up onto the frog; it's not easy, the frog's skin is slippery and slimy and there's nothing to hold on to. When he sits straddling its back, the King helps the Prince up. The frog tenses its thigh muscles, its whole body quivers. Then it jumps. Water splashes around their ears. The frog takes strong strokes with its big hind legs. The shore is quickly reduced to a thin line behind them. The sound of birdsong back on land grows fainter and fainter before disappearing altogether. They're surrounded by silence; there's only the sound of the frog's swimming strokes. The fog settles around them, everything turns white. Then the frog starts to tread water.

"I'm hungry," it says. "I'm really rather hungry."

"You promised not to eat us," the Prince says.

"I prefer to be a full liar," the frog replies, and starts to open its mouth.

"You can have our packed lunch," the Prince says.

The frog considers this and then it nods. Ripples form in the water.

"You'll probably keep for a while longer, anyway."

The King and the Prince open their bags and throw eggs, sausages, and red apples sideways into the frog's mouth. It chews and swallows. Then it swims on. My dad turns off the light, pulls the blanket around me, tucks me in.

"Sleep tight," he says.

MY DAD AND I are standing in the yard outside the workshop.

"Listen, I've got something to tell you," the boss says. "We've got a big order from Germany. The Germans can't get enough of all the old crap we make."

An hour later a van arrives, crammed with furniture for us to distress. Anything we can't find room for in the workshop we leave in the yard and cover with tarpaulin. Then we run out of tarpaulin and the boss goes off to get some more.

When he returns it has started to snow, and we have to wipe down the furniture before we can cover it.

In the afternoon we're still working on the first lot of chairs and tables. We've moved inside the workshop; it smells of wet wood, of varnish and coffee grounds. The boss looks over my shoulder while I use a file to scratch the legs of an armchair.

"Not bad at all," he says.

On his way out he slaps my dad on the shoulder, chuckles to himself, and mutters something about "child labor." Then he laughs even louder.

WE DON'T LEAVE the workshop until late that evening. I sit in the bicycle's basket; there are no stars in the sky. I recognize the soreness in my feet like when we've walked all day, but it's the first time I've experienced my whole body aching. I like the feeling of having worked hard.

My dad brings in the chair from the kitchen. His eyes are heavy, but he says we can't let the King and the Prince sit on the frog all night. Their lips are dry and their stomachs groan with hunger pains. They still can't see the far shore. The frog starts to tread water again.

"I really am terribly hungry," it says. "A king and a prince would taste very nice right now."

"Wouldn't you rather have the meat we packed?" the King asks.

"I thought I ate your packed lunches yesterday."

"Yes, but you didn't get the meat we intend to sell when we get across."

"Give it here," the frog says.

The King takes off his shoes, very quietly so the frog won't hear. The Prince does the same. They tie their shoes together by the laces, then they throw them into the frog's open mouth. The frog munches the leather.

"It tastes funny," it says. "And it's very tough."

"Real meat is always very tough," the Prince says. "So that you can chew on it for much longer."

THE NEXT MORNING a van picks up the furniture we've finished. The wood is now darker than when it arrived, the seats have been distressed with a steel brush. We need to get it all out of the workshop quickly to make room for the next lot.

After lunch the boss says he's had an idea and disappears through the archway. An hour later he returns with thirty brand-new alarm clocks. They're metal and have to be wound up, but the varnish is still shiny and the price tags are still on.

"For the Germans," he says, and explains that every time we send off a van full of furniture, we'll throw in a handful of clocks. "They're gonna love them."

We take the clocks apart and put the hands and the clock faces in a bucket with water and acid.

I'm quickly given responsibility for the clocks. Once the clock faces are immersed in acid, the varnish starts to bubble up and the clocks look like they've been lying in an attic for many years under a leaking roof. The metal casing also needs to be aged. When I'm not busy varnishing an armchair or drilling woodworm holes, I take a new clock from the pile. I smear black shoe polish into the cracks and rub them with sandpaper before putting them outside in the rain.

THE FROG IS still swimming across the lake. The fog grows so dense that the King and the Prince can no longer see each other. Nor can they see the frog beneath them; they can only feel its slimy skin and hear its stomach rumble. It starts treading water again, but it doesn't say anything.

I look across at my dad; he's asleep in the chair. I pull at him until he gets up and staggers over to the couch. I ask him if the King and the Prince will make it.

"Who knows?" he mumbles, and goes back to sleep.

THE BOSS HOLDS up a clock I've just reassembled, one of the first to be finished. He looks moved to tears.

"You need something for it," he says while we eat lunch.

At first I don't realize he's talking to me so I carry on eating; I try to keep the pickled beetroot in place on top of my liver pâté sandwich.

"Hello, boy," he shouts. "Hello, boy! What do you want?"

I don't know what to reply.

"I know I laughed when I called you child labor, but I'm starting to feel bad about it. So what's it gonna be?"

I look at my dad. He nods to give me the go-ahead, for me to just say it. I hesitate. I don't want the boss to laugh at me, throw me out. I want to stay here, be with my dad. Work up a sweat and get splinters in my fingers. They both look at me while they wait.

"A bicycle," I say. "A blue bicycle."

I regret it immediately. I should've asked for something smaller, like a toy car or a new football.

But the boss just smiles. "Well, of course it's got to be blue. You don't want a girlie bike, do you?"

WE RIDE THROUGH the city. The slush splashes up and hits my cheek; it makes the butcher's bike wobble. I lie down in the big basket and look up at the dark sky. I almost fall asleep. Tomorrow we'll make more furniture look old. Tomorrow I'll be allowed to handle nitric acid. My dad has promised me. As long as I'm careful. Tomorrow we'll get lunch from the sandwich shop again. Possibly an egg sandwich with a single herring on top. Or beetroot salad, which makes my lips go pink.

Tomorrow I hope the boss will tell me once again that I'm good.

I'M LYING IN my bed. The frog is still swimming with the King and the Prince. It starts to tread water again.

Before it has time to say anything, the King asks his son: "Why don't we kill ourselves a frog? It's been a long time since the last one."

The Prince replies: "Yes, a fortnight, at least."

"You eat frogs?" the frog says, and tries to turn its big green head to see if the King might have a knife or a small sword. A weapon it might have overlooked when they climbed onto its back. "Do you really eat frogs?"

"No," the King replies. "We've never done that."

"We just kill them," the Prince says. "Some people like flying kites, others love riding bicycles. We kill frogs. It's what we do."

"But not me," the frog says, now sounding more reassured.

"Why not?" the Prince asks.

"Because then you'll drown."

"I agree, I don't think we can swim ashore, either," the King says. "It's too far. The water is too cold, the fog too dense. But we kill frogs. It's what we do; it's what we've always done."

The frog has started shaking a little.

"But perhaps we could make an exception," the King says.

The frog resumes swimming. Faster than before. It makes small, unhappy grunts all the way to the shore.

The King and the Prince jump off its back. They're wet, cold, and hungry, but they can't help laughing out loud. The birds' twittering sounds like hundreds of tiny beaks saying welcome, welcome. You've won. You're here now. You're still alive.

The grass under their bare feet is so green that it hurts their eyes. They hurry away from the frog, still submerged in the lake, only its eyes sticking out of the water.

MY DAD IS standing in the yard, cursing. He has accidentally broken off a chair leg while he was sanding it down.

"Do we have any more panel pins?" he asks.

I shake my head. I used the last ones this morning on a tabletop that had started to warp because it had been left out in the rain for too long.

My dad goes into the workshop. He quickly reappears.

"You're right. I'll just pop out and get some. Do you want to come along?"

I shake my head. I know we're busy. When the boss came in yesterday, he pointed to the chairs and said, "Remember they need to look old tomorrow."

My dad jumps onto the butcher's bike and rides out through the archway.

I press the drill against the wood again. A few more holes and the armchair will be ready. I try not to make a mess of it even though we're in a hurry.

"Where's your dad?" the boss asks. I didn't hear him come in. Perhaps I've finally learned to focus only on the table or the chair that I'm working on.

"He went to get some panel pins," I say.

The boss lingers for a little while and looks at me. "Isn't there . . ." He doesn't finish his sentence, he just shakes his head.

He'll explode in a moment. Scream and shout. I'm almost sure of it. He might have been pleased with the clocks, but I shouldn't have carried on working, not on my own. I should've waited for my dad to come back so he could supervise me.

But the boss doesn't say anything; he just turns around and goes inside the workshop.

I stand with the drill in my hand, not knowing what to do now. A couple of minutes later I start to feel stupid: we're rushed and I'm just standing here doing nothing. I start drilling the next hole.

I have only one more hole to go when the boss reappears. I quickly lift the drill, expecting a walloping. Delayed, but I know it's coming. He's been in the workshop thinking: What did I just see, what the hell was that?

Before he has time to open his mouth, I ask him if he thinks I've done a good job on the armchair.

"Yes," he replies, without looking at it.

His eyes are red, it's probably the cold that has made them water.

"I want to show you something."

He starts walking back to the workshop; he half turns around and gestures for me to follow.

"It's important," he says. "It's important that you see it."

I follow the boss past the wide worktable with the tools and the tins of oil and varnish. I follow him to the door at the back of the room. Today it's ajar; the padlock has been removed and lies on the table.

"In there," the boss says.

I open the door. Behind it is a narrow passage lit up by a single lightbulb in the ceiling.

"You really should go in there and have a look. Your dad will be really proud."

The boss walks right behind me, his wide hips scraping against the rough concrete walls.

At the end of the passage is a small room with no windows; the only light is that which slips past the boss. When my eyes have grown used to the darkness, I can see an oil drum up against the wall. Apart from that the room is empty. Something furry is lying on top of the oil drum.

"Go to it," the boss says.

I take a couple of steps further into the room and now I can see that it's a toy rabbit. It was probably white once, but now its fur is gray from dirt, with dark stains that could be oil or earth.

"It's feeling sad. It needs a home." The boss's voice is barely louder than a whisper. "Pick it up."

The rabbit's fur is damp. It smells sour.

The boss sniffs; he wipes his nose on his sleeve. "I'd promised myself . . ."

He fumbles with his blue dungarees, pulls down one strap over his shoulder. I can see beads of sweat gleaming on his scalp. Then the other strap comes down; he struggles to get the overalls past his stomach.

"Four years, seven months, and six days." His voice is thick.

Then I see a shadow over the boss's head. Like a bird has flown in here and now can't find its way out.

After four blows I see my dad standing behind him, holding the chair leg in his hand. The boss sinks to his knees and gets stuck like a cork in the doorway. With each blow I can see more of my dad. I'm good at counting, but I wouldn't be able to keep up even if I tried. My dad keeps hitting him and the sound changes from the hard whack of wood against wood to a much softer, rounder sound. Like a rolling pin slamming into dough.

"Drop it," says my dad, who is out of breath. I'm still holding the toy rabbit. He lifts me across the boss so my feet won't get wet.

When we're back in the workshop, my dad pulls off his sweatshirt. His black T-shirt clings to his body, his face and neck are covered with red splashes. He wipes the chair leg with his sweatshirt. Then he puts his sweatshirt and the chair leg in separate plastic bags and ties a knot in them. He washes himself in the sink in the corner. He lifts me up so I sit on the worktable.

"We'll be going very soon; I've just got to do a few things."

He puts on a pair of work gloves, gives me a quick peck on my forehead, and starts wiping down the room with an old rag. Just as when he works on the furniture, he looks like he knows exactly what to do.

When he has finished, he crawls under one of the worktables along the walls. He emerges with a big metal box in his hands. He takes an electric drill from the wall, closes the door to the yard, and tells me to cover my ears. Sparks fly from the metal box. When he has finished, he opens it and empties it of banknotes and coins.

ON THE WAY home we stop three times. The first time to throw the plastic bag with the chair leg into a garbage on a street corner. The second time to throw the bag with my dad's sweatshirt into a different garbage. We cycle down a few more streets and my dad pulls in at the curb. He gets off the bicycle and helps me out of the basket. He doesn't say anything; he just sits on his haunches in front of me, looks into my eyes, and holds me tight. His winter coat is buttoned all the way up, but I can feel the top of his wet T-shirt against my neck.

When we get home, my dad says that we have to take off our clothes. All of them. He stuffs them into several plastic bags and ties knots in them. We take a bath; he scrubs us both thoroughly with soap and a sponge. Then he starts splashing water at me, spouting water out of his mouth like a fountain. I can't help laughing.

EVERY MORNING MY dad asks me what I feel like doing. And then we do it. We go to the zoo. We feed the ducks and go to Madame Tussaud's Wax Museum. We go to the cinema and see a film about a racing car that can talk. We see the film three times in one day, and I eat my body weight in popcorn.

When we come out of the cinema or the zoo, I can't remember where we've been. I know we stood in front of the lion cage, I know I saw the lion cubs play. But I can't remember what they looked like. As if it happened to someone else, as if it's something I've only been told about. I nod to my dad, yes, the little monkeys were cute.

My dad stops buying newspapers; we no longer go to the kiosks. He buys his tobacco at the bakery, when he gets bread for breakfast before I get up.

I lie in bed all night, unable to sleep. My eyelids don't grow heavy until the sun starts to rise. And then the dreams come. I keep seeing the boss.

In the morning, I try to draw my dreams, I want to draw a bear in overalls, a big, brown furry bear. I want to look at the drawing, laugh at it, and scrunch up the paper. But every time I try to start it, draw a line on the paper, I stop immediately. I can't draw it, I feel sick the moment I pick up a pencil. I put my paper and my coloring pencils, watercolors, and brushes as far under my bed as I can. So far that I have to bend down to see them.

That night I lie on my bed until sunrise; if I close my eyes, I can see the boss dance.

I don't say anything to my dad; he wants me to be happy.

I'M EATING A giant ice cream cone as we walk through the city. It wasn't easy to find an ice cream parlor in the middle of winter, but we kept looking. We walked down to Nyhavn, which my dad tells me was once a busy harbor. Built by Swedish prisoners of war. The strawberry jam on my ice cream runs down the cone and I lick it off. I start to cry and I can't stop.

It's still dark outside. My dad walks around the kitchen in stockinged feet. He does everything as quietly as possible. I see him tiptoe past the doorway to my bedroom with an unlit cigarette in his mouth, his shoes in his hand, his jacket over his shoulder.

When he realizes that I'm awake, he asks if I want to go back to sleep, he promises to get home before I wake again. I shake my head and he helps me get dressed. Several layers, clean clothes on top of dirty ones.

It's just after four o'clock and we're standing in a parking lot behind a supermarket. Around us, people have congregated in small clusters. My dad pointed them out to me last time. Students in one group: they're the ones with the red eyes. Dark-haired men, many with black mustaches. They speak a language I don't understand. They've brought Thermoses; they drink coffee from small glasses.

"They came to Denmark because they were told there was work for them. Now they find themselves here," my dad says.

The van arrives. People flick away their cigarettes; the groups mingle as they head for the van.

There are rarely enough newspapers for everyone, but my dad's sure to get some even when there's a long line in front of him. The man with the newspapers inside the van waves my dad over.

"You've got to look after your own," he says, and hands him three or four bundles.

I'm well aware that I'm not much use. I'm not nearly as fast as my dad. Once we're inside a stairwell, he disappears. I can hear his footsteps going up; he takes three steps in his stride. The ground floor is my responsibility; I take care not to drop a single section.

In the morning my dad's hands are swollen and covered in newspaper ink. When we walk home, we see people going to work. If we've finished early, we walk around to the back of the bakeries and knock. The price is different before the shops open and the bread is still warm. Some days we get the bread for free; we get the bread they can't sell and we stuff ourselves with misshapen poppyseed buns, crusty rolls, and croissants straight out of the oven.

The next morning my dad tries once again to sneak off without waking me up. When he succeeds, when I open my eyes and the sun fills my room, I lie in bed thinking, Who will deliver to the ground floors for him now?

I EAT BREAD rolls and drink hot chocolate in bed.

When I've finished my breakfast, my dad tells me to hurry up and get dressed: we're going out to get my birthday present.

I drag my dad down the street. I don't know where we're going, but we can't get there soon enough.

I wonder if he has saved up for the fire engine. The red metal fire engine with flashing lights and jets that spurt water when you press a button on its roof. The toy shop is on the corner and there's always an old lady behind the counter. We've been there a few times, bought a bouncing ball or a couple of stickers if my dad had some spare change in his pocket. The last time we were there I was allowed to take down the fire engine and put it on the floor.

Or the bicycle, the blue bicycle with leather fringes on the handlebars which will flap in the wind when you ride downhill. We walk past the window of the bicycle shop almost every day, and every time I hope it hasn't been sold. But I know we can't afford it. So I hope for the red fire engine, the one that squirts water.

I know I don't need either of them. I'm eight years old today. What use is a fire engine to me? It's also quite expensive. But what if my dad has saved up for it?

Or perhaps he'll just take it. The old lady could look straight at him, they could talk about the weather, how the price of butter and milk keeps going up. And he'd still be able to slip the fire engine into his rucksack without her noticing. But I also know that he wouldn't dream of taking anything from an old lady with a small shop.

WE WALK PAST the toy shop and we keep on going. Could it really be the bicycle? I'm almost certain of it until we also walk past the window of the bicycle shop.

We're waiting at the bus stop when my dad asks me if anything is wrong. I shake my head.

The bus takes us to the city center. It's a cold February day; winter jackets brush against coats. I trace the number eight with my finger on the steamed-up window.

My dad leans close to me.

"Today you're going to get a very special birthday present."

I look at him, trying to guess what the next word from his lips will be.

"Today you're going to see an angel," he says.

We walk down Strøget, Copenhagen's main pedestrian street. My dad holds my hand in his, he shows me the way.

We walk through the doors of one of the big department stores and continue up the escalators to the cafeteria.

We have to wait in line for a long time to pay for our hot chocolate, coffee, and plate of Danish pastries. In a corner we find a table covered with cups and cake plates from previous guests.

"This is a good place to see an angel," my dad says, and drops two lumps of sugar into his coffee. He stirs it with a teaspoon. "Angels follow people, I don't know why, but they do. That's why this is a good place; there are lots of people here, and you can drink hot chocolate at the same time."

I look around the cafeteria, but I can't see any angels.

"No," my dad says, and laughs so much that his coffee spills over. "No, angels aren't fat children with wings on their backs. Nor are they tall men holding swords like in the Old Testament. Angels are different; they're outside our world."

My dad takes off his coat and drapes it over the back of a chair. He rolls up his sleeves and takes one of the empty coffee cups from the table. He looks at me and I nod.

"We can touch this cup," he says. "If we smash it, it'll break."

My dad presses the cup into my hand.

"But there's something more. Something you can't get a hold of. Something you can't touch."

He takes the plate with the Danish pastries and holds it under the table.

"Can you see the pastries now?"

I shake my head.

"But that doesn't mean they aren't there, does it?"

He breaks off a piece of pastry and hands it to me.

"There are things in this world you can't touch. Things you can't see unless you know what you're looking for. Most people have forgotten that. Or they're too scared to open their eyes."

We share the Danish pastries and when only crumbs remain, he says: "Finish your chocolate. Do you need the bathroom? No? Good, then let's get started."

He looks around the cafeteria, searching for something. His gaze ends up somewhere to the right of the exit, not far from the woman behind the till and the trays of cutlery and napkins.

"I want you to look over there. Keep looking that way."

I follow his finger; I want to be quite sure that I'm looking in the right direction.

"Try to relax your eyes," he says. "Look, but don't look at anything in particular. Like when we go to the museum."

I look as hard as I can, I try really hard.

"Am I allowed to blink?" My eyes are starting to water.

"Of course you're allowed to blink, as long as you keep looking over there. Look without looking. Forget where we are. Forget the girl at the till; forget the sound of knives and forks and coffee cups."

I don't know how long we sit there. All I hear is my dad's voice.

"Seek and you will find, says the Bible. But it's not true. People who look too hard won't find anything at all. We're not talking about missing keys. See without seeking."

I sit there until my eyes ache and one of my legs has gone to sleep. I open my mouth; I want to ask my dad if we can please go home. Come back another day, perhaps.

But then it happens. If I hadn't known that I was looking for something, and what I was looking for, I would've missed it.

It starts like the color blue. Like smoke floating across people's heads. Then it grows, gets bigger, the blue tones darken and become less transparent.

"Look," my dad whispers.

The blue grows arms and legs. It's between the people; it sticks to them briefly as they walk past, then it lets go and returns to a form which now also has a head, a face with no features, neither male nor female.

Then it's gone. The sound of forks against cake plates, the ringing of the till and hundreds of words spoken simultaneously, all the noises return quickly and violently.

My dad smiles at me. His eyes are moist.

"I knew you'd see it. Happy birthday."

He pulls me up from the chair in a big hug so my feet leave the ground.

WE WALK DOWN Strøget. I feel strangely light-headed. In the bus on the way home I ask my dad if I really saw an angel. I was absolutely sure when we were in the cafeteria. Now I'm starting to doubt.

"Who knows?" he replies. "I think so. But who knows. The important thing is that you saw it."

I WAIT ON the bottom step. I wring out the cloths so they're ready. I run to get clean water for the bucket and I beat the doormats while my dad washes the stairs. I'm no help and I know I'm not.

One day the sun appears behind the clouds. It's early May and I can feel the sunbeams through my clothes.

"Camus was right, starving is easier when the sun is shining," my dad says.

"Not that we're starving," he quickly adds.

We walk around parks collecting bottles. I'm good at that even though I can't carry very many. I don't have to walk far to get a new bottle. People knock back the last few drops or tip them out on the grass so they can hand the empty bottle to me.

In the evening my dad says he's not hungry. He pushes his plate over to me.

"Eat," he says. "It'd be a pity to waste it."

I'M SITTING IN the bicycle basket. We ride past the bus stop and keep going until we're the only ones left on the road, until the road becomes uneven and the gravel crunches under the bicycle tires. My dad stops so I can have a pee in the bushes, then we ride on. My dad stops in front of a rusty old gate. He closes it behind us and we cycle down an avenue with tall trees on either side. The leaves are so dense they look like a green wooden fence. We keep going further down the avenue until I can no longer see the road behind us. Then we emerge from the trees. The house in front of us looks like something out of a Western; it's on several floors and built from broad planks. It could be the ranch of a rich cattle owner.

"The lady who lives here," my dad says, leaning the bicycle against a tree, "she looks a little different, you should know that."

I never know how he gets his jobs; one day he just has them. It's the same this time.

We walk up the steps to the terrace, the boards creak under our feet. As we stand outside the front door, my dad smooths back his long hair. He wipes his mouth, gives me the once over, and then he nods. He knocks three times before he opens the door. We walk through a large hall and enter a drawing room with lace curtains and porcelain figurines. My dad puts his hand on my shoulder. We wait for a few moments before the old lady appears from the darkest corner of the drawing room. Her face is wrong, contorted, but in the middle of her head are two human eyes. I'm on the verge of tears, but I can still feel my dad's hand on my shoulder. I don't look away and I hope he's proud of me.

"Hello," the lady says, leaning towards me.

For a moment I'm scared that she'll take my hand. Surely they can both hear my heart beat; it must make a noise in this drawing room, far away as we are from cars and other people.

Then she starts to walk and it's a relief to see only her back as we follow her out on the terrace.

"I used to play here as a child," she says.

We look across an unkempt lawn that ends in dense bushes and trees.

"I knew the garden better than anyone. Of course, that was before it got so overgrown."

I hear a scraping sound and I think she must be scratching herself.

"I want you to make me a path. It doesn't have to be a nice path. Not everything that's nice is good. I would just like to go for a walk without breaking my neck. Do you think you can do that?"

"Of course." My dad pats her on the shoulder. "But it's going to take some time."

I can tell from the old lady's shadow that she nods.

"And it won't be a straight path. It has to be a winding path, crooked like the trees."

Again her shadow nods.

"That's why I want you to do it."

WHEN THE OLD lady has gone back inside, I follow my dad around the house. Several times I nearly trip over in the strong, yellow grass. My dad opens the door to the garden shed and we hear the sounds of small animals scurrying away from the sunlight. Tools hang on the end wall. My dad takes down the chainsaw. He runs his finger across its body.

"It's German," he says. "It was made more than fifty years ago. It's the best you can get."

My dad wipes the metal label with his sleeve. It depicts a bear with big claws and bared teeth.

"They don't make tools like this today. This saw alone would cost as much as a small car."

He unscrews the chainsaw's gas cap, then takes a small bottle from a bag and empties it into the hole.

"I bet you it'll start," he says.

He pulls the cord, the chainsaw splutters, and then it starts.

MY DAD IS the only man in the restaurant without a jacket; I'm the only one in shorts. The waiter gives us a strange look until we order the most expensive dishes on the menu and my dad counts the banknotes between the starter and main course.

"Our advance," he whispers across the table, and empties a glass of red wine. He orders me another soda.

"Never save up money," he says. "Yes, of course, if there's something you really want. A bicycle, you can save up for a bicycle. But money isn't something you should hold on to. People who cling to their money become unhappy. Spend it. It'll come back to you."

I had a bicycle once. I think about it while we eat soup from tiny bowls with a kind of mushroom I've never seen before. I had a bicycle, and then we had to move to a new town. We washed it, oiled the gears, and pumped up the tires. Then we left it unlocked on a street corner.

AT NIGHT I dream about the old lady. She opens her mouth and a beetle crawls out. It sniffs the world, its antennae whir, then it takes off from her teeth. For a moment the beetle hangs suspended in the air before its dark carapace opens and the wings unfurl. Several beetles follow. They fly around her head. Her eyes sit deep in her head like two black buttons. I don't know if she's crying. I don't know if she's smiling, but I think she's trying.

I DON'T WALK any further into the garden than from where I can still see my dad on the terrace. The orchard begins where the strong yellow grass ends. I pick apples and pears which I eat while I watch my dad work. He has spread a dark green tarpaulin across the wooden terrace, where he sits dismantling the tools. He cleans every single part individually with a white cloth dipped in ammonia. Then he carefully oils all the cogs before they resume their place in the metal casing. The smell of gasoline and oil lingers in the air around him.

"Feel this," he says, handing me a cog from the chainsaw.

At first I can't see why it's anything special. He guides my finger and I can feel that every single tooth is identical. I can find no flaws, not even traces from the cast.

I hear a faint creaking from the planks behind me and see the old lady's shadow.

"You may eat as much fruit as you want," she says to me. "But if you find a fruit you don't know, don't put it in your mouth. The birds are attracted to its color. They can't help taking a bite. You mustn't do the same."

Out of the corner of my eye I can see the toes of her tiny, burgundy leather shoes.

"People think nature's always good, but it can be evil, too."

My dad nods without taking his eyes off the tools.

"Just buy new ones," she says. "I'll give you money for new tools."

My dad shakes his head. "I don't expect you to pay me for sitting here. I would've done it for free."

"Nonsense, I wouldn't hear of it."

When I pay attention only to her voice, she could be any old lady. Like the one who bought pork chops every Wednesday in the butcher's where my dad once worked.

"I've got something that might interest you," she says.

We follow her around the building.

"In there."

She points to a huge bush. It takes a couple of moments before I realize there's a shed behind it. My dad pulls aside the branches to get to the door. The padlock has rusted red. He whacks it with a hammer and then he disappears into the darkness.

I stand very still and hear my dad rummage around inside the shed; I keep my eyes peeled on the door. I don't want to look at the old lady, alone here in the garden with no shadows. I hear something creak and I follow the sound around the shed. The branches give or snap. Two doors swing open and I'm looking into what was once a garage. There's a car inside, gray with dirt. My dad takes a step backwards and admires the car for a long time in silence.

"I didn't know there were any of these left," he says at last.

He finds a rag in his pocket, spits on it, and polishes a circle on the bonnet so we can see the black paintwork gleam in the sunshine.

I EXPLORE THE garden one meter at a time; I'm an explorer again. In the distance I can hear the chainsaw my dad is using today. From where I am, the sound isn't much louder than an angry bee trapped in a jam jar. I watch where I'm going and I don't take the next step unless I'm sure I've got solid ground under my feet. No quicksand, not yet. The trees in the garden are different from anything I've seen before: they don't grow straight, but twist and get tangled up in each other. At first I think it's fun that I have to wiggle my way through them. Then I see the skeletons of tiny birds caught in the branches.

I run back to the lawn, stumble, and get back on my feet, hoping that the trees won't wake up and think I'm a bird or yet another plant they can merge with.

I find my sketchbook in the grass where I left it. I sit down and start drawing. I decide not to go deeper into the garden. I'm going to stay here. Between the old lady in the house and the trees.

I draw myself with a cowboy hat on my head and a six-shooter in my hand. I shoot a snake through its heart. I'm not really sure where a snake's heart is, so I guess.

AT NOON MY dad emerges from the bushes. He has leaves in his hair, aphids in his beard, and small scratches on his neck.

"I look like a troll, don't I?"

Together we walk up to the house. The old lady has set out food for us on a small, white metal table on the terrace. Fabric napkins have been slipped under the plates. The bread we eat isn't rye or white bread, it's dark and sweet. The egg salad tastes fantastic. My dad says the lemonade is made with fresh lemons. Apart from that he doesn't say much, but he smiles while he chews. The chainsaw lies so close that he can reach out and stroke the metal with his hand.

I listen to noises from the house and keep my eyes glued to the front door. The house creaks, but the old lady doesn't appear. She must know that it would be impossible to swallow a single bite if she were standing in front of us.

After lunch I follow my dad to the first row of bushes and find my sketchbook in the grass.

I'M DRAWING WHEN a young man comes cycling down the path and out between the trees. His bicycle is like my dad's, a butcher's bike. He swings his leg over the crossbar and jumps off while it's still moving. He grabs the large wicker basket from the front; he has to lean to the side to haul it up to the terrace. There, another basket is waiting for him. He picks up an envelope, puts it in his inside pocket, and takes the basket. It looks lighter; perhaps it's empty. He walks back to the bicycle, slowly, like someone who has promised himself not to run. His lips are moving slightly, I think he's talking to himself. Then he stops, he has seen me on the grass. He stares at me as if I don't fit in, as if I shouldn't be sitting here, drawing. He takes a few steps towards me. Then he turns around again. As he leaves the garden, he stands upright on the pedals.

THE MIDGES BUZZ around our heads; my dad has just come out from between the trees. He gives me a quick kiss on my forehead.

"We're going home shortly."

He goes to the car in the shed. I hear the sound of tools, hear him talk in there, but I can't make out the words.

I'm waiting on the furthest board on the terrace. I let my legs dangle over the edge. If shadows from the trees reach my feet, the old lady will come and get me. The shadows look like fat fingers, they point at me as they slowly creep up on me. When they're less than half a meter from the toes of my shoes, my dad reappears. He has dark spots on his face, and his teeth glow yellow in the dark.

I FOLLOW MY dad's finger with my eyes. Two men are standing in the archway leading to the courtyard of the building where we live. They're both wearing jeans and windbreakers over their shirts. I nearly fall off when my dad slams on the bike's brakes.

"Look how they stand," he whispers into my ear. "Notice how hard they try to look as if they just happen to be there. Far too relaxed. Smoking casually."

I narrow my eyes, but struggle to see anything other than two men in an archway.

"Do you remember what I told you about the White Men?"

"The Queen's helpers?"

"Yes, them."

"Are they the White Men?"

"I don't know. But I don't think we should try to find out."

We get back on the bicycle. We ride out of city until the tarmac turns into gravel, which later turns into hardened earth. When we can no longer see the city lights, my dad pulls over. He paces up and down, then he sits down against a tree and smokes. I try to be quiet. I don't want to disturb him while he's thinking.

Two cigarettes later he gets up.

"I think we might have to move again."

We cycle down the path to the old lady's house. The colors are smudged. Dark branches reach out for us, like the trees in the fairy tales my dad tells me. Forests filled with trolls who may grant you three wishes, but who'll always want something in return. Trolls who love little boys, keeping them as servants before they put them on the spit and roast them or eat them with wild berries.

My dad opens the door to the garage. The car has been washed since I last saw it. He opens the back door and I get in. The leather upholstery is cold against my bare legs.

"I know you're not ready. I know that. But we need you." He puts his hand on the dark wood of the dashboard. "Afterwards we'll take really good care of you. But do this for us, please."

He turns the key, but nothing happens.

"Just today, sweetheart."

Again he turns the key. The engine growls, then the whole car starts to shudder like a dog shaking off water.

"That's right, you can do it."

Slowly we drive across the uneven lawn, down the path, and out onto the big road.

Sometime later my dad pulls over and takes a woolly blanket from the trunk. He covers me with it.

"Try to get some sleep if you can," he says, and gets back behind the wheel.

I experience that night in glimpses, in the brief moments when I'm awake.

I know we're by the sea, I can hear the waves. My dad stands in the glow from the headlights. He smokes and looks at his watch.

Another glimpse, we're back on the road again. The engine purrs: a calm and friendly sound. I lie staring up at the roof of the car.

Yet another glimpse: we've stopped in front of the archway leading to the courtyard. My dad is busy filling the trunk; he's holding the box with the records.

"Just go back to sleep," he says.

I'm woken up by my head bouncing up and down on the seat. We drive past the old lady's house and into the garage.

My dad empties the car, it doesn't take him long. Every time we move, we have fewer things. The last thing he takes out of the trunk is my easel; in his other hand he has the portfolio with my drawings.

"We can always buy new towels," he says.

We sit in the old lady's kitchen eating crispbread with salami and cheese. I drink fruit punch, my dad heats coffee in a saucepan on the stove.

He talks to the old lady in the hallway; they whisper as if there were other people in the house we should try not to wake. My dad laughs; it sounds as if it was his plan all along to move in here. The old lady wishes us a good night and I hear the sound of her slippers down the hallway.

There's still one last bite of crispbread on the plate, but my eyes grow heavy. My dad carries me up the stairs. He pushes open the door with his foot, our new home. The room isn't big, but bigger than our last apartment. The wallpaper is pale yellow with small flowers, the mattress is hard. My dad puts me down on the bed; the sheet is stiff and smells of fresh air.

I WAKE UP alone in the room. In the distance I can hear the sound of the chainsaw. I stay in bed and read the same comic over and over. I get to know every single cobweb on the ceiling. The abandoned ones and the ones where I occasionally see a black spider darting up and down. I get to know the cracks in the wallpaper; a small flap points down at me. I stand on the suitcase and pee out the window. I'm scared that the old lady is going to come and get me every time the house creaks. Then I hide under the blanket.

At noon my dad comes up to my room to fetch me. We go downstairs and have lunch together. I ask him if he would please wake me in the morning, take me with him outside, I promise to look after myself. He nods and I'm glad he doesn't ask why.

I stay on the lawn until my dad has finished his work for the day. He says good night to the car: "We were too hard on you. But you did well."

In the kitchen a big pot of soup is waiting for us with slices of freshly baked whole-grain bread. Bowls have been set out on the table, a beer for my dad, a soda for me.

At night the wind makes the house squeak and groan, wood rubbing against wood like a ship sailing on a stormy sea.

WHEN I WAKE up the next morning, I'm alone in the room again. I search the suitcases but grow increasingly convinced that my dad packed just a single comic when he cleared out the apartment. I know the words by heart; all I have to do is close my eyes to see the pictures, one by one. I sit on the bed and I cry. I think my dad is doing this on purpose, leaving me here in the room. I'm meant to learn something.

Before I've time to think about it, I'm standing with my hand on the door handle. I let go and race back to my bed. I pull up my feet as if the ground is toxic. I sit there for a while, wiping my eyes on my sleeve. My dad won't be coming to fetch me for a long time. Yesterday morning, I listened out for all the noises of the house, doors opening and closing. I'm almost certain that the old lady doesn't leave the drawing room until she goes to make lunch for us. I should have at least a couple of hours to make it down the stairs and out into the garden.

I OPEN THE door; I hold my shoes in my hand. I walk down the passage as quietly as I can. I've reached the top of the stairs when I stop. One of the doors is ajar.

I notice something inside. It looks like hair, but I'm not sure. I know it'll bug me for the rest of the day if I don't find out what it is. I go back and push open the door. The room I'm looking into is filled with antlers. Not just one or three: it's crammed with them, all four walls from floor to ceiling. No furniture, only antlers from deer, and gazelles, and every imaginable horned animal. I bolt down the stairs and out the front door.

I'M SITTING ON the grass drawing when my dad appears between the trees. He smiles; I think he's proud to find me here.

"This is a strange house," I say to him while we eat liver pâté sandwiches with meat jelly.

"People are much stranger than they're prepared to admit." He takes a bite of a large pickle. "So why shouldn't their houses be?"

THE NEXT DAY I stand at the top of the stairs again. I know that I should just walk down them. Not just walk, but hurry as much as I can without running. Down the stairs, out the door. And yet I stay where I am. I managed it yesterday, I still have all my arms and legs.

I pick the door opposite the room with the antlers. This door isn't ajar, but neither is it locked. A little boy looks out at me from the dimly lit room. When I raise my hand to my mouth, the boy copies my movement. I enter. The room is full of mirrors. From floor to ceiling, in wood or gold frames. I stand in the middle. I see an ear, a nose, a shin, some hair, the shoes in my hand. A little boy who looks like me, cut into small pieces and stuck on the walls. There are more mirrors in the ceiling; the boy looks down at me, very small and a little bit scared. When I leave the room I'm dizzy.

As I walk down the stairs, I promise myself to stop being so nosy. I don't want to take any more chances.

IT'S EARLY IN the morning; I'm lying under the blanket, keeping my eyes closed. I hear my dad get dressed. He walks along the passage and down the stairs. The front door opens and closes. I leap out of bed. I've become a thief who doesn't steal. I explore the house in stocking feet, a new room every day. I find one full of stuffed animals: dogs and cats, beavers and squirrels. Animals with bared teeth, all of them facing whoever enters the room. They stare at me until I leave. In another room there's only a single stuffed bison with its head facing the wall as if it's ashamed. It's much bigger than the doors and windows; the house must have been built around it.

I keep away from the old lady's drawing room, but I investigate the rest of the house, from the ground floor to the loft. I follow the loft beam to the end of a long corridor. I reach a red door. I push down the handle, but it won't open. I rattle it to make sure it's not just stuck.

Not all the rooms are as exciting as the first one I visited, but there's always something to discover, such as Chinese porcelain painted with tiny brushstrokes. A single cup tells a story about dragons and emperors, a mighty battle with hundreds of tiny arrows flying through the air. In another room a whole wall is covered with butterflies on pins. Hundreds of them in as many different colors.

In the afternoon, I sit on the grass drawing whatever room I've visited that morning. I've reached the eighth page of my sketchbook when I realize something's wrong. Something much stranger than anything I've found in the rooms.

I walk around the house and draw it from the outside. Two stories, clad in broad wooden planks. I draw every single window. I try to draw everything as it is; many times, I have to erase everything and start over. It's not until I've finished drawing that I realize what's wrong. The outside of the house doesn't match the rooms inside.

The next morning I make notes in my sketchbook as I walk from room to room. I tap the panels. Where there ought to be doors there are walls with pictures of brown bears with fish in their mouths.

I finish up on the top floor. Again I stand in front of the locked red door. The explanation must lie behind it.

At night I dream about the door. It swings open all by itself; I'm blinded by a light coming from inside. I cross the threshold, then I wake up.

When my dad has risen and gone to work in the garden, I start looking for the key to the red door.

I'm no longer interested in the huge collection of walking sticks with carved animal heads or the curved sabers and the shrunken heads. All I care about is finding the key. The old lady is so tiny that if she had it on her, it would bulge like a bone sticking out.

I'M DRAWING WHEN I hear a noise in the grass behind me. A slither like a rattlesnake or possibly an anaconda. When I turn around I see something that scares me much more than a wide-open jaw with fangs. The old lady isn't hidden by the shadows, nor does she have the blinding sunlight behind her. She stands only a few meters away from me.

Somewhere far away my dad starts up the chainsaw again. I look down at the sketchbook; if you meet a bear in the forest then you must stand very still. Dogs can smell fear. I start drawing a dog eating an ice cream cone; it holds it between its paws as it licks off the whipped cream. My hands are shaking, but I keep drawing, hoping the old lady will disappear of her own accord.

"I've heard you walking around the house," she says to my back. "You think I can't hear you because I'm old."

The hole in her face is a mouth; more words come out of it.

"You think that because you tiptoe around in your socks you won't make a noise. This is an old house. A wooden house. And wood creaks."

I can no longer take my eyes off her, even though I try.

"I've lived here all my life. I've grown old with the house. I can hear you when I lie in my bed. I always know exactly where you are. I hear you in the kitchen, pulling out drawers. I hear you walk up the stairs; I know when you open the cupboard doors, when you rummage around the bottom drawer in the sideboard. I know this house. I could put it on my back like a snail."

I want to run, I want to hide in the garden, but I stay where I am.

"I'm offering you a deal," she says. "I'm going to show you what's behind the red door. I'll go up there with you. I'll give you the key so you can open it yourself. In return you have to do something for me."

I try to keep my eyes on her white hair.

"Do we have a deal?" she asks.

I feel my head move up and down. The old lady starts walking back to the house. Just before the terrace she turns around: "Are you coming?"

I walk right behind her up the stairs, up to the top floor. We go down the passage to the locked door. The keyhole looks at me; it's very big and a little bit scratched after all the different keys I've tried to insert into it.

The old lady holds out a bony fist towards me, unclenches it, and shows me a black key.

"So, do we have a deal?"

I nod.

"You're not a very talkative boy."

I try not to touch the palm of her hand when I take the key.

At first it refuses to go into the keyhole, possibly because my hands are shaking.

I try a couple of times. I'm about to give up, it must be the wrong key, the old lady must be mistaken, she hasn't been up here in years. I feel a certain relief, the deal's off, I'm going to forget all about the door. I'll sit on the grass and draw dogs and ice cream cones, wear down my pencil. My dad will finish in the garden, tomorrow will be like today and we can move on.

I hear a click when the key goes into the lock. I turn it around and open the door.

I blink a couple of times. I'm staring right into a brick wall. There's nothing behind the door, not even a big cupboard, just straight rows of red bricks with mortar in between.

I touch the bricks to be sure. Then I put the key back in the old lady's outstretched hand.

"Now it's your turn to do something for me. That was the deal."

We go back down the stairs and into her drawing room, which I haven't been inside since we first came to the house. We walk past the porcelain figurines and the dark leather furniture. She opens the door to a smaller room with bookcases from floor to ceiling.

"You know how to read, don't you?"

I nod.

"I thought so. You're your father's son."

She sits down in an armchair underneath the window. The sun blinds me so I can only see her outline.

All the books are bound in red leather; the title is printed in golden letters down the spine.

"Third shelf, far right. It's about a huge whale."

I wipe dust off the book's cover, sit down on the chair she points out, and open the book. My voice is feeble and it trembles when I read the first words aloud.

MY DAD'S T-SHIRT is soaked in sweat when he emerges from the bushes. Again he's scratched and covered in leaves. We sit down on the terrace and he looks at the drawings I've done during the morning. Many of them are of whales.

Then I hear the old lady behind us; the fabric of her skirt rustles as she moves.

"How is the garden coming along?" she asks.

My dad makes to stand up.

"Don't get up, you work hard."

He wipes his hands on his trousers.

"I know what it could look like," he says. "Now that we live here as well. But there's more work than I first thought."

"It's a big garden."

"That's not exactly what I mean."

"I know. Last year, another young man came. I told him to take it easy, but he worked every day from morning till night. The first night he grinned like a man who has just survived a shipwreck; a week later, he looked like a convict. Then he vanished for good. I think he gave up. But, who knows, perhaps you'll stumble across him in the wilderness."

She laughs to herself.

I look across at my dad. It's not until now that I notice that his cheeks seem sunken, his eyes have grown bigger. Perhaps I haven't seen it because he smiles all the time.

"What kind of tools did he use?" my dad asks.

The old lady hesitates as if she hasn't quite understood the question.

"His own," she then replies. "He brought his own tools."

My dad nods, runs his thumb across the metal plate on the chainsaw with the image of the bear.

"Tonight I'll put a little extra bacon in the soup," the old lady says.

I follow her inside the house; it's time for me to read to her. Always when the sun is high in the sky and she can sit below the window and be only a silhouette.

Often I lose track of time. I'm on the ship with Ahab. Every day we come close to catching the great big white whale.

Some days I don't stop reading until there's not enough light in the room to make out the letters. Then her face emerges from the shadows. The first few times I nearly dropped the book. I said sorry and raced out of the room. Slowly I've grown used to her appearance. Just like I've grown used to the smell of wood when the summer sun has roasted the house all day long.

AT NIGHT THE water comes. I see it burst through the trees, taking with it big and small plants. The old wooden house releases its grip on the earth and floats away like a ship. Only the three of us are left in the whole world. The birds fly above us. The sky is theirs now and they screech loudly. Cries of joy: no high-rise buildings, no telephone poles, only the open sky. They've yet to discover that they've no place to land.

I READ THE last sentence in the book. I can now look at the old lady for several minutes without blinking.

We sit there, the two of us, neither of us saying anything. The words of the book still linger in the air between us. Then she straightens up in her chair.

"I tricked you. And you know it, you're not stupid."

She wipes her mouth with a white fabric napkin, then she spreads it across her knee.

"All you had to do was ask me for the key, ask me what was behind the door. But you were scared."

I don't say anything.

"And when you finally stood there, staring at the brick wall, you could have asked: 'Why?' It was the only word you had to say, but you were still scared. Didn't you think it was odd, a brick wall in a wooden house?"

I don't know what to reply.

"Of course you thought it was strange. You're not stupid. But you were scared. And sometimes they're the same thing."

She looks straight at me.

"Let's make a new deal," she suggests. "If you carry on reading to me, I'll tell you the story of the house. No cheating this time. I'll tell you everything I know. I think that'll answer some of your questions."

I still make no reply, but I don't think I need to, either.

"Very well. You'll get the story about the house, but not today."

I feel my head nod. This time I'm not scared.

"Fifth shelf, three books in," she says then.

I have to stand on tiptoes to reach it.

I dust off the book. *Twenty Thousand Leagues Under the Sea*.

It won't be the last book we read this summer. The days disappear into the books. When the sun turns red, my eyes are dry and they sting. When my dad and I eat dinner in the kitchen, I sit surrounded by musketeers. Outside the window a man rides past on a donkey.

The next day I'm back in the library reading to the old lady. If I struggle with a word, a word I don't quite understand, she helps me. She doesn't even have to look in the book. I think she must know what it says on every single page.

She leans back in the armchair and says: "This was always my favorite room, being surrounded by books. Now you know why. If we had another year, we could make a start on the great Russians."

It's early evening when I come out on the terrace. My dad is smoking a cigarette. He runs his hand through my hair.

"Looks like you've got yourself a new teacher," he smiles.

THE OLD LADY leans on my arm as we walk down the stairs. The car is parked in front of the house; my dad stands next to it, waiting for us. He's wearing a brown suit the old lady has lent him. It smelled of mothballs when he put it on. Underneath it he has a vest and a tie. He has shaved and smoothed back his hair with soap. He looks like a man who has stepped out of an old photograph.

My dad opens the car door and helps the old lady in. Then he rushes around the car to open the other door for me.

I sit in the back next to the old lady. She wears a hat with a veil that covers most of her face. She could easily appear in the same photo as my dad. I wear long trousers and a freshly ironed T-shirt. We've dabbed the scuffed leather on my shoes with a black marker.

We drive down the avenue. Here, in daylight, the car's interior of dark wood and leather makes it look like a small sitting room.

We reach a country lane; the old lady puts her hat on the seat between us.

"My mother used to say that a lady never takes off her hat, be it in church or in the smallest room. She was buried with hers on." The old lady smoothes the veil. "I've always found hats to be terribly itchy."

The country lane turns into tarmac; we're nearing the town. My dad drives smoothly in the traffic. Only rarely are we stopped by a red light. People turn around to look at the black car, some wave.

"I hope you can find it," the old lady says. "I know my description wasn't very accurate. It's been years since I was last there."

My dad smiles at her in the rearview mirror.

"If it's still there, then I'll find it, don't you worry."

I believe him. My dad once told me about a deer mouse that lives in Wyoming. It's no bigger than the nail on my little finger, but it can travel several days' journey away from its home. The equivalent of 160 kilometers for a human being. And yet it always finds its way back. It needs no signs, never has to ask for directions. It always finds its way home. It's always been the exact opposite for my dad and me.

The speakers in the car crackle; my dad turns the big shiny metal knob on the radio. He keeps turning it past human voices and guitar playing until he finds something he likes.

We leave the town to the sound of a trumpet solo. We continue along the road past yellow clover fields and churches.

The engine lets out a little grunt when my dad turns off the ignition.

"Does this look familiar?" he asks.

We've left the main road and are now in a gravel parking lot surrounded by trees. The old lady looks out the window.

"Yes," she says, sounding as if she can't quite believe it. "Yes . . . this is it."

The old lady puts on her hat and lets the veil fall to cover her face. My dad opens the car door; I can hear the sea. From the parking lot we walk down a narrow path until we reach a half-timbered house in yellow brick. People sit outside at tables with white tablecloths; their knives and forks sparkle in the sun. They turn their heads, their eyes flit from me to my dad in the brown suit and then linger a little too long on the old lady. Then they quickly look down at their food.

A waiter shows us to a table somewhat apart from the others. He fixes a white fabric tablecloth to our table with pegs which my dad says are made from silver. The menus we're given are bound in soft ox leather.

We eat sandwiches, but not the kind you'd put in a packed lunch, the filling squeezed in between a slice of cucumber and half a tomato. Here the fish fillet covers the whole bread slice and the prawns fight for space on top of it, pushing each other out of the way and nearly toppling off the plate in the process. My dad drinks his beer in large mouthfuls, the old lady sips hers and wipes the rim of the glass with her napkin. They toast each other with schnapps.

I can feel people looking at us while we eat. When I catch their eyes, they quickly avert theirs. Slowly they all turn away until we're surrounded by people's backs.

"We used to come here in the summer," the old lady says. "Every summer. I didn't look quite like this back then. It's gotten worse with age."

She dabs her lips with the napkin.

"In those days I never knew why people stared. I thought people always looked at each other like that. I used to stare back at them in the same manner until my father told me not to. I didn't understand why."

For dessert I have chocolate mousse with fresh raspberries. My dad and the old lady drink coffee from small cups. We can't see the sea from here, but when the wind changes direction, we can smell seaweed and salt water. The seagulls fly high above us.

THE OLD LADY keeps nodding off on the way home. Then she straightens up in her seat.

"I thought if only I got to see the garden, then that would be enough . . ." she says. "But today . . . I so enjoyed today."

I can make out her lips under the veil. Now I know what she looks like when she smiles.

WE'RE SITTING IN the library; the old lady in the armchair, me on the chair beside the door.

"We made a deal," she says. "I'm afraid that if we put it off for much longer, I won't be able to keep my side of it."

She takes a tiny sip of water from her glass, barely enough to moisten her lips.

"Today I'm going to tell you a story. Pass it on to you before it disappears. It's up to you whether or not you believe it. That's less important."

She looks at me; she wants to be sure she has my full attention.

"My father was an old man when he built this house, not much younger than I am now. You're too young to protest, fortunately. I know I'm old. Like milk that has been left in the fridge for too long. It has gone off. But this story isn't about me."

She leans back in her chair. Puts her hands in her lap.

"My father was apprenticed to a watchmaker. On the day he finished his apprenticeship, he boarded a ship to

America. Several passengers fell ill. Many didn't survive. When my father went ashore he was yellow all over. Thin and yellow. He walked the streets in the new country, but he couldn't find a job and he deteriorated even further. He was almost dead when he met a salesman from Smith & Wesson.

"The man said he needed someone like my dad. He even paid his train fare to Massachusetts, where Smith & Wesson had their factory. They made firearms and they quickly saw how skilled my father was with his hands. Don't forget he was a watchmaker and used to working with tiny pieces of metal under a magnifying glass.

"He worked for them for ten years. By that point, he'd invented his own rifle. It was called the Johnson—that was how they pronounced his surname. The rifle was very expensive, but it could shoot further and with greater accuracy than any rifle they'd ever seen. For more than thirty years he made rifles for people who wanted to shoot bison. Or at least that was what they said. 'Shoot bison'—even though more often they shot Indians. The bullets in a Johnson rifle weren't as big as in many other guns. A buffalo wouldn't necessarily have died had it been hit, but the bullet would go straight through a human being. It had become a rifle for shooting people. My father became a very rich man. But as he got older, he grew very troubled; he knew what his rifles had been used for. How terribly good and how terribly accurate they had been."

The old lady takes a couple of deep breaths, closes her eyes. The room has grown dark. For a moment I wonder if she has fallen asleep.

Her voice is hoarse when she resumes her story.

"First my father moved to the East Coast, but it wasn't far enough. At night he could still hear the souls of the Indians in the wind. So he moved back to Denmark and built this house, a house like they build in America. He had the cladding brought over from Sweden by ferry. Not one nail was hammered into place without his watching it being done. When he had lived here a couple of years, the housekeeper bore his child. That child was me. Possibly in another attempt to confuse the spirits."

While she was speaking she fetched tiny bits of her story from the ceiling; now she looks straight at me.

"It might sound strange. But that was my father's intention. To confuse the spirits. The spirits of the Indians. Trap them between the walls in rooms with no doors. That's why the house is the way it is. It's an old tradition from before we stopped seeing the things we don't understand. Your father knows what I'm talking about. Your father is a very wise man, never forget that. No matter what people say. I've a drawer filled with clippings, articles he has written to magazines and newspapers. He didn't always cut hedges. But that's not my story and I'm not the person to tell it. It's your father's and yours. Now you know almost everything there is to know about the house."

THE OLD LADY leans on me; we follow the trail of decapitated flowers from the bottom of the steps, across the lawn and down to the first apple and pear trees. There my dad is waiting for us with a rucksack over his shoulder. This morning he filled it with bottles of fruit punch and rolls the old lady had baked.

"Provisions," he declared. "We'll need them."

My dad pulls branches aside and shows us the start of the path he has spent the summer clearing.

Again the old lady takes my arm and we walk in between the trees. The path is about five feet wide; it winds around bushes with white, yellow, and red flowers. The earth underfoot is uneven and knobbly.

"My garden!" the old lady exclaims.

We reach a wooden bench cleared of branches and trailing plants.

"Would you like to sit down for a moment?" my dad asks.

"Not yet."

With her index finger she traces the grooves of letters carved into the back of the bench. They've almost disappeared and are illegible. They make her smile. Then she walks on, she no longer needs my arm, soon she's the one leading the way. She stops only to enjoy the sight of a plant or a bush or wildflowers clinging to a tree trunk.

A rusty child's bicycle hangs in the air, lifted up by the branches that envelop it.

"So that's what happened to it," the old lady laughs.

"I couldn't make myself take it down," my dad says.

WE REACH A clearing between the trees. I don't know for how long we've walked, an hour, maybe more. My dad takes a picnic blanket from the rucksack and spreads it across a tree stump for the old lady to sit on. My dad and I sit on the forest floor. He finds the fruit punch and the rolls. Some are filled with spiced meatloaf, others with mature cheese. When I take the first bite, I realize how hungry I am.

The old lady nibbles her roll and drinks only tiny sips of her fruit punch. I have a pee behind a tree when I've finished eating; my dad helps the old lady to her feet and we walk on.

First I hear a light tapping on the leaves above our heads. Then the rain breaks through the treetops.

"We can shelter over here," my dad says. I hurry under the tree.

The old lady finds a spot on the path, a spot with a clear view of the sky. She stands there while the rain washes down on her, looks up at the sky and laughs with her mouth open.

"Summer rain," she says, looking at us with rainwater in her eyes. "Feel how warm it is." Her dress clings to her body. "Today's the last day of summer. Autumn starts tomorrow. You'll see if I'm right."

When the rain is nothing but a light drizzle, we move on. The garden smells of warm earth and sweet flowers.

"My father brought seeds home with him," the old lady says. Her voice is labored, but she carries on walking. "Others he had sent from South America, Africa, and Australia. People said they couldn't grow here. That they'd never survive the Danish climate. He just laughed at them."

We pass a small bird bath which my dad has cleared. The old lady leans on it.

"The seeds my father sowed came from plants older than mankind. They weren't cultivated by a botanist. They didn't come from plants that just looked pretty or smelled nice, but from plants that refused to die. Kill rather than be killed."

The old lady takes a deep breath and carries on walking. The shadows have grown longer.

On the way back to the house, the path seems narrower. I'm convinced that the trees have started growing again, that they're closing up the path behind us.

My dad holds the branches back; we step out from behind the last bush and we're back on the lawn. The sun is setting behind the house in red and orange hues. Today all three of us have been explorers.

The old lady smiles at me. Her leather shoes are muddy, her dress is still wet from the rain, and she sways slightly. The exertion seems to have made her light-headed.

"Thank you," she says. "I . . . thank you."

She presses my dad's hand, gives us both a peck on the cheek, then says she wants to go inside for a lie-down.

My dad sits on the terrace. He looks across the garden while he smokes a cigarette. I fetch him a beer from the kitchen; he drinks it without taking his eyes off all the greenery in front of us. I've never seen him so content.

WE SHOWER ON the first floor. I scrub my dad's back with a coarse sponge. His neck and shoulders are covered in aphids. He checks me carefully for ticks.

My dad prepares a big plate of open sandwiches: liver pâté, pastrami and meat jelly, cheese with bell pepper. He makes coffee on the stove. When the table is set for three, he asks me to fetch the old lady who, he says, would probably like to join us.

I find her in the armchair in the drawing room. She sits very still; she's still wearing her summer dress. At first I think she's asleep. I take a couple of steps into the room, and then I'm sure that she won't wake up again.

I'm not scared, maybe because she's smiling.

WE WALK FROM room to room. My dad fills plastic bags with the old lady's things. He takes a book from the bookcase; behind it lies a wad of banknotes. He opens the wardrobe in the old lady's bedroom, takes out a broad-brimmed hat which he empties of gold jewelry. In the drawing room he takes porcelain figurines from the windowsill. Three dogs playing with a ball, a small shepherdess. He wraps them in towels. He takes a painting from the wall, an oil painting in a good frame. He reads the back of the canvass, looks over at me before he puts it down. He sits down on the sofa next to me and takes my hand.

"I don't want you to think that we're nicking stuff."

My cheeks are wet.

"When you own a house like this one, with a garden, yes, and a car. And books. The books on the bookcases alone. Then you always have a lot of relations. Even if you never see them."

I can't stop sobbing, he holds me tight. I try not to look at the old lady in the armchair a few meters away from us.

"'Give them a day or two,' she would say, 'and they'll start ripping up the floorboards. Looking for the X that marks the spot on the treasure map.' She would have wanted us to take what we could."

My dad cups my head in his hands, looks into my eyes.

"You made her very happy," he says. "You made her incredibly happy."

We continue through the house. It's like working your way down a shopping list. My eyes are still wet; I wipe them on my sleeve. I've never wanted to stay in a place as much as this. We could smash all the clocks. Break every mirror so the old lady would never have to look at herself. We could stay here until my hair was just as long as my dad's, until I could grow a beard like his. We could drive around in the old black car, go shopping, but never buy a newspaper. No one would ever find us here. This is the first place we've lived where I haven't been woken up by my dad's nightmares.

THE ENGINE GROWLS; the trunk is stuffed with our belongings, new and old.

We're back in the city today. It's just as big and noisy as when we first arrived. My dad parks the car beneath a sign with luminous red letters. The hotel is squashed in between a bar with dark windows and what my dad says is a strip club. He carries the suitcases into reception, hits the bell. We wait a long time. I stare at the carpet; the pattern is hidden under several layers of dirt.

NOW I'M SITTING on the bed. I'm alone. My dad has gone to take back the car. It'll be hours before he returns on the butcher's bike. The suitcase lies unopened next to me. I can hear noises from the street, from the other rooms. New sounds. Our new home.

MY DAD TAKES a bite of his crusty roll, drinks the last drop of coffee, and gets up.

"Do you want anything?"

I shake my head. He walks past a table with two young girls who look like they've been crying. My dad fills his cup with coffee from the Thermos on the table by the wall.

When we sat down in the hotel restaurant I was sure I must have stepped in something. Then I realized that it was the carpet that smelled of wet hand towels, dirty dogs, and cigarettes. My dad piles his plate high with bread rolls, a couple of slices of cheese, and some jam. I try to keep my eyes to myself. A man with a chunky silver chain around his neck sits at the neighboring table. He has drawings on his fingers. His hair is black and cut very close to his scalp. When I asked my dad, he said the man was probably from Bulgaria or Romania. The man forms patterns with matchsticks on the table in front of him. He makes a star. When he has put down the last matchstick, he picks them all up again and begins a different pattern. He meets my gaze and I quickly look down at my plate.

My dad sits down again opposite me. He has spilled a little coffee in the saucer.

"What separates man from any other species," he says, wiping the saucer with a paper napkin, "is his ability to adapt."

I follow his gaze to a man in the corner. He's wearing a suit and tie. On the chair next to him lies a brown leather briefcase. The man's hair is smooth, with a part on the left. On one cheek he has a small cut from shaving. He reads his newspaper, hums to himself, and eats bread rolls.

My dad hands me two sugar lumps to suck.

THERE'S A SMALL cinema close to the hotel. The girl who sells tickets smiles at my dad and brings him coffee while we wait for the film to start.

We watch German, French, Russian, and Polish films.

Often I don't read the subtitles; I look at the screen and decide what they're talking about.

We must build a killer robot in the basement, Alexei.

Or,

When will the killer robot be ready, Alexei?

The robot is always just out of the shot, shining like silver and ready to attack.

THERE ARE FIVE hot dog stands near the hotel. My dad thinks it's important that we try them all, to find out who makes the best hot dog. You can't just eat one hot dog at each stand. You have to come back.

My dad has his hot dogs with everything. I don't like the strong mustard and the raw onions.

"He'll have everything but that," my dad says to Ulla from Ulla's Hot Dog Stand, to Morten from Star Sausages, and to Svend from Svend's Snack Bar. Once we've been there a couple of times, they too know what "everything but that" means.

"You can't eat a good hot dog without getting your fingers sticky," my dad says, ketchup at the corner of his mouth. "And not just your fingers; your hands should be covered in the stuff."

AGAIN I FALL asleep to sounds: the whistling of my dad's nostrils next to me in bed, noises from the street, cars braking hard, tires squealing against the wet tarmac. Drunken people chatting, arguing, shouting beneath our windows.

Every night I hear a couple of fights. The first few times they wake me up, and I go over to the window. I see the doorman from the strip club push a man so hard he goes flying over the hood of a parked car. That, too, has its own sound.

I learn to tell the difference between a police siren and the siren of an ambulance. The hotel also makes noises. Drunken people have a special way of walking and they're bad at whispering.

"How much?" they say. "How much did we agree on?"

I snuggle up close to my dad. When he scratches himself in his sleep, he ends up tickling me. The first few nights the sounds keep me awake; they're more alien and intrusive than in any of the other places we've lived before.

ONE MORNING MY dad says that the summer holidays are over, that it's time to go back to school.

"You're in Grade Two now. You should expect things to get a lot more difficult."

There's a new subject on my timetable, History. We start with the Second World War. My dad says it's a good place to start.

We don't have a table, so we lie on the bed. While my dad talks I see roaring Messerschmitts leave trails of smoke across the ceiling of the hotel room.

On the wall I see Tiger Tanks appear over green hilltops; they're enormous and they plow up the grass. Yellow flames erupt from their cannons.

We spend a whole week on Hitler. We go to the library and look at photographs of Hitler giving a speech. Hitler raising his arm towards the sky, all his fingers pointing. Hitler patting a deer. My dad flicks to a new picture. It's grainy and at first I can't see what it's supposed to be; it looks like black shadows twisted together. They're human beings, my dad says. Then, suddenly, I can make out arms and legs. Naked bodies, as thin as the matchstick men I used to draw when I was little. I start to cry. My dad catches up with me on the sidewalk outside the library.

"There's a reason I showed you that," he says, as he dries my cheeks. "When you see the world, when you really see it and you don't close your eyes like the man over there," my dad points to a man across the street, "or that lady with her shopping bag. When you see things as they really are, you also have a responsibility. Then you have to do something."

My dad takes my hand and we start walking.

"People saw Hitler," he says. "They heard him speak. He was a great speaker. Do you remember the film we saw with him in it?"

I nod; we watched it on a small television with the librarian.

"He looked funny, didn't he? A small, posturing man."

I couldn't help laughing when we saw it.

"But the people in that crowd, they saw hope. They loved him. Even though no one would admit it afterwards."

We continue down the street. We go into the kiosk on the corner and I'm allowed to choose an ice cream, any one I like. I can only swallow a couple of bites.

I'M WOKEN UP by a scratching on the door to our hotel room.

It sounds like a mouse, tiny sharp teeth nibbling. I try to go back to sleep, but the noise persists. I tug at my dad's arm until he wakes up and I stand right behind him when he opens the door.

It takes a couple of seconds before I recognize the man from the hotel restaurant in the suit and white shirt. Now he looks as if he has been in a fight with wild dogs.

"I'm sorry," the man says. "This is all wrong. I'm so very sorry."

He scratches his head with the key.

"But this happens to be my room."

"Which number is your room?"

"212."

"This is 112, you want the next floor."

The man stands there for a moment, swaying. Then he starts to walk down the corridor. After a couple of steps he bumps into the wall and collapses on the floor. When he has managed to get back on his feet, he continues to the next door and again tries to insert his key into the lock.

My dad puts on his trousers, lights a cigarette, and takes a couple of drags before he chucks it into a half-empty cup of coffee.

The man in the corridor is still trying to unlock the door. He's now closer to the wall than the keyhole. My dad takes him by the shoulders and steers him down the hall and up the stairs.

On the fifth step the man lies down and hugs his knees.

"We could always roll him up in a rug," my dad says to me, and grins.

Then he gets the man back on his feet and pushes him in front of him. When we reach room 212, my dad takes the key from the man's hand and unlocks the door. The room is filled with bottles, big bottles that have had babies and made a lot of little bottles. In between lie densely written, scrunched-up sheets of paper. My dad opens the window to air out the room and helps the man into bed; he takes off his shoes and throws the blanket over him.

WE WAKE UP late the next morning. The street below us is buzzing with cars and people. We walk to the bakery to buy breakfast, which we eat on one of the benches by the lakes that divide the city in two. When we've had enough, my dad takes out the bag of stale bread and we feed the ducks. Today we play Hit the

Swan. It's a game we've invented because the swans think they're better than the other birds and because many of them hiss at us and demand more bread. For that reason we're allowed to throw stale bread at them. You get maximum points if you can deliver a soft underhand throw so that the bread lands and stays between the wings.

We walk back to the hotel and up to room 212. The door is open; the man is sitting on the bed. He's wearing a shirt and tie, but no trousers.

"Let's get you dressed," my dad says, picking up his trousers from the floor and tossing them over to him.

It takes the man ten minutes to tie his shoelaces. He does what my dad tells him without protest, without saying very much; he brushes his teeth, splashes water on his face.

My dad looks in the man's wardrobe, rummages through his suitcase which, like the floor, is filled with crumpled notes.

"Do you have any other clothes?"

"I used to, but . . ."

"Not anymore?"

"No. I don't really know what happened to them."

We walk down the street. A couple of times my dad has to grip the man by the shoulders and point him in the right direction. In daylight he looks even worse than last night. We reach a small dry cleaner's; the man behind the counter is talking on the telephone. His shirt sleeves are rolled up; on his forearm he has a tattoo of a lady in a bikini. He looks at the man in the filthy suit and carries on talking into the handset. I think he's hoping we'll get bored and leave, but we stay put until he hangs up.

"How long would it take you to clean a suit?" my dad asks.

"Next week at the earliest." With his eyes he says: *Preferably never*.

My dad leans across the counter.

"I don't know this man very well. We just happen to be staying in the same hotel. But I know what it's like to be in trouble."

The man behind the counter scratches the tattoo.

"This guy was sent over here by his boss in Jutland. He was to meet an important customer and come home with signatures on several contracts. But he runs into the wrong woman and ends up getting a beating in an alleyway. He has lost the contracts and most of his money. He has been drinking these past few days, drinking up the last of his money to get over it."

While my dad speaks, I can see the man in the suit straighten up. He is starting to believe my dad's story.

"Now he's scared to go home to Jutland. And as for the meeting with the big customer . . . just take a look at him, he's not a pretty sight."

The guy behind the counter nods. The suit will now take just over an hour to dry clean. We wait in the shop; I can see the man's naked knees stick out from behind the curtain. When the suit is done, my dad is told to put his wallet back in his pocket.

"This one's on the house."

We leave the dry cleaner's. The man is wearing his suit; once again his shirt is white and freshly ironed. He walks down the street holding his head high. His suit gives off a little steam in the cold air.

When we moved into the hotel room there were bags along all the walls. I played on the floor where hangers from the wardrobe became ships racing each other across the carpet.

My dad would say: "Be careful with that one," pointing to a bag. "I think that's the one with the china."

I wake up at the sound of the door opening. My dad has been up early and yet another bag has gone. Slowly the room has been emptied. He has a comic for me and a pile of newspapers for himself.

We eat sandwiches and spill fried onions on the bed.

"I thought we'd get a bit more money for that stuff," he says.

I no longer have to be careful where I play.

The walls are dark red; the lights are hidden behind colored sheets of glass or plastic palm trees.

Outside the sun is shining, but it could be midnight in here.

My dad helps me up on the barstool; my feet dangle high above the floor.

"You don't have to be a big guy to do this job," the man behind the bar says. "The last thing I need is yet another dumb knucklehead pumped full of steroids. No shortage of those."

Around us, chairs have been put upside down on the tables with their legs in the air. At the back of the room there's a small stage.

"You wouldn't believe how many guys I've had to fire. How many survive only a week or even just a single night. Men with big muscles, but tiny brains and even tinier dicks."

Then he remembers that I'm here.

"Sorry," he says. "What the hell, we're all boys."

He puts a glass in front of me and fills it with orange juice.

"Sure you don't want some vodka in there?"

He laughs and is about to say something else when we hear the door open and footsteps. Two men spill in through the curtain. Their voices are slurred; they lean on each other for support.

The man behind the bar puts down his tea towel.

"Let's consider this your job interview. Can you get them out of here?"

My dad nods, takes a drag on his cigarette, and leaves it in the ashtray. He steps down from the barstool and walks up to the men.

"Gentlemen, I'm afraid I'm going to have to disappoint you," he says. "Unfortunately we're not open yet."

"The door was open, so you have to be." The man who is talking is standing with his legs apart and his chest puffed out.

"I'm very sorry." My dad continues towards them with his arms out like a goalie ready to catch a ball. "If you want to look at naked ladies at this time of day, you need to go down to Istedgade. The girls down there take off all their clothes and give lap dances as well."

The man stays where he is until my dad is only a meter away from him. Then his shoulders slump. The men follow my dad, who holds the curtain open for them.

"Come back tomorrow," I hear him say. "You'll be more than welcome."

The door closes behind them.

My dad takes his cigarette from the ashtray. The man behind the bar chuckles.

"I don't bloody believe it."

He takes my dad's glass from the counter and tips the contents into the sink.

"Christ Almighty, you were born for this job. I think I can take a vacation now."

He takes another bottle from the shelf. Sets out two small glasses and fills them to the brim. The liquid looks like apple juice.

"You wouldn't believe what I charge for this. One single glass and the bottle is paid for."

They clink their glasses.

"Do you think you could tie your hair back?" the man asks. "Put some Brylcreem in it, brush it back?"

My dad nods.

"Then you've got yourself a job." They shake hands on it. "I'll get you a dark suit, don't you worry about that."

THAT FIRST EVENING I follow my dad to work. He smells of soap, and he's wearing his new suit.

One of the other bouncers is already standing outside the strip club, a big black man. The streetlights reflect in his bare scalp. He fills his suit completely; one wrong move and it would split.

"I'll take good care of your dad," he says, and lifts me up so I dangle in the air. "Don't you worry about a thing. I'll take care of him."

I'M SITTING IN the windowsill looking down on the street. I can see one of my dad's shoulders, or sometimes his back, when he takes a couple steps out onto the sidewalk. I see people come and go, see taxis pull up in front of the strip club and men get out. My dad holds the door open for them. Other men come alone; they walk down the street in thick coats. Some are allowed in, others are told to move on.

A young couple with backpacks stop below my window. They stand in front of the hotel for a long time, looking from the number above the door back to the piece of paper the girl is holding in her hands. I can't hear what they're saying; their words are drowned out by the traffic. The young man shakes his head and they carry on down the street.

I keep my eyes on my dad. Whenever he disappears from sight, I start counting. I get to nineteen; I get to twenty-four. I lean out the window, but I still can't see him. When I get to thirty-two, I can see his elbow. Then more of him. He has one arm around a man's shoulder; his other hand around the man's wrist. My dad straightens out the knot of his tie. The man leans against my dad for a little while before he's sent down the street with a pat on the back.

The young couple returns; now the guy is in front, there's distance between them. Their backpacks appear to have grown heavier since the first time they were here; they enter the door to the hotel without speaking to each other.

I look at my dad. As long as I keep my eyes on him, nothing bad can happen.

THE DOOR OPENS, my dad's footsteps across the floor become the sound of raindrops on the roof of a bus that will keep driving all night long and not stop until it reaches a distant country. We get out and feed giraffes; we give the apes tiny pieces of bread from our packed lunches.

My dad turns over in his sleep. I can smell beer and tobacco and I know that all's well now.

Some nights my dad doesn't get back until the sun comes through the curtains, dyeing the room orange. Then he brings me breakfast. Other days he wraps me up warm and we walk down to the lakes and eat bread from the bakery. Some days I have school, other days we go for long walks across the city. When we cross Rådhuspladsen, I don't look up at the clock on the town hall. The hours pass too quickly and soon my dad will have to go to work. I've brushed my teeth and I'm lying in bed. My dad tells me the next part of the fairy tale about the King and the Prince. Every day I hope that he'll forget what the time is, I hope that his eyes will grow heavy, that he'll fall asleep in his shirt so that I can take off his shoes. It never happens. He kisses my forehead, takes his suit jacket from the back of the chair, and I hear the door slam shut.

ONE NIGHT WHEN my dad gets back, he curses all the way through the room. He closes the door to the bathroom behind him and stays in there for a long time. The sound of the tap becomes a huge waterfall; our little boat is heading for the precipice.

I wake up before my dad. The city is still quiet, the sun's on its way up. With sleep in my eyes I go to the bathroom to pee; I turn my head and see my dad's shirt. It's on a hanger on the shower curtain rail. The shirt is wet and crumpled and it's still dripping. On the front and at the end of both sleeves there are big pink stains so it looks like someone spilled fruit punch on him.

WE CELEBRATE CHRISTMAS EVE while the sun is high in the sky. We sit on the bed eating roast duck. We have caramelized potatoes in one foil tray and red cabbage in another.

My dad dragged the Christmas tree up the hotel's back stairs. We dance around it and sing Christmas carols. Then I open my present; it's wrapped in several layers of paper. It's a remote-controlled boat. Tomorrow we're taking it out for a sail.

My dad puts the blanket over me. He's going to work now. I ask him to please stay. Please, just a little bit longer. Please tell me again what's starboard and what's port on a ship, I think I've forgotten.

He says that more men want to see women take off their clothes at Christmas. He doesn't know why; perhaps they're lonely. But they tip him generously. He kisses my forehead and closes the door behind him.

MY DAD HAS the next couple of days off and we sail the boat from when we get up in the morning till the sun sets, interrupted only by a lunch break or to go to the nearest newsstand to buy new batteries. I learn how to turn the boat against the wind so it won't keel over.

When we return to the hotel room, my nose is running and my cheeks are burning. Even in my sleep I can see the boat. I'm now standing on the deck; the boat hasn't grown bigger, I've just grown much smaller. I sail past a giant duck at great speed and nearly crash into an enormous beer bottle floating on the black-and-green water.

We're woken up by shouting and people running down the hotel corridor. My dad and I hurry out of the room, still wearing only T-shirts and underpants. We follow the flow of people. When we reach the landing, we see that everyone is on their way up, not down. We follow them; the second-floor hallway is packed with guests. Everyone is talking at the same time. My dad takes my hand, we push our way through. The door to room 212 is open. My dad tells me to wait outside; I hear the sound of a bottle smashing against the wall.

"Leave me alone," someone shouts from the inside. The voice is strangely thick, but I'm almost certain that it belongs to the man in the suit.

My dad stands in the doorway.

"That one," the voice calls out. "I'm only talking to him."

My dad enters the room and I lose sight of him. I'm pushed around by people craning their necks in order to get a better look. They whisper to each other. A few minutes pass, then a man in orange clothes appears in the doorway. He asks everyone to move aside, first politely, then more forcefully. He's carrying the foot-end of a stretcher. People retreat along the corridor. When the stretcher passes me, I can see the man lying on it; he's wearing the jacket from his suit, but no trousers. His sleeves are pushed up; he has bandages around his arms. My dad holds his hands, doesn't let go even though the corridor is narrow. I follow them down the stairs. They lift the man into the ambulance, they close the back doors, and the ambulance drives down the street. My dad puts his arm around my shoulders. The ambulance disappears around the corner.

MY HEAD FEELS as if it's rolling loosely around the bed. I don't want to wake my dad; he has barely had any sleep since he got the job at the strip club. I drink water from the tap, it tastes of metal, my tongue is too big for my mouth. I sit down and look out the window, I watch cars drive by, I'm hot and cold at the same time.

I feel a little better after I've had a bath. My dad hums while he shaves; today's the last day of the year. My dad has been pointing it out to me on the calendar in the hotel reception, only four days left now, three days, two days.

We sit on the bed and eat marzipan wreath cake. We wear paper hats and we pull crackers. Inside them are small plastic cats, one red, one blue, and one yellow. I put them on the bedside table.

We walk down to the lakes. We've got three fireworks and I'm allowed to light them.

On the way home I throw fun snaps. They make a loud bang when they hit the ground.

We've just walked through the door to the hotel when I start to feel ill again.

The pattern in the carpet in the corridor starts to twist.

I lie down on the bed between the paper plates with marzipan cake. The glasses with orange juice are still standing on the bedside table; the orange color moves up the wall and spreads across the ceiling. I've never seen anything so orange.

I'm sweating and shaking. My dad fetches me a glass of water from the bathroom. I manage to swallow a couple of mouthfuls before I throw up; small lumps of marzipan and juice land on the bed and the carpet.

We haven't used the telephone in the hotel room since we arrived, but now my dad makes a call.

"I can't come tonight," he says into the handset. "My son's ill." Then he listens to the voice down the other end. "Yes, I do know what night it is. No, the money's not the issue, I only have one son." Then he listens again, looks over at me. "Okay, yes, I'll ask him . . ."

My dad kneels down by the bed and looks me in the eye. "Would you like to see where your dad works? See the place at night?"

I make no reply, I'm afraid I'll throw up again.

"If you can last tonight, just for tonight, you'll get that bicycle. We'll buy it for you the moment the shops open again. What do you say?"

I see the bicycle: it floats right above my dad's head and it's incredibly blue. I nod.

My dad gets me dressed and washes my face with a wet hand towel. He takes his suit out of the wardrobe. I hate that suit, I know that now. He wraps me in the bedspread and carries me down the stairs, past reception, and then the few steps along the street to the strip club.

Inside a man in a white shirt is busy taking down the chairs from the tables. Another man is setting out a stack of ashtrays which he cradles in his arms. There are stars and paper chains along the wall. My dad carries me past the stage, pulls aside a curtain, and walks down a passage where dark red paint is peeling off in large flakes. He knocks on the door three times before he opens it. One wall is covered entirely in mirrors. On the wall opposite are racks with cat costumes, bunny costumes, dresses with feathers. An older woman sits with a needle and thread in her mouth. She's sewing buttons onto a dress; a cigarette smokes itself in the ashtray on the table.

"My son's ill, tell the girls to take good care of him."

The woman nods and takes the next dress from the table. My dad puts me on a low, dark green sofa at the back of the room. He wipes my forehead with the inside of his shirt sleeve.

"All you have to do is last the night," he says.

WHEN I OPEN my eyes again the room is filled with girls. They're younger than my dad. Some of them are wearing only bras and panties. They put on makeup and spray themselves with perfume. I can hear music from the stage; I recognize it from my nights in the hotel bed where it never gets louder than the sound of a fingernail against a glass table.

The girls laugh and shout to drown out the music and each other. They drink from bottles on the table; they fill the glasses until they overflow. When they walk out the door, they look as if they're going to a party in their glittering dresses, strings of pearls around their neck, their high heels making clacking sounds against the concrete floor. When they come back, they're dressed only in their panties, the clothes now a small, crumpled bundle in their arms.

They sweat; beads of sweat have formed between their breasts and trickle down their stomachs before collecting in their belly buttons. They dry themselves with white hand towels, then they walk around in tiny panties before they take another dress from the stand.

The room smells of sweat, perfume, and cigarettes.

The girls take turns coming over to me. They ruffle my hair and pinch my cheeks.

I keep seeing the bicycle over their heads, the bicycle I'm going to get soon. Blue—or red, possibly. Red is a girl's color, but it's also the color of fire engines and mailboxes.

One of the girls says her name is Camilla; she gives me a glass and fills it from one of the bottles.

"Champagne," she says, as she tops up my glass with orange juice.

One of the other girls asks her what she's doing, but Camilla doesn't reply. She hands me the glass and whispers in my ear: "It'll make you feel better."

When I'm halfway through the glass, it no longer tastes quite so disgusting. I drink the rest in big gulps.

The girls laugh and I laugh with them. They stand in front of me and use me as their mirror.

"Do I look good now?" They jiggle their breasts before they walk out the door again.

The girl whose name is Camilla refills my glass, not quite so much orange juice this time.

"Tell your dad I think he's cute, won't you, sweetheart?" Her perfume smells of apples and flowers. "He probably knows me as Candy."

I empty my glass.

IT'S EARLY IN the morning when my dad carries me through the strip club. The air is so thick with smoke that my eyes water. The tables are covered with bottles. Broken glass crunches under his shoes.

My dad lays me down on the bed in the hotel room. He puts a wet towel on my forehead; it helps a bit until the towel's just as warm as my skin.

My dad supports my head and holds the water glass to my mouth. I manage three mouthfuls.

My dad sits on the edge of the bed, running his hand through his hair so it sticks out. He throws down the jacket; it lands on the floor. He smokes two cigarettes while he stares into the distance. The streetlights fall on his cheek, ear, and some of his neck. He looks older now. Not just a couple of years, but much older.

"I think it's time we move," he says.

· 1989 ·

I'M SITTING ON the floor, up against the wall. I read my comic with a flashlight. The man in the comic can make himself invisible. My dad sits behind the lighting desk, smoking; he turns some knobs, presses some buttons. There's a hole in the wall in front of him. When he doesn't look down at the desk, he looks out of the hole.

Sometimes he turns to me and we mime along to the voices from the stage.

My dad says: "Hello, Ivan, have you also come outside to enjoy the morning sun?"

Then I say: "Oh, dearest little Olga, these days the morning sun is the only joy I have left."

We've been here for two weeks now. I don't know how he got a job in a theater.

THE MAN IN the comic only makes himself invisible in order to help others; he catches robbers and thieves who steal handbags from old ladies. He never takes anything for himself. He doesn't trip up people he doesn't like though it would be incredibly easy for him to do so. Even when he catches the bus, he puts money down in front of the driver, but he never gets a ticket.

I don't understand him. I follow the drawings with my finger.

At the end of Act One, my dad gets up and goes over to the cassette player on the wall. He places his finger on the button, tilts his head, and listens. When the woman on stage has said: "But you'll never understand. You're in love with your art, Ivan, you don't love people," my dad counts: "One Mississippi, two Mississippi, three Mississippi," and then he presses the button. The sound of seagulls screeching and waves crashing fills the auditorium below us. My dad gets back into his chair, quickly presses a couple of other buttons, and slowly pushes up the big handle in the middle of the desk. The reddish glow of a sunset creeps through the hole in the wall and into where we are.

The auditorium is never more than half full. My dad says the tickets are expensive, that must be the reason. When the play is over, the applause is scattered and out of sync. A few people clap hard and long. He smokes a cigarette while the auditorium empties. Then he turns on the light and I switch off my flashlight. He cleans up after himself, empties the ashtray, and rewinds the cassette tape so that it'll be ready for tomorrow.

There's a knock on the door and the theater manager pops his head around. He's a small man with dark hair that sticks out as though he has just woken up. Even though this is his theater, he grins apologetically. The first time I met him, he told me to help myself to some sodas. He repeats this offer every time I see him, just pop over to the bar and help yourself to a soda.

Today he doesn't notice me. He pulls up a chair next to mine and sits down. He's wringing his hands more than he usually does.

"About that contract," he says.

"Yes?" My dad organizes some papers, the ones that tell him what the actors have to say.

"There are just a few outstanding details, but you will get it, of course." The theater manager looks down at his hands. "I know I said I'd have it ready for you today . . ."

My dad lights a cigarette and offers the packet to the theater manager, who carefully accepts one. "As soon as I sign that contract, you're obliged to pay me for the whole season even if you have to close the show tomorrow."

The theater manager is still looking at his hands. "I know you're not a fool."

"Let's forget all about that contract," my dad says. "As long as I get paid on time, that's all I care about."

The theater manager holds his breath as if he can't quite believe what my dad has just said. Then he gets up and shakes my dad's hand, pumping it up and down.

"You're all right, you are," he says, producing a white envelope from his inside pocket. "Don't forget to report this on your tax return."

They both laugh. The theater manager leaves quickly, as though he's afraid my dad might change his mind.

My dad locks the lighting box after us and we walk down the narrow passage to the stairs. Sara comes towards us. She has changed out of her costume and into jeans and a dark red knit sweater. Her hair's pulled back in a ponytail; she still has beads of sweat on her forehead.

"Promise me you'll come. Stay just for one drink."

My dad looks at me, it's my decision.

THE WET COBBLESTONES shine in the streetlight. We walk with the actors. Before the performance they're always very serious. They hardly speak, but drink coffee and smoke cigarettes. Afterwards they laugh out loud, they laugh at absolutely everything.

The bartender greets us when he sees us come through the door.

"The actors are here," he calls out. "Lock up your daughters."

He starts pouring beers. An older man gets up and makes room for us. It's the least I can do, he says. We sit down at a table in the middle of the room. One of the actors is always telling stories or rude jokes or gossiping about the others.

I'm sitting next to my dad, drinking orange juice through a straw. I'm here with them. People at the other tables listen in. They would just love to sit here, too, I can tell from looking at them even though they try to hide it. Kim and Margrethe sit at the head of the table. They both used to be quite famous, my dad has told me.

Margrethe is the oldest of the actors. I haven't seen any of her films, even though she has acted in quite a few. She drinks white wine; I can see traces of her red lipstick on her glass and on the cigarette she holds between the tips of her index and middle finger. In my mind I draw her; I draw the bar, the dark wood that stops halfway up the wall, the tables which all have cigarette burns. There are photos on the walls of people I don't recognize. They smile or raise their glass in a toast. At the bottom of the photographs little greetings have been written in black ink.

Kim falls out with Margrethe. Once again he has said something that makes her turn away and pretend that he isn't there. Kim gets up, pulls a chair over, and sits down next to me.

He plays the world-weary doctor who looks across the fields and talks about the city.

"Are you ready?" he asks, and takes three coins out of his pocket.

"Three Fly," he calls this trick. Another one is called "Find the Lady." He turns cigarettes into paper napkins; coins disappear and reappear under my juice bottle.

I hear the bell ring and I see my dad standing at the bar with the bell rope in his hand. I know this means he's buying a round. He takes the white envelope from his pocket. He asks if I want another juice; I shake my head. I need the bathroom and I'd like to go home, but I don't tell him that. I see the money come out of the envelope and disappear across the counter. I see beer glasses fill up. Schnapps and vodka. People pat my dad on the back.

WHEN WE GET home, my dad tips the rest of the money out of the envelope. There's hardly any left.

He looks at me. "You're wondering why I bought everyone in the bar a beer, aren't you? Why I bought drinks for people we don't know."

I nod.

He squats down on his haunches in front of me. I'm fairly certain that I'm at school again.

"You can't make a living from being invisible," my dad says. "That man in your comic, how does he earn his money?"

I'd never thought of that.

"No one gives him money for being invisible, do they?"

No, I'm pretty sure that they don't.

"I wish I could drive a car without a number plate, that my feet didn't leave footprints in the snow. But that's not possible. So you have to trust people. Not always and not unconditionally. But you have to trust that if they like you, then they'll do a lot to help you. And that's worth much more than the money which was in that envelope."

I help my dad unfold the camping beds and we find our sleeping bags.

Our new apartment is the smallest we've ever lived in. One of the stagehands at the theater knows the landlord and said he would have a word with him. The next day we moved in. When we need something, a jacket or a pair of shoes, we take it out of a suitcase and afterwards it goes back into the suitcase.

The walls in the apartment are sloping. My dad says that we can hear it if a bird lands on the roof. He can't stand upright. While he fries sausages, he leans to the right. While he drinks a cup of coffee and smokes a cigarette, he leans to the left. While he washes up, he leans backwards.

EVERY SUNDAY WE visit Sara and bring cakes. She lives in a small apartment, not far from the theater. Sara and my dad drink coffee; Sara makes hot chocolate for me in a saucepan on the stove. My dad talks, Sara nods and smiles. On stage you can hear her all the way to the back of the auditorium and she doesn't even have to shout; on stage it's hard to take your eyes off her. But in the street and here, in the apartment, she's very small and practically transparent. Like some girls you meet on the sidewalk who'll always move, step right out into the bicycle lane if you just carry on walking.

We go for a walk in a park nearby. The weather is cold and we're wrapped up warm. We feed stale bread to the ducks. My dad and I play Hit the Swan, but Sara thinks it's mean. She takes his hand.

"I can't wait until the summer," she says. "I can't wait until I can come here and eat ice cream."

"Would you like an ice cream?"

"It's too cold, isn't it?"

"It's never too cold to eat ice cream."

Sara and I wait on a bench while my dad goes to get us ice cream. Sara pulls her coat around her, moves a little closer to me.

"You're lucky," she says.

We both look at my dad's back; he's walking up the path towards the exit.

"You're lucky you've got a dad like him."

She keeps her gaze fixed on the gate he has just walked out of. Then she sinks into herself. I can feel her through my clothes.

When she sees my dad again, she comes alive, claps her hands. She rips the paper off her ice cream and laughs when it sticks to her bottom lip, frozen.

MY DAD IS sitting behind the lighting desk. He looks at his watch and then puts his fingers back on the buttons in front of him.

Below us the auditorium is less than half full, as usual. The audience has long since stopped talking and coughing, but the curtain has yet to go up.

My dad checks his watch again, then he asks me to please go backstage to see what's going on.

I walk through the narrow passages that run along the auditorium, the ones the audience never sees. My dad calls them the theater's arteries. They remind me of the strip club, they're dark and scary and the paint's peeling.

The actors and stagehands are standing outside the dressing rooms, talking to each other in hushed voices.

A door opens and the theater manager appears.

"I don't know what we're going to do," he says. "Why the hell did you have to go and . . ."

Kim's hands hang limply by his sides. "Do you want me to talk to her, perhaps I can . . ."

"I think you've said enough."

"But everyone knows she screwed her way to all those film roles. That's what you did in those days."

The theater manager looks as if he's about to shout at him or possibly hit him. Then he heaves a resigned sigh and rummages around in his pockets for cigarettes. Waves of smoke waft under the low ceiling.

Sara squats down in front of me. She puts her arm around my shoulder and whispers into my ear. I look at her; she nods and gives me a little push. I go to the door, the actors fall silent; I can feel their eyes on me. One more step and I take hold of the door handle. Again I look at Sara; she smiles and nods. I enter, closing the door behind me.

Margrethe spins around and nearly throws a hair-brush at me, but stops in mid-movement. Her face is red, as though she has been trying to hold her breath. She has black stripes down her cheeks. She lets herself collapse into the chair in front of the dressing table mirror.

I sit down next to her.

"It's only theater," I say, the words Sara told me to say.

At first Margrethe looks at me in surprise, then she starts to laugh. She laughs until she begins to cough and then she laughs even harder.

"Yes, darling, it's only theater." She looks at herself in the mirror and lights a cigarette. "So, what do you think: should we do it?"

I nod.

"It's only theater," she repeats to herself while she lays out her makeup.

"The others are a bunch of assholes," she says.

She removes the old makeup. Her hands work automatically.

"But then again, all actors are, or most of them, anyway."

She dips cotton balls into a jar, removing layers of stage paint, briefly revealing naked skin before new layers are applied. She drips a bluish liquid into her eyes, blinks a couple of times. Then she smiles to herself in the mirror and turns to face me. In a very short amount of time she has a whole new face with no trace of tears.

I SIT IN row three; Margrethe has said she would like to see me in the auditorium.

The first few times I saw the show, my dad asked for a ticket for me. Now we know there's no need.

Act One is long and boring. The actors smile and drink tea and look across a field which lies somewhere beyond the stage. Towards the end they argue a little, but still using impressive and clever words while they fling out their arms.

In the play Sara's name is Olga. Every time I see them perform, the light on her is a little brighter.

During the intermission I drink orange soda from the bar and I don't have to wait in line.

"Is that little boy alone in the theater?" I hear someone say, but I ignore them.

AFTER THE INTERMISSION the stage walls are dark gray and grimy. The family has lost all their money. The table in the middle of the room is dirty. The floor looks as if a thousand muddy boots have trodden on it. Now they live in a basement. The actors look sad and poor, but I don't quite believe them, they're hiding too many kilos hidden under their ragged clothes. Sara's the only one who looks like she knows what it means to go hungry. When she sits on the filthy bed and her back convulses in silent sobbing, I want to climb up on stage and put my arm around her.

I DRINK JUICE, my dad plays pool, and the actors take turns patting me on the shoulder. Kim and Margrethe are sitting at the end of the table. After the show they walked down the street arm in arm. Now they look like old friends again. Kim says something that makes Margrethe laugh and cover her mouth with her hand; he spreads a deck of cards out in front of her.

"What you did today was impressive," Sara says to me. "When things go well, actors drink a lot," she says. "To celebrate. But when they play to empty houses, as we do now, then they drink even more. They argue and they drink. They scream and they shout."

I hear a sharp bang when my dad hits a pool ball and it bumps into another ball. Sara looks into the air; I try to follow her gaze.

"I would've been happier working in a shoe shop," she says. "Selling shoelaces and pressing the toes of people's shoes when they're not sure if the size is right."

She shudders slightly as if she's cold, then she smiles and looks at my dad's back. He leans across the pool table and shoots another ball. I hear it hit the sides and I'm almost certain he pockets it.

"Do you think he'll win?" Sara asks.

"Yes," I reply.

WE MOVE INTO an apartment a couple of floors further down. The old man who lived there has died; they found him in a chair in the middle of the living room. Next to him was an overflowing ashtray. The caretaker says that after the man lost his wife, he just sat in his chair smoking one cigarette after another. That was all he did. Once a week the grocer's delivery boy would turn up with a plastic bag containing a box of crispbread and four cartons of cigarettes. I think the caretaker must be exaggerating until I see the apartment. Every piece of furniture is covered with tiny burns. The walls are yellow and the smell of smoke is so overpowering it makes my eyes sting.

"We used to worry he'd fall asleep with a lighted cigarette and set fire to the whole building," the caretaker says.

We leave the windows open for two days, we walk around the apartment with our coats on, we sleep in them. The smell of tobacco refuses to go away. My dad opens a bag of ground coffee and tips it out onto three plates: one he puts on the kitchen table, another on the windowsill, and the third on the floor in the hall. It's an old trick real estate agents use to sell properties, he says. Everyone likes the smell of coffee.

Only old people live in this building. We pass them on the stairs; at night we hear their televisions mumble. It won't be long before another apartment in the building becomes available, then we'll probably move again. I hope we can stay here. Just for a little while. Move from apartment to apartment; move whenever my dad feels like it without ever leaving the building.

EVERY TIME WE leave Sara's apartment, the sky has grown a little darker. One day we stay longer and eat with her. From then on we no longer come for coffee, but for dinner. My dad spends hours in her kitchen, preparing food that goes in and out of the oven. We have old-fashioned roast beef, we have lamb chops, borscht, and veal. After dinner, when the red wine bottle is empty, they drink coffee. I sit on the floor with my back against the bookcase as I draw them. I draw the table they sit at, the coffee pot, which my dad says is called a Madam Blå. I draw the ashtray and the smoke from a cigarette Sara hasn't quite managed to stub out. She laughs at something my dad says. My dad always makes her laugh. Otherwise I don't think I've seen her laugh. Yes, on stage, but that's because she has to, it says so in the papers that lie in front of my dad. And in the bar with the other actors. But she doesn't fool me. I've seen people slip on the ice in winter, get up with grazed palms, and laugh, No, they're fine, it's nothing.

I draw my dad as a zebra sipping coffee from a tiny china cup. I draw Sara as a lioness. I'm about to draw her mane when I remember that lionesses don't have manes.

"We deserve a little something with our coffee." Sara walks over to the bookcase where I'm sitting. "I got this after last night's show."

She takes a bottle from one of the shelves. Then she looks down at my sketchbook. My first thought is to hide it; my dad is the only person who has ever seen my drawings, and perhaps she'll get mad because I've drawn them as animals.

"Mind if I have a look?" she asks.

I hesitate before handing her the sketchbook.

"That's really good," she says, and my dad beams with pride. "Why don't you try drawing us while we're on stage?"

I'VE A CHARCOAL pencil in my hand. Not too hard or too soft. The red glow from the emergency exit sign lights up my paper. Should it become necessary, I can sharpen my pencil halfway through Act One. That's when Olga gets bad news and drops the teapot.

I draw the two Janus masks mounted above the stage, then I draw tables and chairs, the pitcher with water, and the display cabinet. I can feel my palms getting sweaty, as though someone is looking over my shoulder. I know I can draw dragons, trolls, strange animals whose shape I can decide. I'm good at buildings and trees with lots of leaves. I've drawn cowboys, but I always focus on their guns. Drawing real people is difficult. The actors on stage keep moving. They walk and talk, they fling out their arms before disappearing off stage. I close my eyes. Like a camera taking a picture. Then I draw them as they were. A single moment. The hand raised, the mouth open. I draw as much as I can remember before putting my pencil down.

The next day the actors stand in their usual positions and I carry on drawing. Raised eyebrows, palms open.

I draw six days in a row. Sunday is our day off. We go to Sara's for dinner. I don't look at the drawing; that would be cheating. And I think I'm also worried what I might find. On Monday I'm back in the theater with my sketchbook, sketching in the glow from the emergency exit. I put the last few lines on the paper; the drawing is done. I don't look at it until the intermission. The stage might be a little too big. The folds in the curtain could be more accurate, but then again they change every night. Then I look at the actors. They look like people, but they're not. They stand far too still. Like stuffed animals, their eyes look like glass beads. I scrunch up the drawing, throw it into the garbage among the empty cigarette packets and plastic cups.

I TELL MY dad I'm not feeling very well. He has his coat on; we're going to the theater. I tell him not to worry about me, I just want to stay in bed, I'm tired. When he has gone I lie there staring at the ceiling. I hate that piece of paper. It's underneath me, as far under the bed as I could hide it.

My hands move under the blanket, draw lines in the ceiling. I try to stop.

THE NEXT EVENING I'm back in the theater with my sketchbook on my lap. I've made up my mind that it's the last time I'm going to draw. I no longer care about likeness; it's not as if anyone will ever get to see this drawing. I draw so hard that the pencil goes through the paper. So hard that the point snaps and I have to find my pencil sharpener. An older man turns around and looks at me, but I ignore him. I'm not drawing the actors; I'm only drawing their movements. The head is the last thing I draw; eyebrows, mouth, and eyes no longer matter. The table, the chairs, and the samovar, I know they're about to be knocked over soon and then they, too, will be in motion. I draw without looking at the paper, I draw through the whole of Act One and when we reach the interval, my wrist aches. During Act Two I just watch them talk. I don't want to draw any more, it's over. The easel my dad gave me, there must be another use for it. We could hang clothes on it.

I'M SITTING ON the barstool drinking apple juice; the straw makes a slurping sound near the bottom of the bottle. My dad asks if he can please see my drawing. I hand him the sketchbook. He can look at it now and then neither he nor Sara will ever ask me to draw again. My dad puts down the sketchbook on the bar in front of him, his hand finds the beer glass, he empties it. He taps the ash off his cigarette without hitting the ashtray. Then he waves over the bartender and pushes the sketchbook towards him. Perhaps to teach me a lesson, like house training a puppy by pressing its head into its mess. The bartender looks at the drawing. He has tattoos on his forearms, a ship with tall masts and a naked lady. The tattoos have been made by someone who really knows how to draw. I bite my bottom lip and try not to cry.

The bartender looks up at me.

“Can I buy it?” he asks.

I nod; of course he can buy it. He can have it for free. He can tear it up and throw it away if that’s what he wants.

“Please, would you write your name on it?”

I write *Peter* in the bottom right-hand corner. The bartender opens the till and takes out a banknote and puts it in front of me. Then he tears the drawing off my sketchbook with great care and puts it up on the mirror behind the bar.

My dad keeps pointing to the drawing for the rest of the evening.

He says, “My son did that.”

People stop, they look and smile. But no one laughs.

That night when we walk home, the banknote is in my pocket. I can feel it against my fingertips, the kind of thin, slightly stiff paper that can only be money. I know I’m never going to spend it.

A COUPLE OF hours before the performance my dad and I are alone in the auditorium. My dad has a long wooden pole with a metal hook in his hands; he uses it to adjust the stage lights, nudging them a little to the right, a little to the left. He takes a couple of steps back, fiddles with them a little more before he's satisfied. He takes down some lights to replace the lightbulb or attach new filters or gels. Gels are thin pieces of plastic that you put in front of the lightbulb. They come in red, green, yellow, or blue. One night, during Kim's long monologue in Act One, my dad showed me how they work. It's when the country doctor says that life always happens elsewhere. My dad let me dim the yellow and red lights. Kim grew very pale, he looked like he'd eaten something that disagreed with him or had received very bad news. Kim kept on speaking; he still had many words to go.

"Why don't we try green?" my dad suggested.

He put my hand on another button; I was allowed to turn it up slowly. Kim looked as if he wouldn't get to the end of his speech before collapsing. Possibly never leave the stage alive.

MY DAD RAISES the pole towards the stage light again; this time he's on tiptoes. "Why won't the damn thing . . ."

I sit with my feet dangling over the edge of the stage. I remind myself not to whistle. There are rules. You're not allowed to wear your coat on stage, either. Both bring you bad luck.

I hold up a gel in front of my eyes. The whole world turns blue. We're in the middle of a snowstorm.

The door at the end of the auditorium opens and the theater manager comes running in. He sprints down through rows of seats. Polar bears are on his heels. Panting, he asks if my dad has heard the news, heard about the critic. My dad shakes his head, carries on working with the pole and the light in the ceiling. The theater manager says that it might just be a rumor, but he has heard that Erik Schmidt is coming to review the show tonight. The theater manager wipes his forehead with his shirt sleeve.

I find the red gel and hold it up to my eyes. That's better: The whole world is red now. We're surrounded by flames, no wonder the theater manager is sweating. He says it's important that everything goes smoothly and jumps up and down on the spot to avoid his shoes catching fire. I feel sorry for him and find the green gel.

Now we're inside a humid jungle. Big birds with long crooked beaks perch in the treetops above us. The theater manager's voice drowns out their chirping.

"Tonight everything must be perfect, it must be absolutely perfect," he says, wiping his forehead with his sleeve; again he grins nervously and hurries back up the aisle. His feet sink into the soft forest floor. He reaches the door without being eaten by predators.

MY DAD TURNS on the lighting desk one button at a time until the whole board is buzzing. If he's nervous, it doesn't show. He does everything he always does: he puts out the book, he flicks through the pages to make sure they're in the right order. The cigarette packet and the lighter are in place next to the ashtray.

I, too, have my comics ready on the floor beside me. I switch my flashlight on and off a couple of times.

My dad brings each lamp up and down to make sure that none of the bulbs have blown while he adjusted the lights.

Sara enters.

"With lots of luck for your final performance," she says, and kisses my dad on the back of his neck.

"Is it really that bad?"

"Erik Schmidt either loves or hates a show. He's not going to like this one."

Sara takes a cigarette from the packet on the table. "Everyone has been saying, 'If only the critics would come, if only we got some reviews then the show would sell out . . .'"

My dad takes her hands in his. He usually has something to say in any situation, but now he's quiet.

"I only hope someone's prepared to sleep with him." Sara laughs a little too loud. "Someone from the cast, the theater manager, Kim, anyone. Otherwise we don't stand a chance. As long as he gets . . ."

Then she looks over at me. I get very busy rearranging my comics.

Sara turns in the doorway, forms her hands into a cone, and says in a stage whisper to my dad: "As long as he gets laid! Laid! Laid! Laid!"

I hear the sound of her heels down the narrow passage.

My dad checks the tape recorder, making sure the tape is in the right place. Then the door opens again and Kim enters. He wears a gray woollen vest over a baggy white shirt.

"The country doctor's here," he says, and laughs. "Where's the patient?" His doctor's bag clinks as he sits down on the chair next to my dad. "I can't stand being in the dressing rooms. Everyone's going crazy. Margrethe is crying into her lap. Mikael is walking around in circles. I'm scared he might hit me if I should bump into him."

Kim takes two beers out of the doctor's bag. He puts one in front of my dad and takes a cigarette from the packet on the table.

My dad has told me that people get nervous if you don't drink with them. They clink the bottoms of the beer bottles against each other.

"We're going to get slaughtered," Kim says, taking a deep swig of his beer. "Completely slammed." Then he smiles. "But if you know that failure is the only option, then there's really nothing to be scared of."

Kim empties the first bottle and finds another one. When he has finished that, he grabs the handles of the doctor's bag, which still clinks.

I stay in the lighting box during the performance. It feels wrong to go down to the auditorium. My dad and I once saw a car crash and he told me that I must never rubberneck. That I should just carry on walking if I can't do anything to help. I'd really like to have seen the theater critic, to know what someone like him looks like. Someone who can make grown people cry and sweat.

I read comics about the man who can make himself invisible. He fights a giant spider that throws road signs and cars at him. I can hear the actors on stage. Today they speak faster and louder than they usually do.

After the performance Sara returns to the lighting box. The other actors left without talking to each other; they were out the stage door before the last members of the audience had even left the theater, she says.

My dad offers to walk her home, but she says she'll take a taxi while she still has a job.

THE WHITE ENVELOPES lie in a pile on the dining table.

My dad wanders around the apartment, takes a banknote out of his jacket pocket, and discovers another one that has hidden itself in his shirt pocket. A third one has been used as a bookmark.

He shakes a shoe and I hear coins rattle. Then he borrows one of my pencils. He drinks coffee while he arranges the money in small piles, coins and notes separately. He writes numbers on a piece of paper in front of him. I know this math problem: How long can we manage before he needs to find another job?

A RAPPING ON the door wakes me up. Seconds later my dad appears in the doorway to my bedroom.

"Get dressed," he says.

When I come out to the living room, the camp bed has been knocked over. My dad quickly pulls a sweater over his head and rushes over to the table, where he sweeps the money and envelopes into a carrier bag with his forearm. Some coins end up on the floor, but he doesn't pick them up.

"Don't forget your winter coat," he says, as loudly as he can without raising his voice.

He grabs the clothes that lie nearest, throws them into the suitcase on the floor. I manage to add a couple of comics before he slams it shut.

My dad has opened the door to the back stairs when we hear Sara's voice.

"Wakey-wakey," she calls out.

My dad freezes. Then he reverses back through the door and puts down the suitcase. He lets her in. Sara hasn't been to our apartment before, but we walked past it once and my dad pointed it out to her and told her we lived there. He quickly shut his mouth and I could tell from his face that he regretted it. Now Sara stands in our living room taking little steps on the spot. Her eyes are wide open, the cigarette in her mouth is unlit and bent.

"Read this," she says, and hands my dad a crumpled newspaper.

He quickly skims the page, then gives her a big hug.

"But that's great," he exclaims. "That's really great!"

He lights her cigarette. I sit down at the table with the newspaper. The review is written in a column in a difficult language full of words I don't understand.

When I get to Sara's name, I spell my way through it.

She portrays Olga with greater authority than I have seen in any previous production. That the director has chosen to use her as the driving force of the production is bordering on genius.

I carry on reading. I can tell from looking at Sara and my dad that it's a good review, that they haven't been slaughtered as Kim predicted. When his name appears, I try again, word by word, to make sense of what it says.

. . . Making the world-weary country doctor a profoundly alcoholic character is a brave decision. Rarely have I seen alcoholism depicted so realistically, from the shaking hands to the slow but deliberately clear diction. Nothing is overplayed, nothing is superfluous. When the doctor drinks from his teacup, the audience wonders how little tea and how much vodka it contains. When he puts it down, the audience crosses its fingers that he will find the table.

"What happened here?" Sara says, looking around the apartment, rubbing her eyes and nearly burning herself with the cigarette in the process. "Was there a break-in?"

She looks at the clothes that didn't make it into the suitcase, the bowl of porridge oats I ate last night—knocked over in the rush and now lying broken on the floor, the milk seeping down between the floorboards.

"Fire drill," my dad says.

AFTER THAT NIGHT'S performance we're dragged out of the lighting box. We've no choice, of course we're coming with them.

The beers are ready and waiting, the bartender grinning. The newspaper review has been put up on the wall.

The bell rings many times that night, many rounds are bought. Kim performs magic tricks not just for me, but for the whole bar. Margrethe sings a ballad; at first she doesn't want to, but the others persuade her. The song is a little rude and everyone laughs.

"The actors are celebrating tonight," my dad says, helping me into my coat. We can still hear them shouting and laughing as we walk down the street.

THE ACTORS AND the stagehands have gathered in the theater foyer. We see them through the windows as we come down the street. We're late today: my dad stopped to buy new gels for the lamps and more lightbulbs.

The actors look ill. My dad says they must have been drinking all night. Even Margrethe struggles to hide it under several layers of makeup. We're told we're waiting for the theater manager.

Kim leans against my dad: "If he's going to pull the show, his timing is lousy."

People in the street stop and stare at us before they move on.

The theater manager rushes in. "I wanted to tell you in person to avoid any misunderstanding."

"Speak up!" someone calls out.

The theater manager coughs into his hand. "I'm afraid we're going to have to cancel tonight's show. Nothing terrible has happened, not really. Water damage in the basement. A pipe has burst in one the dressing rooms."

I hear people say *A blessing in disguise* or *It's bad luck*.

The theater manager holds up his hand again to speak. "The good news is that the costumes weren't damaged. We should be able to re-open in a couple of days. The tickets are selling like hotcakes."

People break up into small clusters.

Kim asks out into the room: "Am I the only one who's thirsty?"

THAT NIGHT SARA and my dad go out for dinner.

Sara squats down in front of me; she says that I have to pick the restaurant. That I have to come with them or it won't be a good evening. I tell her I'd rather stay at home and do some drawing. I follow them down to the takeaway on the corner where we buy half a roast chicken and french fries for me. I wave to the taxi as they drive off.

I EAT RAW porridge oats with milk while my dad is still asleep on the camp bed in the living room. With every mouthful I take, my spoon hits the side of the bowl a little harder. My dad sits up, rubs his eyes, and asks me if I want to see something exciting. He takes me to the theater. From the top step we can see men in rubber boots that go all the way up to their waists. They splash through the gray water and have to shout at each other to drown out the sound of the trunk. There must be an elephant right outside, sucking up the water. It's very thirsty.

I'M DRAWING IN my room. Through the door to the living room I can hear Sara talking to my dad. She's convinced that Kim caused the water damage. She has been thinking it over and now she's sure of it. My dad doesn't reply so she tries to convince him, telling him that Kim acted strangely in the bar that night. At first he was happy. Then he was on the verge of tears. Then he disappeared and was gone for hours. Then he came back and sat there nursing a whisky.

"It would make sense," Sara says. "He's never gotten that much applause before. Not in the last fifteen years and not without him wearing a funny hat or dressing up in a monkey costume."

My dad asks if I feel like going out. We could go to Langelinie Promenade, throw coins at the Little Mermaid statue and eat ice cream.

I tell them again that I'd rather stay at home and do some drawing.

My dad doesn't wake up until late the next day. He hums as he tidies up.

"Music," he says, "let's have some music. We'll buy a record player, you can choose the color. Or we'll just paint it."

He drums solos with his fingers on the table.

"Are you sure you don't want to come?" he asks.

I hear his footsteps down the stairs; he takes them three at a time.

I TAKE OUT a tennis ball from one of the drawers. The block we live in is nice and very clean. No chewing gum wrappers or tricycles thrown into the hedge. No hopscotch lines on the courtyard floor. Only old people with walkers and signs saying "Watch out, steps."

I throw the ball up against the wall and catch it. I say *Try again, throw higher, you can do it.* The second-floor window opens and a lady with white hair and lots of wrinkles sticks out her head. She looks around, searching for something. She blinks a couple of times before she spots me.

"You're not allowed to do that," she says. "No ball games in the courtyard. Can't you read the sign?"

"No," I reply. "I'm blind."

She looks at me, baffled. "No ball games allowed."

She withdraws her head, but leaves the window open. I'm sure she's sitting right behind it, ready and waiting in case I throw the ball again.

KIM IS SITTING on a chair in the dressing room with a wet towel around his neck. He's clutching a cup of coffee with both hands; his body is shaking so violently that his trousers are covered with brown stains.

"He has been drinking ever since the pipe burst," Margrethe says. "I don't think he has slept since Tuesday." She holds his head, looks into his eyes. "Are you sure you can go on?"

Kim nods; more coffee stains appear on his trousers.

"If not, now's the time to tell us."

Kim swallows a big gulp of coffee that must surely burn his throat. "I'm fine."

"You heard him," Margrethe says, clapping her hands, and the actors carry on doing their makeup and getting into costume.

Kim groans faintly.

THE AUDITORIUM IS so packed that I have to sit on the steps between the seat rows.

On stage the actors talk about the harvest festival, they pour tea from the pot. Today the sun shines more brightly than ever on Sara. Her last line lingers in the air. This is the cue for the country doctor to enter. The actors stare down into their cups, they fiddle with their costumes. Margrethe examines the teapot as though there's something wrong with it. I count one Mississippi, two Mississippi, and have got to twenty-two Mississippi before Kim staggers on stage. He doesn't have his doctor's bag with him. A couple of meters in he stops. I think he's having second thoughts and is about to leave the stage. Then he goes over to the table. Sara quickly pulls out a chair for him.

"Have you been waiting a long time?" he asks.

The play carries on. Kim has a cup of tea which he sips. When the other actors talk to him, he mumbles his lines, but everyone pretends to understand what he's saying.

We reach the end of Act One; my dad slowly dims the lights. A summer evening. Now Olga and the country doctor are alone on stage. Kim gets up; for a second, it looks as if he's about to fall over. Then he moves downstage and stops a few centimeters from the edge. He scratches his face. The auditorium is completely silent. The country doctor says that life didn't turn out the way he thought it would. Then he goes blank. He takes a few steps back. Sara looks at him. Everyone in the auditorium is looking at him, their mouths hanging open. Kim scratches his face again.

He starts speaking again. The country doctor says that Olga has grown up, that she's a big girl now. Once she was so small she could fit in a pocket. Kim speaks for a long time and with many pauses. He stumbles through his words. Not everything he says makes sense, can be heard or understood.

When he finally stops, there's total silence in the auditorium. A young man gets up and starts clapping so hard that it must hurt. He's quickly followed by others until the whole auditorium is echoing with the sound.

ARE YOU HUNGRY?" my dad asks me.

We've just left the theater and we're walking down the street.

"Isn't Sara coming with us?"

"Not today."

We cross Rådhuspladsen, we carry on walking. We end up in front of a place that looks like a bar from the outside. When we've entered through the large wooden door, I can see white fabric tablecloths and gleaming cutlery. A waiter shows us to a table in the middle of the room. Two men in suits are sitting a few tables away from us; apart from that we're alone in the restaurant.

The waiter returns with the menu, he brings a large beer for my dad and a soda for me. My dad flicks through the menu. He asks me what I want, have anything you like. Then he puts the menu down and looks at me.

"Something's bothering you."

"No . . ."

"Yes."

"I want to go to school."

"You do go to school."

"A real school."

He nods, shakes a cigarette out of the packet. The waiter returns and my dad orders for both of us. When we're alone again, my dad looks at me.

"You'd like to go to a school with other children?"

"Yes."

"Then you shall."

We eat roast pork with parsley sauce on large white plates. Between us is a bowl of boiled potatoes with a sprinkling of chopped parsley on top. My dad crunches some crackling.

"It's a bit complicated," he says, and looks as if he needs time to think about it. "I'll need to check out a few things. But you will go to school." He cuts a potato in half, dips it in the sauce before he puts it in his mouth. "After the summer . . . after the summer you can start Grade Three."

One of the men in suits gets up. He leans on the back of his chair for support before he starts walking. On his way to the bathroom, he knocks a fork from one of the other tables. He bends down, picks it up, and puts it back on the table very slowly and carefully.

"Do you think I'll be able to keep up?"

I had a dream I was in a classroom, the other pupils were laughing at me, told me to spell "idiot," write it on the board.

My dad stops chewing.

"I mean, the others have been going to school for two years. Five days a week. Are you sure I'll be as good . . ."

Then he starts to laugh. He laughs so hard that the beer in his glass sloshes and I think I can see tiny ripples on the surface of the sauce.

"You're not as good as them," he says, wiping his eyes with the napkin. "You're much, much better. Take the best pupil in any class you join and you'll be better than him or her. Just remember this," he says. "It's okay that you're better than the others. But try not to be too clever. Try not to show it. People will only start to ask questions."

I promise—even though I find it hard to believe him.

My dad orders more pork, says eat up. Eat until you burst. I get another soda, too.

"We'll carry on with our own school, perhaps just on Sundays when we've nothing else to do. You don't need to be as stupid as the rest of the world."

WE'RE SITTING ON a picnic blanket in a big park. I've been here before, collecting bottles with my dad. Today we're the ones tipping out the dregs and smiling as we hand the bottles to men and women with dirty hands. We're surrounded by people walking, standing, and sitting down again, disturbing the grass so I can see that the soil is filled with worms and old bottle caps.

It's May Day, and Sara says she's cold in her summer dress. My dad gives her his denim jacket to put on. It's too big and her hands disappear inside the sleeves. Sara stays on the blanket while we wait in line at a food stand. I get a sticker from a man and put it on my T-shirt. It's big and round. I ask my dad if it's very important that we leave the European Community. He smiles. "I don't think you and I were ever in the EC."

We buy grilled sausages that have split and are a little burned on one side; we sit on the blanket and eat them off paper plates. We can hear music from the stage: a man is singing and I hear the word "peace." The rest of the lyrics are drowned out by drums and guitar. Sara gets tomato sauce on the sleeve of my dad's jacket; she promises to wash it, promises that it'll wash out. My dad just laughs. After we've finished eating, he comes with me to the bushes to have a pee. I have to watch where I put my feet. Many of the leaves are already wet and there are small puddles all over the place.

My dad has a pee, too. He aims his willy at me and says, "I'm going to pee on you, I'm going to pee on you."

I try to escape, I trip, fall into a bush and scratch my cheek a little, but I'm still laughing when he helps me back to my feet.

I drink fruit punch. My dad rests his head in Sara's lap. Sara says she likes my sticker.

She looks at her watch. "If we're going to get to the front of the stage, we have to leave now."

My dad nudges the plastic bag with his foot, it clinks. "There's still some beer left."

Sara starts to rise so my dad has to sit up; the lap he was resting on is gone. "I want to hear her speak."

I help my dad fold the blanket.

The area in front of the stage is already packed with people, hundreds of them.

Two men are walking around the stage picking up empty bottles and cigarette stubs and rolling out cables. When they leave, a blonde woman appears.

Her name is Monika: I know that from the placards people are holding up. She wears jeans and a T-shirt and her hair is in a ponytail. She smiles and steps up to the microphone. People clap, some whistle. Even though we were at the back a moment ago, we're now surrounded by people. I can no longer see anything, only their backs. My dad lifts me up and puts me on his shoulders.

The woman on the stage laughs as if she can't quite believe so many people have turned up just because of her. But when she starts to speak, she sounds neither hesitant nor shy. I look at the people around us; everyone is listening to her. It's the first time today that the park has fallen completely silent; all we can hear is Monika's voice from the big loudspeakers. She says it's not about Left or Right, but about people and the future. Her eyes shine while she speaks. My dad stands very still underneath me. He doesn't rummage around in his pocket for cigarettes or shuffle his feet like he usually does when he's bored.

When Monika has finished talking she takes a few steps away from the microphone; again she smiles apologetically. Everyone around me starts to clap and refuses to stop.

I think my dad has forgotten I'm still sitting on his shoulders; he just stands there staring at the empty stage. It's not until Sara touches his arm that he lifts me down, picks up the plastic bag, and we leave.

"I told you she's not like other politicians," Sara laughs.

I'M WOKEN UP by a loud bump in the kitchen and then I hear my dad swear. He has stubbed his toe on the table leg again. Shortly afterwards he appears in the doorway to my room.

"I'll be back soon; I'm just going out to get some bread."

My dad didn't wash up last night, so I fill up the washing bowl. When he comes back, he has a big pile of newspapers in his arms, but no bread. I don't say anything; we have porridge oats and milk in the fridge.

My dad pours himself some coffee and takes the first newspaper from the pile. He sits hunched over the pages. When he finds something interesting, he reaches for the scissors.

When I've finished my porridge oats, I try to draw the ghost of the old man who lived in the apartment before us. I draw him just as transparent as the smoke that comes out of his mouth.

I take my sketchbook and go down to the courtyard. I draw birds sitting in the tree. I draw cats slinking around as they hunt for rats by the bin shed. Then I draw a cat's head on one of the pigeons and I'm pleased with my drawing. I draw a cat jumping from a garbage can; it has the head of a pigeon with its beak open.

A couple of hours later I return to the apartment. My dad's still at the table reading newspapers. I empty his ashtray for him. The last bit of coffee has burned black and stuck to the bottom of the pot on the stove so I put it in the sink, fill it with water, and leave it to soak.

The sun is starting to go down, so I switch on the lamp above the table. My dad massages his eyes, takes his jacket from the back of the chair, and says that we'd better be going.

That evening his movements at the lighting desk are slow. I don't know if the actors notice, they're probably too busy remembering their lines. But I see it. His hands are usually resting on the buttons while he counts to himself or whispers the lines as they're spoken on stage. Tonight his eyes are half closed and he forgets the cigarette in the ashtray. I smell the filter burning.

After the performance he kisses Sara good-bye and tells her that he's tired. We leave the theater together with the last members of the audience. There are tiny droplets in the air; they settle on my cheek, they make my hair damp. I ask my dad where we're going.

"We're just going for a walk," he replies.

We eat at a hot dog stand. I'm still chewing my last bite of hot dog when my dad looks at his watch and says it's time to go. The first newspapers come out just after midnight; he buys them from a newsstand at

Hovedbanegården, Copenhagen's central railway station. He also buys a pile of magazines, cigarettes, and a comic for me.

When I go to bed that night, my dad's back at the table. I fall asleep to the sound of scissors.

THE SCREEN SHOWS red deer in a forest, the leaves are yellow. A man steps out in front of the animals, he's wearing green clothes, he fills most of the picture. He points to the red deer behind him. The volume of the TV is turned down, but it looks as though he's whispering.

My dad goes from television to television, takes a couple of steps back, and narrows his eyes. He presses buttons, steps back again, and studies the screen.

He says: "Look at the colors."

He says: "Isn't that picture a little blurry?"

At last my dad takes out a white envelope from his pocket and empties it. The television we buy is big, my dad carries it home. A lock of hair falls in front of his eyes; he blows it away. I'm sad there are so few people in the street today. People who'd have to move out of our way, who'd have to step out into the bicycle lane. I wish they could see what we've bought.

I decide to watch TV all summer. I want to be ready for the school playground. I'm convinced that other children watch a lot of TV, that they watch TV nearly all the time.

I make rye bread sandwiches while my dad reads the manual. I hand him a liver pâté sandwich; he presses the remote control and mutters *why won't it work*? He doesn't get the television to come on until late that night.

From then on the television is on all the time. Mostly with the volume turned down, but when the news comes on, my dad turns it up so it's just as loud as the televisions of the people who live around us. I could shout "Fire!" and he wouldn't hear me. When the weather forecast begins, he drains his coffee cup and smiles at me as though he has just come in the room. He turns the volume down again; I ask him why he doesn't turn off the television completely.

"Emergency broadcasts," he says. "If something important happens, they'll interrupt the program with an emergency broadcast."

He tells me to look out for them as well. Then he carries on with today's newspapers.

I THOUGHT I'D enjoy watching children's TV, but now I'm expecting every program to be interrupted by a man in a suit announcing an emergency broadcast. I'm scared of sitting very still and not being able to call out to my dad if it happens, like in those dreams where the bear comes closer and closer and I'm rooted to the spot.

I practice. When my dad goes down to the kiosk for more newspapers, I shout "Emergency broadcast!" out into the room. When I go to the bathroom, I whisper it to myself. Just before I fall asleep, I say it into the blanket, *Emergency broadcast.*

MY DAD STARTS to tape his newspaper clippings to the wall. He rearranges them. He draws lines with a black ballpoint pen, arrows going both ways and winding their way across the wallpaper.

In nearly all the clippings I see the woman whose name is Monika, the woman we heard speak in the park. Her name is in big letters, she smiles down at us.

My dad says: "Just give me a couple of days . . . I could be wrong." He draws another line with the pen across the wallpaper. "Perhaps the devil isn't as black as he's painted."

"I'm hungry," I say to him.

"Right." He swaps two clippings around. "Why don't you have a go at cooking today?"

"But what if . . . ?"

"Just give it a go. And if something catches fire, there's water in the tap."

I find saucepans and take out food from the fridge. The margarine sizzles in the pan. I drink a glass of water and pretend it's beer. That night I cook spaghetti with fried raisins. We eat in front of the television. It doesn't taste very good, but my dad clears his plate. "Delicious," he says, never once taking his eyes off the screen. Tomorrow I'll try adding some spinach.

I never cook the same dish twice. I cook rice with fried onions. I cook potatoes with cod roe.

I TELL MY DAD that the fridge is nearly empty. He points to the coffee can on the kitchen table which has money in it.

I've been to the corner store before; a couple of times my dad has waited outside while I've gone inside on my own to buy an ice cream.

Now I stand there looking at packets of gravy powder that you mix with water. I see cans of fruit, peas, and carrots. Jaka Bov Pork Shoulder, it says on one of the cans. If I buy it, I won't be able to carry much else, it's that big. And it's quite expensive. But you can fry the meat and eat it cold in a sandwich. I stare at the can for a long time until the grocer in his coat comes over to me and asks if he can help.

I jingle the coins in my pocket, afraid he might think I'm going to steal something. He merely smiles and moves on.

I stand by the till trying to count the money. I sweat on the one-krone coins; I've never had to count anything with other people watching me before, no one except my dad.

"Would you like me to help you?" the grocer says.

My dad has always said never mix money and people. Money makes people strange. And yet I put the coins on the counter. The grocer counts them slowly so I can keep up.

I fry the pork on both sides and put peas and carrots on top. Today I have dinner on the table before the news begins.

When they show something about Africa, my dad tells me to look away.

When they show something about the politician whose name is Monika, he holds a finger to his lips. The reporter asks people in the street what they think of her.

"I haven't voted for years, but Monika gets my vote next time."

I notice how most people call her "Monika" as if they've just been to her house.

Other people call her "the Swede" because her parents are from Sweden. It sounds like a nickname, but some people snarl as they say it: "That Swede thinks she can save the world."

Monika doesn't get cross, she laughs. "I don't care, as long as they listen to what I've got to say."

I like her voice.

I tell my dad that she seems like a nice woman.

"Yes," he replies. "Yes, she does."

He makes a note on a pad in front of him and then he turns his attention back to the television.

ARE YOU LOOKING for anything in particular?" The librarian seems to think it's funny that I'm standing next to the bookcase labeled 64.1. The cookbook section. I feel like kicking him in the shin and running away.

"I cook dinner at home," I say, but it doesn't make the librarian stop smiling.

"We've some nice cookbooks over in the children's section with really great pictures. Perhaps *My First Cookbook* would be . . ."

"Are these proper cookbooks?"

"Er . . . yes." He stays where he is, shifting his weight from foot to foot. "If I can be of assistance, just ask." Then he's gone.

I take the first five cookbooks on the shelf and carry them to the nearest table. I flick through them. I quickly discover that I prefer books with color photographs so I can see what the finished meal is supposed to look like. I make notes on a piece of paper: how to fry a good steak, how to make a basic white sauce. I've made up my mind to be a good cook. I've tried putting too much salt into my dad's food. So much that I couldn't eat it myself. But he just shoveled it into his mouth without looking away from the television or up from the newspapers.

I'm not going to do that again. Now I'm going to cook good food from a real cookbook. "Cooking to make the angels sing"—an expression my dad sometimes uses when we've been out for dinner. It tasted so good it made the angels sing.

I return the books to the shelf. I take another one; it's bigger than the first five and so heavy that I nearly drop it. I drag it over to the table. I'm only a few pages into it before I know that this is the book I've been looking for. It contains every dish I want to make: pork meatballs, beef stroganoff, sausage rolls, and onion soup. All with big color photographs.

MY DAD'S SITTING in the reading room surrounded by newspapers from the last couple of years. A small cave of paper. When I put the book on the table, he looks up from the newspaper he's reading.

My dad turns over the cookbook so he can read the title, then he looks up at me. "You know we don't have a library card, don't you?"

Since we arrived people have gone up to the counter, boys and girls my age, grown-ups, and very old people clutching books with big letters. They've taken out books, lots of books.

“I can give you some money for the photocopier if you want to copy some of the recipes . . .”

“I really want to take this book home.”

I try not to cry. I don’t want to cry in the library. I can feel the tears coming, my eyes start to blur. I want to go to school like everyone else; I want to borrow this book. I try to say this to my dad, but only manage loud sobs.

He gets up. “Of course you can take this book home. Wait here.”

He picks up the book and disappears behind the bookshelves.

My dad’s gone a long time, I wonder if he’s getting a library card. Perhaps he’s talking to the librarian right now. Holding her hand.

When he comes back, he doesn’t have the book with him.

“Done,” he says, taking his denim jacket from the back of the chair and gathering up the newspapers. “Let’s go.”

When we pass the counter, the book isn’t lying there waiting for us. I’m about to say something, but my dad drags me out.

We leave the library and my dad rummages around the pocket of his jacket. I half expect him to produce the book like a magician, but all he takes out is a crumpled packet of cigarettes.

He carries on walking. I follow him around the library. My dad looks into the bushes and then he sticks his hand through the leaves. The cookbook appears. My dad brushes leaves and soil off the cover. Above us I can see the open window from which it must have come. My dad hands me the book.

I RUMMAGE AROUND suitcases and cupboards; I even search odd places like the freezer compartment in the fridge and my dad's boots in the hall. I keep looking, but I can't find my lunchbox, my drinking bottle, or my ruler. None of the school supplies my dad once bought me.

"They've probably been misplaced," he says.

"Misplaced" is code for things we've lost in between moves.

I wanted to lay them out on the kitchen table so they'd sit there every day to remind my dad of his promise that I can start school at the end of the summer.

My dad looks up from his clippings. "We'll just buy some new stuff," he says. "You should have new things, since you're starting at a new school."

We walk from shop to shop and I point out the items I want. We buy a new pencil case and pencils. We buy binding paper for the books I'll be given on my first day. Today we don't take anything without my dad paying.

We buy a lunchbox and a metal drinking bottle. Then we move on to the next shop.

The lady shows us the shelf with school bags: green, yellow, red, and blue. I choose a blue one with space for my lunchbox and my gym clothes.

"We sell a lot of those," the lady says. "It's a really good rucksack."

She takes it down so I can try it.

"Is that the one you want?" my dad asks.

I can tell from his face that he wants me to say no. I ask him if there's anything wrong with it.

"Well, everyone will have one just like it."

He makes it sound as if that's a bad thing. A whole playground full of boys with identical blue school bags. The girls have red ones. Write your name on it so it won't get lost. I keep my mouth shut and nod. I know he could easily talk me out of it. I adjust the straps: the rucksack feels good over my shoulders, I could fill it up with books and it would still be easy to carry. I don't take it off until my dad has paid and we're back outside in the street.

"It's very nice," he says. He zips it open and puts the items we've bought inside.

"Only one thing missing now," my dad says. "If you're going to continue cooking for us, you need the right equipment. If you want to bang nails into the wall, you need a hammer."

The assistant in the kitchen shop unlocks the glass display cabinet with the knives for us. "If you look after them properly, they'll last a lifetime."

The shop assistant's hand becomes a knife that slices smoothly through meat, vegetables, and fish. Then he leaves us alone with the knives. My dad takes them out, weighs each of them in his hand in turn. He shows me how you can feel their sharpness by running your fingertip very carefully along the blade. I can't imagine myself with a knife like that in the kitchen; I'd be terrified I might chop off both my hands. My dad just laughs and says that dull knives are far more dangerous than sharp ones. With a dull knife you have to put all your weight into it, you end up leaning over the knife and that's when they slip. That's how they end up in your thigh.

My dad takes a bus ticket out of his pocket. It looks like a magic trick: one moment the ticket is whole, the next it's cut in half. It barely touches the blade before it's sliced apart.

This is the right knife; this is the one for us. The handle is made of dark wood, it's broad and not quite as long as the others. He hands it to me. Even though the knife frightens me, it feels good in my hand, like a small sword I could use to slay a dragon.

The knife comes in its own dark wooden box. The shop assistant also puts a piece of cloth in the bag. It's very soft and is the only thing you should ever use to dry the knife with.

My dad buys the smallest apron they have. All the chef's hats are too big and fall over my ears.

He takes out his wallet and pays. When we bought the school supplies I was proud, but now I can't help feeling a little nervous. The knife is expensive and I'm starting to see the bottom of the coffee can at home; it now contains only coins.

"I'm looking forward to my packed lunch," my dad says as we leave the shop.

I forgot to bring something to drink so we go into a kiosk and buy a beer for my dad and a soda for me. We walk past several benches before my dad finds one he likes. I've wrapped our lunch in paper with an elastic band around it, like they do in sandwich shops. My dad's salami sandwich has lots of mustard on it; apart from that they're identical. He eats it in big bites and drinks his beer with it.

"Delicious."

He licks his fingers. In front of us lies a palace fit for a king and queen.

"Christiansborg," my dad says. "That's where the politicians decide everything." He wipes his mouth. "Or they think they do. We could go there one of these days and have a look around."

THERE'S A KNOCK on the door. I'm about to open it when my dad pulls me down with him on the floor. I sit on his lap.

"Don't ever open it," he whispers in my ear. "Don't let anyone in unless you know who they are."

There's another knock, harder this time.

I point to the stove and my dad lets me go. I rush over and turn off the gas for my casserole with potatoes, sausages, and cabbage. My fingers are on the stove's round knob when there's another knock. It's not a ghost, it's just another human being, I'm almost sure of it. Fingers, hands, knuckles hitting wood. Even so, I rush back to my dad. He hugs me.

"I know you're in there," we hear through the door and I recognize Sara's voice. "No, I don't know if you're in there. But if you are . . . just open the damn door . . ."

I can feel my dad's arms around me.

"Open the door so we can talk."

My dad covers my mouth with his hand. "She wouldn't understand," he whispers.

The words keep coming through the door, I can't turn them off.

"I just want to talk to you. I do understand . . . no, I don't understand anything. Please, just open the door."

I can feel my dad's muscles through his clothes; his breath is warm against my neck. "She won't understand now. Later, perhaps."

Sara continues to knock on the door.

"It's never easy," my dad whispers. "Remember Jonah? He kept on running and what happened to him?"

"Was he the one with the whale?"

My dad nods; I can feel it against my body. He holds me tight and we both nod, we rock back and forth on the floor.

Sara says: "I don't care about the theater, if you're there or not, whatever the hell you're doing now or if you've just decided to walk away from it all."

It grows quiet out there again. I can feel my dad's heartbeat against my back.

"I really don't care that everyone at the theater is pissed off at you. Please just open the door."

Her voice comes from somewhere below. I think she must be sitting on the doormat now.

I can hear her crying through the door. I look up at my dad. He covers my eyes with his hand.

MY DAD HAS spread newspapers over the living room floor and is sitting on a chair in the middle of the room.

"How do you want it?" I ask him.

"Just nice."

I start combing his hair. In some places it's so matted the comb gets stuck. Slowly I start cutting it, scared that he might suddenly shout stop. But he says nothing, so I keep going. The hair starts covering the newspaper pages underneath us.

"It's quite short now."

He touches his head, pulls a strand forward from behind his ear.

"Just keep cutting, it'll grow back."

I try to visualize men I've seen in the street, how their hair looked, men with briefcases under their arms. Men who were in a hurry, who had trains to catch, meetings to attend. I try to cut my dad's hair a little shorter on the sides than on top. When I start school, he'll look like all the other dads and I'm pleased about that.

When I'm too frightened to cut off any more, he goes to the bathroom and looks in the mirror.

I hold my breath until he says: "That's really rather good." He fiddles with it a little before he's satisfied. "I'm not saying that you should become a hairdresser, but that's really rather good."

He makes a center parting with the comb and smiles at his own reflection in the mirror. Then he makes a side parting, first to one side, then to the other. Now he looks like a man who wears a tie, works in a bank, and comes home every day at the same time. Next time I go shopping, I could buy him a tie. If I smile when he opens his present, I know he'll wear it. My only fear is that he'll wear it over a sweater.

He puts more water in his hair.

"An extreme side part," he says, and flattens his hair completely.

In the kitchen he finds the tin of shoe polish. He unscrews the lid and sticks two fingers into it, draws a straight line under his nose that stops at his upper lip.

"Can you tell who I am now?" he asks.

"Hitler!" I call out.

My dad parades around the living room. He walks stiffly, as if his legs were made of wood, and his right hand points up in the air. He shouts *"Arbeit macht frei!"* while he kicks tufts of hair off the newspapers. He shouts: *"Die Endlösung der Judenfrage!"* Spit flies out of his mouth and he squints.

I laugh so hard my tummy hurts.

THAT NIGHT WE have Swedish sausage casserole for dinner; I found the recipe in the big cookbook from the library. I can't help laughing every time I look at my dad. He has scraped and scrubbed, but he hasn't been able to get the black line off his upper lip.

"When food tastes this good, you're allowed to slurp it," he says, and swigs a mouthful of beer.

I'm proud: it's the first time I've cooked something that resembles the picture in the book.

The wall behind us is blank again. My dad took down the newspaper clippings while I cooked. Only the blue pencil lines on the wallpaper remain.

MY DAD HAS already made packed lunches. My rucksack is waiting for us on the table. I've just woken up.

"We're going on a trip today," he announces.

"Put on your best clothes," he says through the doorway to my bedroom. "We're not going to the woods."

My dad wears a white shirt under his denim jacket, his black shoes shine, he has combed his hair.

He helps me get the rucksack on my shoulders. "You need to get used to walking with it. School is about to start."

I tighten the straps.

We walk down the street.

"It's not too heavy, is it? I put the drinking bottle inside it."

I shake my head. I know it'll be much heavier once I get new books.

My dad takes long strides and looks at his watch. I'm forced to jog to keep up with him.

"Sorry," he laughs, and slows down. "Do you want me to carry your bag?"

I shake my head.

While we wait for the bus, he smooths my hair with a comb and spit until he's satisfied.

"We're going to Christiansborg so it's important we look smart."

MY DAD LOOKS out the window of the bus. He strokes his knee; he keeps running his hand over the denim. I pull his sleeve. He turns to me and cradles my head in both hands. He kisses me on my forehead before looking out at the street again. He has stopped moving his hands.

I didn't have any breakfast before we left home and I start to feel it now. The woman on the seat across from us is eating bread from a baker's bag, tiny bites. She nibbles it like a bird at a feeding table. Yet another tiny piece of bread, pinched between her fingers.

I'm about to pull my dad's denim jacket again, ask him about the packed lunch, ask about all the politicians, how you become one and why they're so important. Something, anything, because he's far too quiet. Then he turns to me and smiles.

"Exciting, isn't it." He takes my hand in his.

WHEN WE GET off the bus, I tell my dad that I'm hungry. He pats my rucksack.

"Soon," he says.

We walk across the cobblestones towards the palace. My dad holds one of the big wooden doors open for me. Instead of knights in armor, two policemen are standing inside. They smile at us. We walk down a long corridor and up some stairs. I stop in front of a painting. A bird, a crow perhaps, is surrounded by other birds. It looks ill; its beak is open and its head is slumped down. It has spread its wings, and between them it says: "He who understands the language of birds can become a politician."

My dad grins, takes my hand, and drags me along past the other paintings.

THE ROOM IS filled with people, and when we enter they all turn around. They have cameras with long lenses and tape recorders in their hands.

They look at us briefly, then they carry on chatting to each other. My dad says that the big camera on a stand in the middle of the floor belongs to the television company.

A door opens and everyone in the room surges towards it. I can only see their backs now.

People start talking on top of each other, asking question after question. I hear cameras clicking.

My dad takes my hand and pushes us past all the arms and elbows. Right up to the front so we can see her, see Monika. She smiles and gestures to signal that the questions will have to wait.

She's on her way to the rostrum when she stops and looks down at me.

"Hello, you," she says. Her eyes are very green. I hear more clicking from the cameras around us. She touches my hair. "Have you come to hear me speak today?"

I nod.

"Well, in that case, I'd better make an effort."

She steps up to the rostrum and taps the microphone lightly with her index finger.

"Thank you for coming."

She talks for a long time. At first I try to understand what she's talking about, but soon I just listen to her voice. I look at her mouth as it shapes the words. They sound like music.

Pencils against notepads make up the chorus. A couple of times I'm convinced that she's looking straight at me. She speaks the language of birds and I'm the only one who knows it.

MONIKA THANKS EVERYONE for coming again. She answers a couple of questions and gathers up her papers. She's on her way down from the rostrum when my dad opens my rucksack, which I still have on my back. He takes something out of it and it gets a little lighter. It must be the drinking bottle, he's thirsty. But I don't hear the sound of the cap; instead I see my dad make his way through the cameras and outstretched microphones. He holds something in his hand, I can't see what it is, but it doesn't look like my drinking bottle.

Then all the backs get in my way and I lose sight of him.

A woman starts to scream, then lots of voices shout.

I run towards the sound. I'm not afraid, I know that my dad's there somewhere, I know I'll find him. It's not difficult to get through the crowd; everyone is standing very still now, a forest of arms, I brush through them like branches.

Monika has stopped screaming, but her mouth is still open, her eyes wide. My dad is lying on the floor in front of her. One man has flung himself across his back; another man presses his shin against my dad's outstretched arm. Not far from my dad's fingertips lies the kitchen knife. I recognize the black handle. Yesterday I chopped onions and carrots with it.

· 1996 ·

I'M SITTING AT the kitchen table drinking orange juice.

Through the glass door I can see the back garden. It's February and the swimming pool is filled with brown leaves that have almost rotted. Behind the pool the garden rises towards the railway tracks.

I sit in the kitchen, waiting. I'm sixteen years old and I'm in my final year of school.

The front door opens, Karin and my stepdad are back. Michael switches on the television in the living room and turns down the volume. He reads the news on Text TV. A habit from way back when he was a journalist. Today he's a press officer for a pharmaceutical company.

Karin comes into the kitchen. She has dark blonde hair, teaches at a high school, and writes educational books.

"Are you ready?" she says. She gave up trying to make me call her "Mum" years ago.

I nod.

"Has the babysitter arrived?"

"She's upstairs with Clara," I reply.

MY SISTER STANDS in the doorway, waving as we get in the car. The big houses we drive past are similar to Karin and Michael's. Some have a sunroom rather than a garage, a flagpole in the garden rather than a birdbath.

The school is a low building which could easily be a public swimming pool or a library. In the reception are pictures, painted by a local artist in strong, bright colors, of young people with books, skateboards, and Walkmans.

We walk down long corridors with exposed redbrick walls. Posters made by pupils in the earlier grades are on display. We pass a picture of a squirrel eating a nut. In the next picture that same squirrel lies drowned in a pool of oil.

THE ARTIFICIAL LIGHT doesn't reach the corners of the classroom. Two student desks have been pushed together in the middle; cups and a Thermos have been set out. Today my Danish teacher has combed his hair and put on a formal shirt. He shuffles the papers in front of him. Glances at his watch.

"Karsten Eriksen should be here in a minute. He wanted a word with you as well."

"Sounds pretty damn serious," Michael says, and laughs.

My Danish teacher merely smiles down at his papers. Then he starts pouring coffee into the small cups the first-grade children use for juice.

Karsten Eriksen, the principal, enters; he's in his late fifties and wears a dark suit jacket over a pair of jeans.

"Thank you for coming," he says, and shakes hands with Karin and Michael.

He sits down and pours coffee into a cup with a picture of an elephant.

"All the cups in the staff room were gone," my Danish teacher says to him.

The principal scratches his chin with his pen. "Well, this is the thing . . . Your son has been seen smoking cannabis on school premises and . . ."

"Why didn't you tell us?" Karin straightens up in her seat. "You could've called . . ."

"He wasn't caught in the act. Someone thinks they saw him smoking in the parking lot, but that's not why I wanted to talk to you."

They had come and taken me out of class. I followed them through the school and no one spoke a word. We stood around the big desk in the principal's office while they emptied my bag of candy wrappers and scrunched-up notes. Four books and a comb. A forgotten sandwich that must have been over a week old was inside a plastic bag no one felt like opening.

Then they found the folder: stiff cardboard with an elastic band around it. A folder that could easily contain a couple of squashed joints, so they opened it. I could tell from their faces that they regretted their action immediately.

THE PRINCIPAL TAKES the folder out of his briefcase and puts it on the table. At first Karin stares blankly at him, then she opens it and starts flicking through the drawings. Michael looks over her shoulder. Everyone looks gravely at a drawing of my English teacher having intercourse with an Alsatian. The dog wears a straw hat with little holes for its furry ears. Karin turns it over; in the next drawing my math teacher sits on his haunches in front of a horse with his mouth open. Michael tries hard not to laugh.

That's until we reach the drawings of blood and intestines hanging like paper chains. I've colored them in.

Karin pushes the pile away. The principal asks if I've anything to say for myself. I shake my head. He puts the drawings back in the folder and closes it.

"This falls outside what we'd regard as normal behavior. Several of these drawings could almost be considered a threat. I can't rule out expeling him."

"Expel him?" Karin looks up from the folder and across to the principal. "But that means he'd have to retake his final year. His exams are coming up, he'll never be able to . . ."

"We're not sure that an ordinary public school is the best place for him."

"Just because of a few drawings?" As always when she gets agitated, Karin flushes and spots appear on her cheeks.

The principal coughs briefly into his hand. "It wouldn't be purely because of the drawings, of course, but we see them as an indication of very unfortunate developments . . ."

Up to this point Michael has been fiddling nervously with the steel strap of his wristwatch; now he looks up.

"You searched his bag."

"Yes . . . yes, we did." The principal no longer sounds quite so confident.

"Is the bag his property or the school's? Even in a public school, students still have some basic rights, don't they?"

The principal rubs his hands over his knees. "What I'm trying to say is . . . I don't want you to view this as a punishment." He pauses briefly. "It's clear that your son is struggling to fit in. Many of his teachers tell me they find him hard to teach."

Neither Karin nor Michael says anything.

"This is what I propose." For the first time the principal looks directly at me. "I think you should go home and think about whether this school is the right place for you. Whether you want to be a student here. If you decide you want to do something else, we'll be happy to support you. Help you find an alternative school."

I study the hairs in his nose, coarse hairs stained yellow by nicotine. If he has a wife, she must have asked him to trim them.

"But if you choose to remain here, it must be a positive choice. And it's on the condition that you see the school psychologist once a week for the rest of the school year."

The principal flicks through his Day-Timer; he circles a date with his pen. I'm given a fortnight to think about it. If I want to stay at the school, I have turn up at his office two weeks from today before twelve noon.

The Day-Timer is closed; the decision has been made. When Karin starts talking again, I can hear that she has given up the fight.

"Won't he fall too far behind?"

"We're not worried about the academic side," my Danish teacher says.

WE DRIVE HOME in silence. Michael operates the steering wheel, the gears, and the pedals as if he's engaged in mountain driving that requires his full attention.

I hear small sobs from the passenger seat, Karin holding it back, holding it in. I know it's not just because of the drawings or my potential expulsion. The last few years would have been easier for them without me around.

THE BABYSITTER HAS already put on her coat. She's sitting on the steps to the first floor, waiting.

"Clara has just nodded off. She refused to fall asleep until you came home."

Karin finds some money for her and offers to drive her home. We noticed her bicycle in the drive on the way in, so the offer is made purely out of politeness. The girl turns around in the doorway.

"An old lady rang. She sounded a little confused. She seemed to think she knew you."

"It's nothing," Karin says. "She's called before. Probably just some crazy old lady who rings people at random."

Karin closes the door behind her, takes off her earrings, and walks up the stairs without looking back.

Michael puts his jacket on a hanger.

"Can I have a word?" he asks.

We go into the kitchen. Michael takes two beers out of the big silver fridge, opens them, and drops the bottle opener back into the drawer. He gives it a push with his elbow, it glides shut without making a noise. All the cupboard doors are black gloss. He wipes off his fingerprints with his sleeve. Then he hands me one of the bottles.

"I won't claim to understand you. Not at all. But I respect you. Possibly more than you think." He picks at the label on the beer bottle, his fingers missing a cigarette. "Your Danish teacher's an idiot . . . and your principal's an old hippie. But that's no reason for you to piss away your future. Take the damn exam. Get it over with. You'll find university easier. I'm sure of it."

Michael looks down at his beer, shrugs his shoulders. "I'm not telling you to do what we did. God forbid."

THE DOOR TO my sister's room is ajar. She hugs her teddy bear in her sleep. I have to stand very still in order to hear her breathe. Her dreams don't make her run in her sleep. In her world, Goldilocks and the Three Bears end up friends. My sister is completely surrounded by princes and princesses. By horses and enchanted castles. From the posters on the wall to the plastic jewelry and the dolls on the floor. She gets anything she wants, and when she develops a new interest, her parents follow her around the toy store. Yet I can't help admiring how deeply she has immersed herself in a world of her own devising.

She turns over in her sleep as if she can feel my gaze on her. I want to kiss her on the forehead, but I'm afraid of waking her up.

I SIT ON the windowsill in my room, smoking a joint out the open window. The house is quiet. The neighborhood is quiet. The last drop of red wine has been drunk, the murder on the TV screen has been solved. Tomorrow is another day, not much different from today. But it'll be a good day, a new day organized with small magnets on the fridge. Don't forget to feed the rabbit. Whose turn is it to vacuum? Lasagna for dinner.

The smoke reaches my lungs. I suppress the urge to cough and I feel the heat rise up my throat and across my eyes. Like a thin membrane that turns the glow of the moon more yellow and the fog that lies across the railway tracks into big balls of blue cotton wool.

THE MAN STICKS his arm right down into the terrarium. He holds his hand still until the grasshoppers forget that he's alive. Then he reaches out and catches one of them, his fingers delicately pinching its body. It joins the others in a white plastic tub which used to contain Neapolitan ice cream. The man who owns the pet shop is in his early fifties. Perhaps he has a wife and children; perhaps he has old friends and flies south, to the Mediterranean, for his holidays. But I find it easier to imagine him in a house lit up by aquariums, sitting in an armchair with reading glasses on his nose and a book about saltwater fish in his lap.

He hands me the plastic tub. I ease open the lid, take out the first grasshopper, and drop it into another terrarium.

The monitor lizard stands so still it looks as if it is stuffed. Then its tongue shoots out, lightning quick, blink and you'll miss it. It crunches grasshopper wings and legs before it swallows.

I drop another couple of grasshoppers down to it, but the monitor lizard has lost interest.

"It needs a home," the man says. "I take good care of them, but they go a little stir crazy if they stay here for too long. Not enough room and too many schoolkids tapping on the glass."

He rests his hand on the rim of the terrarium. "Think about it if you want it. At that price it's a giveaway."

I WALK DOWN the main street, past the pizzeria, the florist, the post office, and the pharmacy. My class is doing German now. Right now our teacher is walking around, looking down at the open exercise books.

He can spot an incorrectly conjugated verb at a glance.

I walk through the town center to the park, which has benches and a metal sculpture whose spikes spear fallen fruit in the autumn.

I can hear voices and people laughing before I reach the skateboard park.

There are never more than a few people skateboarding, sometimes none at all. Most of them sit on the ramp, smoking joints and drinking cheap beer from the nearest supermarket. I say hi to Søren. He was adopted from Korea, but everyone calls him the Inuit.

"Have you seen Christian?" I ask him.

"Not today." He flicks his cigarette into the bushes. "But if you see him, tell him I've got some money for him."

I go back to the residential neighborhood. A couple of streets from Karin and Michael's house I turn left and walk down the road to where Christian lives.

His mum opens the door. She's blonde, wears an apron, and has a dab of flour on her cheek. Christian's mum keeps in shape. She appears in many of the locals' wet dreams.

"Oh good, another guinea pig," she says, and laughs.

I follow her down the hallway and can easily imagine a film crew waiting for her in the kitchen: Hold up that packet of flour, smile, yes, that's it.

"I'm experimenting with something for Maja's birthday. Healthy birthday buns." She lowers her voice, her perfume is sweet. "Maja is getting a little chubby, you know."

Christian is sitting at the dining table. "If I knew you were coming, I would have warned you about the buns."

His mum brings us each a glass of juice. Then she disappears back into the kitchen.

"You've been smoking," Christian says to me.

"Is it obvious?"

"Not to my mum. And, anyway, she already thinks you're dangerous. That you belong to some sort of sect. But . . . I think she likes you."

These days I barely notice all the mothers smiling at me with exaggerated warmth. Since I came to live here, they've paid for all my movie tickets. I'm "the other," someone their children would undoubtedly benefit from meeting.

Christian looks at me. "Can you still write?"

His mum enters with a plate of bread rolls and a butter dish.

"Fortunately you two don't have to watch your weight." She sits down opposite us. "Eat," she says, resting her chin in her hand and looking at us expectantly.

The bread rolls are dark gray. They need a thick layer of butter not to stick to the roof of your mouth.

"I'm so proud that Christian is helping you. I know it sounds silly, but I'm really proud. I told his teachers and they think it's really great, too. A couple of years ago he wasn't particularly academic, remember? But you two have fun together, don't you?"

When we've eaten the bread rolls, we go to Christian's room.

He removes a couple of books from the bookcase and slips in his arm.

"I'm afraid that's all I've got," he says, putting a small brown nugget on the table in front of me. It's one gram maximum. "I know I owe you. I'm out right now. If you come to the party on Friday . . ."

"Party?"

"The party one of your little friends from school's having. You're probably not invited. I'm only going there to deal. If you turn up, I'll have the rest for you."

Christian turns on his computer and I sit down in front of the keyboard. He produces his homework from his bag, a five-page essay on Pelle the Conqueror for tomorrow.

"Roll me a joint," I say to him.

He opens the window and finds the pine-scented room spray. He's about to pick up my nugget from the table, but I slap the back of his hand with the mouse.

"Screw you," he says, rubbing his hand.

"I know you've kept some for yourself, roll it out of that."

Christian pretends to sulk and finds another lump from the bookcase. Then he locks the door and starts to roll. He lights the joint, takes a couple of drags, and passes it to me.

"They want to throw me out of school," I say to him while I smoke and write.

"So you'll be reduced to working your ass off at the supermarket."

"They want to send me to another school, as far away as possible."

"Full of hyperactive kids and girls who cut themselves?"

He grins right until it dawns on him what it means. Not for me, but for him. The last couple of years I've written all his essays. He has gone from getting fives to sixes. Then from sevens to eights and nines. Despite his poor exam results, he managed to get into university. It was my idea that he should see a therapist who specializes in performance anxiety. Ever since then, his teachers have been forgiving when he writes incoherent essays during exams and gets tongue-tied in front of an examiner.

"I hope you'll stay," he says.

THE FIGHT STARTS in the bedroom, where Karin is putting on makeup, and continues down the stairs, through the living room, into the kitchen, and back into the bedroom. When they argue like this it's always about me. I know it even though I can only hear the odd word here and there and my name is never mentioned. I go to Clara's room; she's sitting on the floor engrossed in her plastic ponies.

Her parents are now standing at the foot of the stairs; words reach us, angry and suppressed. The ponies jump into the air, they flick their pink manes, Clara hums loudly to herself.

The row ends where it started. The babysitter has canceled due to boyfriend trouble and Karin's mother still isn't fully recovered after a blood clot in her leg, so if they want to go out tonight and not waste 1,000 kroner's worth of tickets to the Royal Theatre, I'll have to look after Clara.

Eventually Michael comes up the stairs. I can tell it's him from the footsteps: heavier than Karin's, but with a certain lightness. Every Sunday he goes for long runs in a nearby forest; he comes back dripping with sweat in his tight-fitting Lycra running clothes.

He puts his arm around my shoulder in a matey fashion he's tried a couple of times before, then he takes it away again. He has stuck up for me.

"Is that okay?" he asks, knowing that I must have been listening in. "There's money on the kitchen table so you can order a pizza. You can take a beer from the fridge if you like."

I nod; Michael hesitates for a moment before he goes back downstairs.

"Right, Clara," I say to my sister. "What do you say we torch this place while your folks are out?"

She looks up from her ponies and grins.

"What does 'torch' mean?" she asks me.

I go down with her to the front door so she can wave good-bye to her parents.

Karin is wearing a dress in a dark, shiny fabric and a string of pearls around her neck that matches her earrings. Michael wears a suit and a shirt with no tie.

"Have you got the tickets?" he asks.

"Have you got the car keys?" she asks.

As she walks out the door, Karin smiles anxiously at us. "If the phone rings, don't pick up. Let the answering machine deal with it."

Michael sends me a trusting I-know-you-can-do-it look.

Then they run outside to the dark blue station wagon. Karin traps her dress in the car door, opens it, and slams it shut again. The headlights come on and they're gone.

I take my sister to the kitchen. The pizza leaflet is stuck to the fridge with a magnet, a laminated picture of a saint they bought on holiday in Rome.

"Who ever heard of putting pineapple on a pizza? What next, apples and pears? Or how about banana? A big banana pizza? A monkey pizza?"

Clara stands with her hands on her hips like I've seen her mum do. She's not budging.

"I want a princess pizza." That's what she calls it.

When the doorbell rings, she races out into the hallway and jumps up and down. She still finds it hard to believe that you can say some numbers into a telephone and a pizza appears as if by magic.

We eat and watch a cartoon Clara has seen twenty, thirty times before. A film with princesses and princes and horses the princesses can ride on. When it's finished, we watch the first twenty minutes of *The Exorcist* until Clara is too scared to peek out from behind her cushion. I show her where her parents hide the sweets, the good sweets, the stuff with artificial coloring and preservatives.

When she has stuffed herself, I take her to the bathroom on the first floor.

"Everyone has to brush their teeth," I say.

She shakes her head, refuses to open her mouth.

"Have you ever seen a princess with black teeth?"

"A black princess."

"You muppet, black people don't have . . . Get a move on or I'll wee all over you."

She looks at me; she laughs and takes the toothbrush.

I help her put on her pajamas.

I read *The Little Prince* to her, but there aren't any princesses in it so I read three picture books to her afterwards.

"I can't sleep," she says, when I turn over the last page. She looks at me, her eyes wide open.

"Do you want me to read you another book?"

"I can't sleep." She grins; she knows full well that it's my problem. That I have to do something about it. I look at the clock; Karin and Michael won't be back for another couple of hours.

I pull her out of bed. First I put her into a warm sweater, then trousers and a winter coat on top of her pajamas.

It's cold outside, and dark. She presses against me. Slowly we walk down the road, moving our legs in unison.

After a couple of houses she stops and points to a large white building. We both know this game.

I say: "Are you sure you want me to tell you?"

She nods.

"And you promise not to tell anyone?"

She nods.

"The people who live in that house landed on Earth in a spaceship a couple of years ago. They're green all over, but they're dressed up as real people when you see them. They were actually trying to get to Copenhagen, but they must have misread the map. They keep their spaceship in the garage. They work on it on weekends and during holidays; they hope to go home soon."

We walk on. A couple of houses later she points again.

"The people living there? Are you sure you want to know?"

She squeezes my hand.

"Okay, but I did warn you."

Clara looks up at me.

"It's actually quite gross. But you're a big girl now. So . . . Last Christmas, they couldn't get a duck. They tried everywhere, every supermarket and butcher's, but everyone was sold out. So they ended up eating the next door neighbor's dog. With caramelized potatoes and red cabbage. The next day they picked the bones clean. Now they're hoping no one will ever find out."

We walk on, more houses, Clara points.

I'M JUST TAKING the key out of the lock when we hear the telephone ring. Clara is faster than me. When I enter the living room, she hands me the receiver.

The woman on the other end tells me she's my paternal grandmother; she pronounces every word very clearly, as if I wouldn't be able to understand her otherwise.

She says she's tried calling several times, but got no reply.

Clara looks at me quizzically. I gesture for her to go out into the hallway and take off her coat. The woman on the telephone says she has to see me, that it's important. When Clara comes back, I'm still standing with the telephone receiver in my hand.

"What's wrong?" she asks.

I shake my head.

I lie next to Clara and look at her closed eyes. Her hands reach out for something that isn't there.

I sit on the sofa waiting for Karin and Michael to come home.

I find it hard to concentrate on the television.

I hear the key in the lock. They're both giggling. They've had a couple of glasses of wine and were probably relieved not to find cars with flashing lights on the roof as they came home. Karin asks me if anyone called. I shake my head.

THE CINEMA HAS a glass front; the small café inside sells sandwiches and foamy coffee. There's only one screen. I don't ask what they're showing, I just buy a ticket and take my seat. In one of the back rows an older man is polishing his glasses. Two little boys sit at the front; they throw popcorn at each other and laugh, then they fall silent and glance over their shoulders. They're scared to be caught skipping school, like in that cartoon with Donald Duck and his nephews. When the ads have finished, the lights go down and the film begins. It's about a policeman who can talk to his dog. Together they look for some stolen paintings.

After ten minutes the darkness in the theater fills with faces I can't name anymore. I've stopped thinking about my dad, that's what I tell myself, but perhaps I think about him all the time.

I don't know very much about what happened. I got an explanation, disjointed and child-friendly. The rest is just fragments, words I've heard through doors left ajar.

I know that he went to university, like Karin.

He studied theology, like his father and his grandfather before him.

I know that he was working on his Ph.D. when it went wrong. Those aren't my words. Nerves, stress, I've heard it called several things, but it went wrong. So they moved. I was very young. They moved to the countryside, a place where my dad could finish his doctoral thesis in peace. Only that's not what happened, it went wrong. Karin was going to take me and leave, but my dad beat her to it.

Whenever I've asked about him, it has always ended with Karin running upstairs to cry in the bedroom. I stay down with Michael, who tells me it hasn't been easy for her. Sometimes he tells me only with his eyes.

The dog on the screen keeps talking, the boys in the front row laugh. I get up and leave the theater. The washrooms are next to the café. I stand on the toilet seat and find a joint in my pocket. I open the window a little and blow smoke outside so I don't trigger the alarm.

When the joint is finished, I go back into the theater.

The man behind me is snoring, the boys are laughing. I sit with my eyes half-shut. The dog on the screen talks and keeps getting the policeman into trouble. It ruins a big cake at a birthday party and farts so that everyone in the elevator has to pinch their noses. At the end the two of them catch the art thieves.

I CAN HEAR the party as soon as I turn the corner. The bass is so loud it makes the windows rattle. Outside the house, stacks of bicycles are leaning against the hedge.

I walk up the garden path. A boy from my year comes running around the house; he hasn't got a shirt on and his chest is scratched. He trips over a coiled garden hose, his hand brushes the ground. Then he continues to run around the house.

I walk past a girl sitting on the steps crying, the jacket she's wearing is inside out, her friend has her arm around her. The hallway is filled with coats and beers in plastic bags. The floor is shaking; inside the living room people are jumping up and down, lit up by flashing red and blue lights.

I drink a glass of punch that tastes of vodka and pineapple while I look for Christian. He's on the sofa, leaning over a girl, one hand resting on her shoulder, the other somewhere between her legs.

I pull him to standing. At first he looks as if he might punch me, then he follows me.

"Do you know how old that Amanda is?" he asks me when we reach the hallway.

"You mean Amalie?"

"Yes, Amalie. She has turned fifteen, hasn't she?"

"Like you care?"

"I do a bit."

"Do you have something for me?"

"Erm, I didn't think you were coming. You didn't sound as if . . ."

"Do you have something?"

"You should've been here a couple of hours ago. I've sold out."

"You're an idiot, Christian."

"I know it's not cool. But I could easily have sold another ten grams."

He takes two bottles of beer from a plastic bag on the floor. Opens them with his lighter and hands me one.

"On Monday I'll definitely have some again, I promise."

He raises the beer in a toast and goes back into the living room.

I drink from the bottle. I'm about to start looking for my jacket in the pile on the floor when I hear a voice behind me.

"I hope you're enjoying my beer."

I turn around and see Camilla from my class. "Sorry," I say.

She laughs. "I don't care, they're not mine." She walks past me and stops in the doorway. "I've got a joint we can share."

I follow her through the house. Camilla only comes up to my chest; she has blonde, messy hair that looks as if she never combs it. I'm quite sure it's intentional, and it must be a real struggle to find child-sized Doc Martens. We walk through the kitchen, where mini-meatballs have been used as ashtrays and carrot sticks have been stuffed into condoms. Camilla opens the kitchen door and we walk out onto a covered terrace.

We sit down on the steps leading to the garden. There's no swimming pool here, but a small pond with bamboo. Camilla takes the joint from her inside pocket; it's lying in a transparent, pale-blue plastic bag.

"I didn't think this was your scene," I say to her while she lights the joint.

"I was bored at home. I decided to give our classmates one last chance. I'm regretting that, obviously."

She passes me the joint, I take a drag, the cannabis is stronger and better than the stuff Christian sells at school.

Camilla takes a blanket from one of the garden chairs and spreads it across our knees. Every time she raises the joint to her lips, I can see a small drawing of a spider on the back of her hand. I've been in the same class as her for five, six years now, but I don't know her. She rarely says anything during lessons, not unless she's made to. I know that she plays bass in a punk band. One day she showed the other girls the blisters on her index finger.

They gave her advice on which hand lotions to use and Camilla fell silent again.

"You're stoned," she says, having caught me staring at her. "That didn't take long."

I look across the garden at the swing moving back and forth every time there's a gust of wind. There's a discarded tricycle on the lawn, its front wheel is pointing up to the sky. At the bottom of the garden is a wooden playhouse painted red. I can't stop myself from giggling; perhaps the joint is kicking in.

Camilla looks at me.

"Is Viktor throwing this party?" I ask.

She nods, but looks puzzled.

"He wanks off in that playhouse."

"What, right now?"

"No, but at least once a day."

"I don't know if I should believe you," she says.

"He told me down at the skateboard park. After five premium beers and a couple of joints. It's his big secret."

"Which you'll take with you to the grave."

"I don't really like him."

"I'm with you there."

Again I accidentally look at her a little too long. I've never noticed the slight gap between her front teeth before.

She stubs out the joint, flicks it away; it flies in a long arc across the lawn and lands in the small pond.

"Stay where you are," she says. "I'll go get some beers."

I'm pretty sure she won't be coming back. I decide to sit here for a couple more minutes and then walk home through the suburb, piss in a hedge. I'm about to get up when I hear the kitchen door open. Camilla clinks two bottles against each other.

"So why did you come tonight?" I ask her while she makes herself comfortable under the blanket.

"You don't believe my story about giving my classmates one more chance?"

"No." I can feel her knee against mine.

"Today's a kind of anniversary." Now she, too, is looking across the lawn. "I don't really know how old my baby sister would have been. She had Downs and a heart defect. My parents are going on a mini break tomorrow. Today they walk around the house, my mum lights candles and they don't say a lot."

WE TAKE TURNS going back inside the house for more beers from the many bags in the hallway. We stay on the steps. We talk about our classmates. About the teachers. We discuss music for a long time. Inside the party reaches its peak, things get broken and people shout.

IN THE EARLY morning hours we walk down streets from which all life has been eradicated as if by a deadly virus. Soon the first cars will reverse out of their garages for fresh bread and juice. They'll drive to one of the neighborhood's two bakeries. Which of them is the better is discussed at length at dinner parties.

"I hear they're about to throw you out," Camilla says, her voice husky from cigarettes and beer.

"Yes. If I don't apologize."

"Are you going to?"

"I haven't made up my mind yet."

The sun is rising, the birds start to chirp.

"This is where I live," she says. We're standing in front of a large house. "I'm glad you walked me home. Now you know where to come tonight."

I'M EATING CORNFLAKES and drinking orange juice. Karin and Michael smile at each other, happy that I've done something normal, that I've been out drinking all night.

Karin puts my little sister's coat on her; they're going shopping for her birthday party. Clara's birthday is the same week as Christian's little sister's. The last couple of years it has turned into a competition: they show each other their presents and clothes and one of them invariably ends up in tears.

While Karin looks for Clara's woolly cap in the hallway, Michael asks me if I'd like to come with him to the home and garden store.

"We're getting your sister a swing," he whispers. "I need you to help me carry it."

"Just like in the cartoon?"

He grins and nods. We've both been forced to watch that film many times, the one where the princess sits on her swing and the frog comes jumping past.

Karin and my sister get dropped off at the shops and we drive on.

"Tell me if you want me to shut up," Michael says, tuning the radio. He finds U2, "Sunday Bloody Sunday." He turns up the volume and the music fills the car.

We both remember what happened last time.

It was just after New Year's and someone had thrown fireworks into our mailbox and blown it up, so we had to get a new one.

"How are you really?" he'd asked, as we stood in front of several rows of mailboxes.

He then spent an hour trying to extract even the tiniest bit of information from me. Some fragment, a tiny, shiny nugget he could put in his pocket and proudly show to Karin when we got home. I made the boy talk, he's gay, he's depressed. He wants a dog, a hamster, an annual zoo pass.

I gave him nothing.

After one hour we bought a red mailbox, the exact same model they'd had before.

We join the motorway.

"I don't want to trap you in the car and make you talk to me," Michael says, turning down the radio. "Your principal called me at work. He said that if you go to his office, he won't ask you to apologize. He doesn't want to humiliate you. He really doesn't want to expel you."

We drive through an industrial estate with gray warehouses.

"So the man's a hypocrite. So am I. It's another word for growing up." Michael turns his head. "Sometimes you smile in the wrong places, did you know that?"

WE PARK IN front of the home and garden store and walk down long aisles with tall metal shelves on both sides. We pass big yellow signs with special offers for smoke detectors and hammer drills.

"Fingers crossed they'll have a swing with princesses on it," Michael says.

It's not the season for swings, so they're hidden away at the back. A middle-aged man with a folding rule comes over to assist us. Michael adopts the same tone with him that he uses to talk to builders and mechanics.

"So is this one galvanized?" he asks. "Does it meet all the safety requirements?"

"Everything we sell does."

Of course we don't buy the cheapest model because it's bound to rust. Michael laughs along with the man with the folding rule. They laugh at the fools who think they're saving money. People who don't understand it'll only cost them more in the long run.

"Do you have one with princesses on it?" I ask. The man from the home and garden store looks at me.

"Oh, it's for you is it?" he grins, resting his hands on his belt.

"Yes," I reply.

"No, not at the . . . No, we don't."

ONCE WE'VE GOT the swing up on the rented trailer, we buy hot dogs from a stand in the parking lot.

I tell Michael I'd like to visit a girl tonight, maybe stay over at her place. He licks ketchup from his fingers.

"Who is she?"

"Camilla from my class."

"That small one . . . I'll need to talk to your mum. But I don't think it'll be a problem." I'm always allowed to do normal stuff.

We get back before Karin and my sister. The swing lies unassembled on the trailer and we quickly carry it inside the garden shed. Michael drives off to return the trailer; I fill a rucksack with clothes.

I WALK UP the garden path and ring the doorbell. It's late afternoon. The house looks bigger than it did this morning; its dark windows watch me.

Camilla opens the door. She wears a faded T-shirt and ripped black jeans.

For a moment I'm scared that I misunderstood her invitation or that she might have had second thoughts. She turns and gestures with her hand for me to follow her. Her bare feet are small and light.

She has opened a bottle of wine and poured some for herself in a water glass on the kitchen table.

"My dad says you should always drink Sauvignon Blanc while it's still young, so I think we should help him."

She jumps up to sit on the kitchen table and offers me a cigarette from an open packet. Then she looks down at her feet, which are dangling far above the floor.

"I'm not small. I'm just very far away."

After a couple of glasses of white wine it no longer feels quite so awkward to be alone with her in the big, empty house.

"I bet you're hungry," she says and takes out a sandwich toaster, the kind you close around two slices of bread, from a kitchen cupboard.

"My parents worry about me."

She plugs it in and a red button on the machine lights up.

"But I can't be bothered to cook so I've been living on toasties for a year and a half now. We never eat anything else when we rehearse. And when I get home at night, it's the easiest thing to make."

She takes a plate with cold chicken from the fridge, along with a jar of barbecue spices and a red bell pepper; she puts the food on the kitchen table.

"My parents took me to see a dietician to find out if you can really live on toasties alone. If it makes you ill. They paid for several appointments."

Camilla's laugh starts in her throat and ends up somewhere in her nose. It sounds weird, but I like it. The kind of laughter you can only have if you don't care or you're used to laughing with other girls dressed in black in an old, damp, soundproof shipping container.

"Or we could order a pizza. This is just a bad habit."

I shake my head. I'm more curious than hungry.

"If it fits between two slices of bread, then it's a toastie. That's the rule."

When the food is ready, we carry it into the living room. She takes the plates; I bring the glasses and the wine.

We put everything on the coffee table.

"I'm just going to get something."

She returns with a videotape in her hand.

"Dario Argento," she says, tapping the cassette. "A girl from my band thinks Argento's films are essential viewing. All of them."

We eat and drink the rest of the wine while we watch *Profondo Rosso*.

Women scream and are murdered with a meat cleaver on the screen. Camilla sits only a few centimeters away from me. Not wrapped in a thick winter coat this time. No noise from drunken people behind us.

When only crusts are left on our plates, we smoke a joint.

"It's very hot in here, don't you think?" Camilla says when the credits roll. "Perhaps we should take our clothes off."

THE DUVET HAS been kicked to the end of the bed. We're both naked. I open the curtain, small drops of water have gathered on the inside of the windowpane. Camilla's room is dark red: outside, the sun is rising. There's a plastic clock shaped like a skull on the chest of drawers. It's early in the morning, but I'm running late.

I find the bathroom and splash water on my face. I borrow a blob of toothpaste from a tube and rub it on my gums.

I can't have been asleep for more than a couple of hours. Maybe just the one.

My underwear and socks are lying on the floor, tangled up with her clothes. Camilla rests on her elbow; she watches me while I put on my underwear.

"I need to go away for a couple of days," I say, taking the joint lying on the windowsill, the one we didn't get round to smoking yesterday. I hold it up and she nods, I can have it.

I kiss her. On my way down the stairs I find my T-shirt. In the living room are my trousers and my hoodie. My rucksack is in the hallway where I left it.

The cold morning air makes me shiver. The sidewalk is wet and smooth. I walk as quickly as I can until I reach the street where Karin and Michael live.

I find pen and paper in my rucksack and use a white Citroën for support. The hood of the car is wet from morning dew and the pen keeps going through the paper and onto the paintwork. I'm as brief as I can be. I write that I'm going away. I tell them not to worry about me. I'll be back in a couple of days.

I don't explain why. Karin knows where I've gone. She must know: she spoke to my grandmother on the telephone and chose not to tell me about it.

I post the letter through their mailbox and think about my sister. She's lying up there, she's so very small. When she sleeps, she drools a little; not very much, but enough to leave snail traces on her pillow.

I run down the street, past the road where Christian lives. Down the main street and past the pet shop.

I sit in the empty train carriage, trying to catch my breath.

The train pulls away from the station. I lean my head against the cold window, my breath steams it up, I watch the houses go past.

I GET OFF at Hovedbanegården. The sidewalks are littered with cigarette butts and squashed chewing gum. I have twelve minutes to buy my ticket and find the right platform.

THE CARRIAGE FILLS up with young people with gym bags and beers. A couple of stations later a family gets on.

"Do you think Granny will have some sweets for us?" a little boy asks.

His mum nods, yes, absolutely.

I show my ticket to the ticket inspector and sink back into my seat.

THE TRAIN DRIVES on board the ferry. I stand on the deck during the whole crossing. The air is cold, my eyes water. I get splashes of salt water in my face and I laugh, but no one can hear me over the ferry's engine. When I get back inside the train, I can no longer feel my fingers or toes.

The passengers around me change as I travel through the country.

I still have many hours' traveling ahead of me, but it doesn't matter. When I half-close my eyes, I'm back in Camilla's room. She has a birthmark on her shoulder and her hair smells of smoke and apples. I can feel her fingers on my arms. Her bare feet are cold against my back. The candles on the windowsill drip wax onto the carpet.

During the night we go down to the kitchen to make more toasties. The house is cold; we're naked and the sweat dries on our backs. She sits on the marble kitchen table, says she's scared of getting frozen to it, and I kiss her on the lips.

The train steward's trolley bumps into my knee. He apologizes. I buy a sandwich with halved meatballs and red cabbage even though I'm not hungry.

Outside, towns glide past. Some small, others bigger.

WE REACH THE last stop; the day has passed on the train. I'm one of a handful of people getting off. I walk through the railway station where the newsstand is closed, continue through an underpass, and then reach the bus station. I find a shelter; I tighten my jacket around me. Half an hour later the bus arrives.

The light inside the bus is so dim I can barely see my hands. Other passengers sit scattered around. When they get on, they nod to the driver and perhaps to a fellow passenger, but none of them speaks. We drive past fields and through small towns that I recognize. Or towns that look similar. Places I lived when I was a child.

The water appears a couple of times to my right like a black line. We drive past large, square buildings with pigs and corn silos. The bus driver goes outside and smokes a cigarette. He looks at his watch, then we drive on.

When we reach the final destination, I ask the driver where the harbor is. He points and says it's not far.

THE ISLAND IS dark. I can't see from the ferry deck how big it is. On the map it looked like a seagull colony that someone had gone to the trouble of naming.

A single car sails with us. The engine splutters to life, the driver presses the accelerator and disembarks.

I walk across the cobblestones. Past a closed snack bar, a small wooden shed with pictures of French hot dogs, meatball sandwiches, and fries.

An old woman in a green wool coat is standing next to an old Opel.

When I reach her, she gives me a quick hug. She signals with her hand for me to get in.

"I'm glad you came," she says, and puts the car in gear.

We drive down a narrow street with low houses. Any window that isn't dark is lit up by the flickering glow of a television.

We drive past the hotel. My grandmother makes a small nod with her head.

"Don't go in there," she says. "Not even if you feel like it."

We leave the town behind. We drive past tangled shrubs and a few low trees.

She slows down as we pass the church.

"They'll never find another priest," she says. "It'll be left to rot now."

THE VICARAGE IS the biggest house I've yet to see on the island. My grandmother parks outside and unlocks the door. She switches on the light as we enter; we pass many closed doors.

"It's expensive to heat," she says. "Mind your head."

We take three steps down to the kitchen. It's big and sensibly laid out. If she had help in the house, she could cook for a big family here.

The table I'm sitting at is covered with a red-and-white checked vinyl tablecloth. My grandmother serves me split pea soup.

"It's not exactly a feast," she says, putting two fat slices of bacon on the edge of the soup bowl. "But you've been traveling for a long time. You need something to sustain you."

She watches me while I eat. Around us the house is cold and quiet.

"I saw you when you had just been born," she says. "And later, at a railway station. Your father called me. Gave me a time. I bought an ice cream, you ate half, then the two of you caught the next train. You won't remember."

When the bowl is empty, my grandmother escorts me past several closed doors and up to a room on the first floor.

"The bathroom's at the end of the passage. Here on the island the day starts early, so I suggest you get some sleep."

I hear her walk down the stairs. Slowly, one step at a time.

The bathroom is freezing. Four dead flies lie on the windowsill. I turn on the tap; it coughs a couple of times before the water comes out, rust-colored at first, then it runs clear. I wash, brush my teeth, and go back to the room. It's not very big. It's so dark outside that the glass on the window might as well be painted over.

I sit down on the bed; the mattress is hard and it creaks. I look from the crucifix on the wall, carved in hardwood, to the drawings of a bicycle hanging over the desk. There's a leather football in the corner. It takes me a moment or two to realize that this must be my dad's old bedroom. Unchanged in a large house where no more children followed him and his sister. I open the desk drawer and find exercise books with equations, essays, and several drawings. The subject is the same in all of them: a racing bike. The drawings in the drawer are drafts of the ones on the wall. The bicycle isn't in motion; it's not going over a hill. It's a bicycle drawn in detail, as accurately as possible. With each drawing the tires get rounder and the proportions more realistic. As I'm about to close the drawer, I feel something scrape against it. I pull the drawer right out; underneath it I find an old, yellowing catalog. It still opens to the last pages, those with pictures of ladies in satin underwear that cover everything from their hips right down to their thighs, suspender belts and bras whose purpose is purely functional. The models don't look at the reader: their gaze is turned away, their smile is friendly, but not inviting. I put the catalog back under the drawer and go to the wardrobe. It's old and made from rare wood with tiny woodworm holes. The doors catch at first, but then open with a squeak. The wardrobe is empty. My dad must have taken his clothes with him. He went to university, and he wouldn't have been able to do that on the island. There's a sweater at the bottom of the wardrobe, forgotten or deliberately left behind. I pick it up; I feel the wool against my fingers. It smells oily, like spoiled lamb meat.

I kick off my shoes, turn off the light, and lie down on the bed. I still have the sweater in my hands. I press my face into the coarse wool. I can now also smell sweat and tobacco: the smell of my dad when he was my age. I don't remember when I last cried.

THE COLD WAKES me up. There's hoarfrost on the inside of the window. The water in the shower never gets properly hot. My hands are shaking as I put on my jeans.

I walk down the stairs and through the house, trying to remember which way we went last night. I open the door to a sewing room and walk into a big cupboard before I find the kitchen.

My grandmother pours me coffee from a pot on the stove. I butter a slice of toast.

"I hope the wind didn't keep you awake," she says, and I detect a hint of a smile around her lips.

WE DRIVE TO the harbor. Today the island is colored in shades of gray and the faded green of old army vehicles.

"Nothing can grow here," my grandmother says. "People on this island have always made their living from fishing. Or at least they used to . . ."

My grandmother drives at her own pace. She drives so slowly that we're overtaken by a moped. The driver is my age, cigarette between his lips and leaning into the wind. I see him again as we drive onto the ferry.

My grandmother doesn't pay for our crossing. I don't notice this until we sit in the lounge and everyone who walks past us nods to her or presses her hand. They all stare at me with curiosity before quickly looking away again.

There are white traces of salt on the window; gulls fly around outside. My grandmother gets up, but before she reaches the coffee vending machine, a man in a thermal jacket has put in some coins. He carries two plastic cups of coffee over to our table.

WE DISEMBARK. I see the town from yesterday in daylight, a mixture of old houses and new buildings, ice cream parlors closed for the season. A supermarket and a snack bar practically identical to the one on the island. My grandmother parks on the main street.

"You only have city clothes," she says.

I follow her into a menswear shop.

A family man who is trying on a pair of jeans is left to fend for himself as the shop assistant measures me and stacks up clothing on the counter as directed by my grandmother.

The boots and a thick winter jacket are the only items I'm told to put on straightaway.

"He'll need a suit. A black suit and a white shirt," my grandmother says.

The shop assistant rings up the items on the till. The legs of the suit trousers need to be taken up, but they'll be ready in a couple of days. I'm looking for my wallet when the shop assistant asks if he should add it to the account.

My grandmother swallows.

"Yes," she then replies. "Put it on the account."

WE GET BACK in the car and drive through an area that's neither town nor country. We pass a gas station, a crazy golf course, and the ruins of a hotel my grandmother says burned down a couple of years ago.

We join the motorway. My grandmother drives in the middle lane, still going at her own pace. The speedometer never goes above 70 kmh. If she sees the cars behind us, she isn't bothered by them. Twenty minutes later, we turn off and drive down towards a large, square concrete building. Inside, the light is dim; there's a newsstand and a hairdresser's with their opening hours displayed in the windows. We follow blue arrows along the floor down a hospital corridor and take the elevator up.

MY GRANDFATHER HAS almost disappeared under the blanket. He was a tall man, I can tell from the bump his feet make at the foot of the bed. My grandmother puts her coat on a chair.

"He'll wake up one of these days," she says. "The doctors don't agree with me. But I know that he'll wake up, that he wants to talk to you."

She looks down at the man in the bed.

"Your grandson's here. Don't keep him waiting for too long."

The man's face makes me forget the hospital smell, forget the pale blue walls and the tubes connected to his body. The man in the bed looks like a very old version of my dad. Much older than I remember him. Much older than the years that have passed.

I LOOK OUT the window, I look at the machines keeping my grandfather alive, but I avoid his face. My grandmother sits next to me, looking expectantly at her husband.

A couple of hours later she takes her coat from the chair.

A woman is waiting in the corridor.

"My name's Merete," she says, holding out her hand.

I'm told she's my aunt. Her hair is reddish, her skin gleams with moisturizer. The boy sitting on the bench by the wall is my cousin. When he sees my grandmother, he quickly takes off his headphones. The music keeps playing, the sound of a drum being hit over and over. He fumbles in his pocket and finally manages to switch it off. His sister is thin and has black hair; her natural reddish color is growing in at the roots. She looks down at herself as if she has just spilled something.

"Are you going in to see him?" my grandmother asks.

The woman shakes her head. "We've been waiting for you in the cafeteria."

We follow the blue arrows and return to the parking lot.

"Please, could Louise go in your car?" asks the woman who's my aunt. "I haven't got the energy to listen to her and Frederik bickering all the way."

MY COUSIN SITS in the passenger seat in front of me, as close to the car door as she can get, ready to throw herself out if necessary.

"It's been a long time since you last visited," my grandmother says to her. My cousin doesn't reply; in the mirror I see her gaze move around the car. "But I suppose you're busy at school."

The dark blue station wagon with my aunt and my other cousin overtakes us.

WE SIT IN one of the booths in the ferry lounge. My aunt gets coffee from the vending machine.

"Have you thought about what we discussed?" she says, putting a plastic cup in front of my grandmother. "I'll deal with the practicalities. Ring round."

My grandmother lifts the cup to her lips. She blows on the hot coffee.

"There's no point in waiting till the last minute."

My grandmother looks across the plastic cup.

"You don't bury people while they're still alive," she says, in a dialect that's now so broad I can barely make out the words.

My aunt lights one of her long, thin cigarettes and looks out the window.

WHEN THE FERRY has docked, we quickly lose sight of my aunt and her dark blue car. They must have gone through the town in seconds. We're driving down the main street when the door to the hotel opens and a big man staggers outside. Equal parts muscle and fat packed inside a dark blue sweater with holes in the sleeves. He stops in the middle of the road with his back to us. My grandmother brakes and waits a few moments before sounding the horn. The man turns around, the muscles in his back tense up, he's about to shout and take a run at the car. Then he sees who's behind the wheel. He steps aside and gestures with a bow and a big, sweeping arm movement for us to please drive past.

"They used to drown," my grandmother says. "That was before the fishing quotas and . . ."

My cousin tries to muffle her laughter in her sleeve. My grandmother glares at her until she falls silent again. We drive past a house with a hole in the roof and an upended fridge in the front garden.

THE DOORS TO the dining room have been opened. A small woman with gray hair sets out salt and pepper shakers on the table. The room is furnished so simply it seems almost modern. A couple of plates with fishing motifs hang on the white walls, but there's not a lace doily or a china figurine in sight. We sit down at the table, my grandmother folds her hands, her lips move silently. Frederik weaves the white fabric napkin in between the teeth of his fork.

I try to catch Louise's gaze. I don't succeed.

The gray-haired woman puts a bowl of chopped parsley on the table before disappearing again.

"Do you still not pay her?" my aunt asks.

My grandmother shakes her head.

"If it's about the money then I don't mind . . ."

"It's not about the money." My grandmother looks across to me, then she smiles. "She needs something to do. Otherwise she'd just be sitting at home."

We eat lamb with a white mustard sauce and small, yellow potatoes.

My grandmother raises a wineglass to her lips, but it's difficult to see if she actually drinks from it. My aunt is on her second glass of white wine, and she pours me a glass without asking. Frederik stares at my glass; neither he nor his sister was offered wine. They've been given orange soda.

I hear only a single car on the country road outside the house during the meal. I see one gull fly past the window.

My aunt says, "I'd almost forgotten how good lamb can taste," and pours herself more white wine.

Louise's hands are thin and scratched. I look at them while she cuts a slice of potato and puts it in her mouth.

Frederik leans over the table, whispers to his sister: "What a shame about all this delicious food, eh? It's wasted on you."

The girl drops her cutlery and it hits the plate. She runs out of the dining room, we hear footsteps on the stairs.

"Why can't you be nice to her?" my aunt sighs.

AFTER LUNCH I tell my grandmother I'm going out for a bit of fresh air.

"If you meet anyone, tell them you're my grandson."

I put on my new clothes, the boots and the thick jacket.

I haven't gotten far when I hear footsteps. Frederik comes up beside me.

"They thought it best I come with you. I know the island better."

I make no reply, I carry on walking. We walk past the first low trees. I use the inside of my jacket as a shield from the wind while I light the joint.

"Can I have some?" my cousin asks.

I walk on. The landscape is flat and deserted. I wouldn't be able to get away from him even if I started running.

He comes up beside me again.

"What's wrong with your sister's hands?" I ask.

"Every time she eats something, she sticks her fingers down her throat. The stomach acid eats the skin on her knuckles."

I hand him the joint. He takes a deep drag and forces himself to keep the smoke in his lungs.

"You can screw her if you want." The smoke slips out of his mouth with the words. "It's not difficult. Like Open Sesame."

He takes another deep drag; the flame flares up and eats its way through the loosely rolled tobacco. I take the joint from him and carry on down the road.

I've been walking for a couple of minutes when I start to wonder why I can no longer hear footsteps behind me. I don't turn around; I just carry on walking while I finish smoking the joint. I get so close to the sea that I can taste salt on my tongue before I turn around.

Frederik is sitting at the roadside, staring into the distance.

I pull him to his feet. He stumbles along the road and I catch him each time he's about to fall. He groans, mumbles, and struggles to focus his eyes.

I sit him down on the bench opposite the vicarage.

In the kitchen I find his sister sitting at the table. She has started drawing a fine mesh pattern on a sheet of paper; she's halfway down the page, tiny lines gripping each other. Behind her, the gray-haired lady is doing the washing up.

I ask Louise to help me with her brother. She looks up; her eyes are still red. I stay there until she gets up and comes with me.

When she sees her brother sitting on the bench, she grins into her sleeve, the same grin I saw in the car.

She leads the way, keeping a lookout while I help Frederik through the house and up the stairs. She opens the door to his room, a small attic with no windows.

I throw Frederik on the bed, I take off his shoes. If anyone looks in, he's having an afternoon nap.

WE CATCH THE first ferry. My grandmother and I are alone today. We follow the blue arrows. My grandmother talks to the nurse and is told there's been no change since yesterday.

"However, the consultant would like to talk to—"

My grandmother has already walked away.

The man in the bed has grown slightly smaller; his skin is stretched more tautly across the bones of his skull.

"He was never a very talkative man," my grandmother says. "He saved his voice. Every Sunday he had to shout down the wind. He could shout, believe you me, he knew how to shout."

A couple of hours later we go to the cafeteria. We drink coffee from a pot that has been stewing for too long, my grandmother eats half a slice of cake, I have an egg salad sandwich. Then we go back and sit down beside the man in the bed. I listen to the machines that breathe for him and I flick through a four-day-old newspaper.

I GO OUT to the coffee and juice trolley in the corridor, put a couple of kroner in the jar for coins, and return with two cups of coffee. I walk as slowly as I can. I'm just about to push open the door with my shoulder when I see a junior doctor coming towards me. He takes the last couple of steps running, touches my elbow, and smiles.

"You're his grandson?"

I can tell from his accent that he's from Copenhagen. He's in his early thirties; he must have been posted here.

"I don't know if you could have a word with her. There's absolutely no chance that he'll wake up."

"Not today?"

"Not today. Not in five days. I don't wish to sound harsh."

The T-shirt under his coat is faded. I feel the hot coffee start to burn through the cups.

"I feel sorry for your grandmother," the doctor says. "And I feel sorry for him because he has to just lie there."

He looks at me, hoping I'll say something, a small nod of the head. A sign.

"Obviously you're not the one who has to make the decision, but perhaps you could talk to her?"

When I enter the room, my grandmother is standing at the foot of the bed, again resting her hands on its metal frame.

"The doctors are wrong," she says, as though she heard us in the corridor. "He'll wake up."

I put down the cups on the table next to a cardboard box of pale yellow latex gloves.

"Your father should be here." She wipes her eyes with the back of her hand.

"What happened to him?"

"Nothing." She keeps her gaze on the man in the bed. "Old age. That's all."

THE NURSE IS gentle the first time she tells us that visiting hours are over. The second time less so. My grandmother takes her coat from the chair, we follow the arrows.

The parking lot is empty. We walk across to the old Opel.

"What happened to my dad?" I ask, as we drive down the motorway.

She straightens slightly in her seat; the lines around her mouth grow deeper.

"People say he got ill," she replies.

"Yes . . . Do you know what happened?"

"No." She keeps her eyes firmly on the road ahead of us.

WE CATCH THE ferry back and stop at the island's only shop. A general store selling rope, engine oil, and alcohol. There's also a small selection of groceries and paperbacks with faded covers.

The man behind the counter has a full beard and weighs at least 150 kilos. He smells strongly of tobacco. My grandmother buys milk and cheroots.

"Any news about the storm?" she asks, and puts some coins on the counter.

"It'll be a bad one this time."

The prices the man rings up on the till are lower than the prices on the labels.

"My dogs are running around in circles, they keep snapping at each other. Perhaps the storm will come tonight. Perhaps it'll come tomorrow, but it'll come, all right. It's going to be a bad one this time."

MY WATCH IS lying on the bedside table. Children will be born and learn to play the piano before the minute hand ticks again.

Then the watch stops completely. I have to shake it to set time back in motion.

I've been smoking every day for a year and a half.

It makes the square pegs fit into the triangular holes. My mouth is dry; I can feel the touch of Rizla paper between my index and middle finger. I get dressed. The house is quiet. I walk down to the ground floor, opening doors. I know my grandmother's asleep in one of the rooms, so I'm careful, I make no noise, I sneak a peek into every room before I close the door again. My grandfather's study looks almost exactly as I'd imagined. There's a desk made from dark wood. I'd imagined an old-fashioned typewriter, but instead there's a pen on the desk next to a stack of papers, yellower and heavier than the sort that goes in a photocopier.

The bookcases are of the same dark wood as the desk. There are a few leather-bound classics, the rest are theological works. Three volumes are standing slightly askew from the others, their spines don't line up. I take them out; behind them I find a half-full bottle of schnapps. I twist off the cap and raise it to my mouth. The clear liquid tastes of alcohol; a few mouthfuls later the warmth starts to spread.

I walk across to the desk, drinking from the bottle while I go through the drawers.

The first one is filled with sheets of paper of the same pale yellow as those lying on top of the desk. There are hundreds of them, all dated. Each sheet contains only a few words, cues in a handwriting I can't read, and then some numbers. I start looking them up in a Bible from the bookcase, but there are too many for me to find a pattern.

There's an old cigar box in the next drawer; the label is peeling off. It's filled with banknotes in large and small denominations. A bank on an island where nobody takes credit cards.

The last desk drawer is practically empty; all I find inside it is a small stack of photographs, pushed into a corner, and a key.

I look through the photographs. The first is of the vicarage, another of the outside of the church. Then a photo of my dad in his cassock, shorthaired and clean-shaven. He's standing in front of the church, smiling. Again I have to remind myself that this must be my grandfather. Perhaps his first day as a priest, a young man who has promised himself to be serious and doesn't quite know what to do with his hands.

The remaining photographs are all of a small boy. They're black and white, but I think that his blond hair must be reddish. The boy is building a sandcastle. The boy is pulling a sled down a country lane white with snow. My dad as a little boy: this time, I'm sure it's him. I put the photographs back and take the key from the drawer. It's big and attached by a short string to a piece of polished wood. I take another sip from the bottle and put it back in the bookcase. I return the books.

THE DOOR IS ajar when I hear my aunt's voice. She's talking on the telephone in the hallway. I switch off the lights behind me and remain in the doorway.

"I hope it's over soon," she says in a low voice into the handset. "I can't stand it any longer. Please come?"

She listens to the voice on the other end.

"I know," she says. "No, I know. I'll be back soon. I can't do this anymore. It's got to end soon."

I FIND IT hard to tell the days in the vicarage apart. Every day we rise early and catch the first ferry.

Some days my aunt comes with us. She drives her own car. She looks down at the man in the bed, seeing him as a nuisance, a puppy that has soiled the rug right before the guests are due to arrive. I never leave her alone with the doctors. Only when she goes to the bathroom do I fetch coffee from the trolley.

After lunch I go out. Every day I hear my cousin's footsteps behind me. He asks me if I'm sure that I don't have any more cannabis. Just a little bit. He looks at me as though I might be smoking in secret, taking a big drag of an invisible joint when he's not watching.

Most of the rooms in the vicarage are freezing cold, so we sit in the drawing room or the kitchen. Frederik turns over the tape in his Walkman, Louise fills page after page with arabesques. My aunt reads the same newspaper or she goes out, running errands, she claims, and is gone for hours.

Every now and then there's a knock on the kitchen door; fishermen arrive, big men in filthy clothes with ruddy skin. I think I recognize the man who stood swaying in the middle of the road.

They speak softly inside the kitchen; every movement is cautious and exaggeratedly slow, as if they're scared they might break the table in half or pull off the door handles. They bring crates of fresh fish, boxes of eggs. They bring a leg of lamb and my grandmother welcomes them with small nods and instructions about where they can put down the food.

EVERY DAY I leave the table early. I leave while there are still potatoes and fish on my plate and I thank my grandmother for the meal. My boots and my thick jacket are waiting for me in the hallway. Every day I try to make it out the door before Frederik has a chance to follow me.

Today I hear not one, but two sets of footsteps behind me.

"Don't you have to cover paper with your crappy patterns?" I hear Frederik say.

I carry on walking.

"Are you going out to smoke?" Louise asks. "Next time we'll throw you in a ditch."

"Go away."

"We can't, there aren't enough roads on this island."

"Why don't you go into town and chat up a fisherman?"

I turn around and they both stop. Neither of them meets my eye. "Fuck off, both of you."

They make no reply.

When I walk on, I can hear two sets of footsteps behind me again.

A couple of kilometers later they come up alongside me. They argue over which way we should go. I decide to follow Louise; Frederik comes with us reluctantly. We walk through what was once an apple orchard. Now all the trees are dead or dying. You only have to look at them to see why, to see the white salt that's covering their leaves.

We continue towards the sea. I hear the waves before we reach the cliff: large, black, crested waves. There are abandoned bird's nests along the cliff. My cousins start kicking them; twigs and feathers whirl up in the air.

"We're outside the nesting season, obviously," Louise says. "It's more fun when there are eggs in the nests."

Tiny tufts of down stick to her boots. My cousins jump up and down and they laugh.

"We've been doing this since we were kids," Frederik says.

"Shitty little island," Louise says. "Shitty little island."

They fall down beside me, gasping for breath. Their faces are red.

I FOLLOW MY aunt outside the vicarage.

"The key should fit here," she says and inserts it into the lock.

The door to the shed sticks; it's dusty inside and covered with cobwebs. I have to move rakes and spades before I can get to the racing bike, the one my dad kept drawing. I carry it outside and lean it up against the wall.

"Your dad loved that bicycle," my aunt says. "It's a genuine Monark."

The bicycle is dark blue with white leather around the handlebars.

"He saved up for it for years. I used to make fun of him; I said, 'You won't even be able to ride it here!' There are cobblestones in town and the roads on the rest of the island are uneven, beaten earth."

It's not until now that I notice the front wheel is warped.

"He was so proud," my aunt says. "He spent more time pushing it around than riding it. A man on a tractor found him. He was unconscious, he'd suffered a concussion. He lay in bed and wasn't allowed to read. That's when Dad locked the bicycle in the shed. I haven't seen it since."

I return the bicycle to the shed. My aunt locks the door after us. Again I follow her. She sits down on the bench opposite the vicarage and pats the space next to her.

She lights one of her long, thin cigarettes, offers me one. I can smell schnapps or possibly vodka on her breath.

I follow her gaze across the bleak landscape, directed at some point far beyond the pale gray horizon.

Her makeup has become heavier in the past few days. She leaves the drawing room and returns with a new layer. Her language has also changed. At lunch she articulates every word as clearly as possible. In the evening her dialect is just as pronounced as my grandmother's.

"You look like your dad," she says. "Your hair's darker than his. But you have his eyes. The same eyes as your grandfather. And I don't mean the color."

"What happened to my dad?"

"He got ill. Surely your mum has . . ."

"But why did he get ill?"

I think she's about to say something, then she takes a drag of the thin cigarette.

"He's probably not the first to go a little peculiar from spending too much time with his head stuck in a book."

She gets up and goes inside.

THE HOUSE BEHIND me is dark. I stayed in my bedroom until I was sure everyone was asleep. I follow the lane up to the church. In my pocket I have the key from my grandfather's study. The gate squeaks on its hinges; I hear the gravel crunch under my feet.

The key doesn't fit the church's large double doors, so I walk around to the back. I take a couple of steps down to a dark-red wooden door and here the key goes in without any problem. The room inside is cold and dark; the light flashes a couple of times before it comes on. There's a coffeemaker on the table by the wall, his cassock hangs in a cupboard; apart from that, the room is empty. I walk up the steps to the nave. After fumbling around for a few minutes I find the switch and a couple of sleepy bulbs light up the inside of the church.

The walls are whitewashed. I've yet to see enough people on the island to fill even half the worn wooden pews. I walk down the aisle.

Jesus on the cross looks like the crucifix in my room. The same eyes follow me around, like surveillance cameras in a clothing store.

I stand on the pulpit and look out over the empty pews; I stand where my grandfather and great-grandfather have stood before me, Sunday after Sunday.

"Hey!" I shout out into the room.

"Bloody hell," I shout, but there's no response.

The sound of my voice reverberates between the walls and it takes a long time for the echo to fade away. I lie down on my back in the aisle. I can feel the cold stones against the back of my head and my neck. From here Jesus and I can look each other in the eye. He doesn't blink, no matter how hard I stare at him.

His eyes still follow me when I leave the church.

I'VE JUST STARTED walking down the lane when the first drops fall. The strength of the rain increases a few steps later; it becomes a thousand fingers tapping on my scalp and my shoulders, hitting the uppers of my boots hard. Then the wind arrives as if the rain has been merely a prelude.

This is the storm the grocer talked about, the one the fishermen mentioned when they brought the food. I'm bent over as I walk the last few steps to the vicarage. I try not to fall over, my hand brushes the ground, I straighten up again.

When I get back to my room, my clothes are soaked. I lie on the bed. Outside the storm is building: it has long ceased to be weather as in *Nice weather today* or *What's the weather going to be like tomorrow?* The storm is now an uncontrollable fury that rattles the windows. It's no longer fingers, but fists battering the roof.

I find the plastic holster from Camilla's joint in my jacket pocket. I unscrew the lid, pressing the tube to my nose. The sweet smell of cannabis brings me back to Camilla's bed.

Right now she's sleeping in a faded black T-shirt with a skull on the front. In a couple of days I'll go to the principal's office. I won't make the date he wrote down, but I'll tell him about my grandfather's milky eyes and he'll love me because I haven't forced him to become what he hates the most.

Camilla's bed will still be there. After the summer I'll go to university, I'll buy a record player. I'll buy a stack of records and some good cannabis. It seems like a plan and I take it with me to sleep.

MY GRANDMOTHER ZIGZAGS around the fallen trees.

In town, tiles are missing from several roofs. Smashed windows have been boarded up with chipboard. I have my rucksack on my lap. I packed it before we drove off; I took my dad's drawings of the bicycle. The catalog with ladies in lingerie lies under my sweater.

I'm leaving today.

The car deck on the ferry fills quickly; my grandmother says everyone's going to the mainland to buy materials and tools to repair their houses and boats.

When we get up to the lounge, all the tables are taken. People get up and offer us their seats, but my grandmother declines and we go back down to the car. We sit right next to the sign telling passengers to leave their cars during the crossing. No one knocks on the windscreen or tells us to get out.

"Please, would you do an old lady a favor?" my grandmother asks me as we disembark. "Would you visit your grandfather one last time? Say good-bye?"

I nod. We drive past the bus stop, through the town, and out onto the motorway.

THE MAN IN the bed no longer looks like a human being. His skin is waxy. He has blue and purple spots on his face and on his arms. His body thinks he's already dead. We sit there for twenty minutes; my grandmother looks expectantly at him. Then she gets up, puts her coat on.

"Your grandson has been here," she says. "I know you wanted to talk him. But he has been here and now he's going."

We walk down the corridor.

"You need something to eat," she says. "You've a long journey ahead of you."

I follow her to the cafeteria. I get a cup of coffee and a liver pâté sandwich. Around us people with IV drips dangling from stands are eating. My grandmother takes tiny bites from her cake.

The nurse comes running. Her eyes are so big we can see the white around her pupils.

"He's awake," she says.

We walk as quickly as my grandmother can manage. Out of the cafeteria, we take the elevator up, we hurry down the corridor.

My grandfather's eyes are open, but blurred. He lies very still. At first I think the nurse must have been mistaken. Or that perhaps he died while we were still in the elevator. Then he moves a tiny bit. My grandmother helps him up on the pillow, holds a glass of water to his mouth. He opens his lips, moistens them.

"I'll leave the two of you alone," my grandmother says, and closes the door behind her.

THE MAN IN the bed looks straight at me, fixing me with his gaze. A man who is nothing but eyes. I don't think I could look away if I tried.

"You came." His voice is hoarse and croaky. "I don't have many words left so I hope you'll just listen."

For a moment I don't think he'll speak again.

"I wanted to be a good person," he says. "I tried. But I wasn't good to your father."

His eyes move towards the glass on the bedside table. I hold it up to his lips, he struggles to drink.

"I told myself that it was necessary. A kind of punishment. But I knew very well that it was wrong. I hope that you can forgive me."

"For what?"

"It was wrong. Isn't it enough to know that?"

"No."

"Forgive me."

"What did you do?"

"I can't . . ." His eyelids are half closed; his voice is reduced to a whisper. "Can you forgive me?"

On the windowsill I can see a glass of fruit punch I left there a couple of days ago. On the chair lies the newspaper I was reading.

His eyelids never fully close.

My grandmother is waiting on the bench in the corridor outside. She seems smaller now, sunken into herself. She goes inside to her husband, reappears a couple of minutes later. She avoids my gaze.

We drive down the motorway, through the town. My grandmother slows down when we approach the bus stop.

"I'll stay till after the funeral," I tell her.

MY AUNT WALKS from room to room. She says we'll have to move the furniture, that we mustn't forget to buy plenty of beer, that if there's not enough beer they'll just start on the hard stuff. My aunt speaks the loudest, but I've no doubt that it's my grandmother's few telephone calls and sparse words down the handset that set the funeral in motion. The next morning my new black suit is hanging over the back of a chair in the drawing room.

THE PRIEST FROM the mainland is young. He stands on the pulpit and looks down at his papers. His hands are shaking. He tries to keep them on the pulpit so that no one will notice.

He was late. His tires careered across the gravel when he parked. He looks up, looks around at the fishermen. Big men with big hands, shifting in their pews, making the wood groan. No one's listening to him; halfway through the sermon he realizes this and stops. His gaze seeks out the family that must have come to hear his words. He finds us in the front pew. My grandmother has folded her hands; she looks down at herself. I, too, look away now. Refusing to help him through his sermon. His words lose their conviction as he talks about the priest who devoted his whole life to this island, who never left, who understood how important it is that people can share in God's mercy wherever they are. That this might be the challenge. Staying rather than going. That you can bring God's words to Africa, but you should never forget a small island in Denmark.

The priest keeps his eyes firmly on his papers until he reaches the last full stop. Then he quickly gathers them up.

MY GRANDMOTHER AND I walk in front, then my aunt and her children.

The women follow us, a small group with dull faces and hands with no nails. They carry dishes. Finally the men, the fishermen, heavy-footed; a small army marching out of step on their way home from a battle they didn't win.

The vicarage has been cleared, just like before a child's birthday party that could become boisterous. In the drawing room the armchairs have been moved and replaced with folding chairs. The sideboard has left a mark on the wallpaper. The dining table has been covered with a tablecloth. Here the women put down their dishes; they remove tinfoil and reveal pies, cold cuts, meatballs, and salted fish.

The men walk awkwardly around the room in worn suits with too-short sleeves and old shoes shining with fresh shoe polish. Their dialect is so thick I don't understand them when they speak. They eat food from paper plates. They empty their bottles of beer in three gulps without swilling.

My aunt positions herself so close to me I can feel the weight of her breast against my arm.

She whispers into my ear: "They're animals. That's what Dad used to say. He was their shepherd. He meant it literally; the men on this island are animals."

One by one the women go over to my grandmother, take her hand, and say a few subdued words. The men follow suit; they stand with their heads bowed like children who've been caught out.

A couple of hours later the food has been eaten and the women pack up the serving plates. They say goodbye to my grandmother and leave the vicarage.

The men are talking more loudly now. The floor creaks under their feet.

OUT IN THE passage my aunt is having an argument with Frederik. She orders him and his sister to go upstairs, to go to their rooms. Do it now. They're not to open the door even if someone knocks. Frederik refuses, he's standing on the bottom step. When he sees me, he points and asks why I'm allowed to stay. His voice is high-pitched and whiny. Eventually he trudges up the stairs in a sulk, his sister following.

"I can't tell you what to do." My aunt and I are alone in the passage now. "But watch yourself. They're not drunk yet."

THE MEN DISPERSE from the dining room, where the folding chairs sway under their weight, and head for the kitchen, where they sit around the table. They drink clear alcohol from coffee cups and water glasses. The table is covered with bottles from Poland and Germany that have probably been smuggled here.

When my grandmother passes the doorway to the drawing room or the kitchen, they quickly lower their voices. Once she has gone to bed, the house becomes theirs.

I stand half-inside the dark passage, looking down into the kitchen where my aunt waits on the men. She empties ashtrays and clears away empty bottles. She smiles all the time and keeps edging away from hands reaching out for her. She drinks with them and when her white wine runs out, she fills her glass with schnapps and beer. She sits on the lap of one of the fishermen and giggles as though she were younger than her daughter. When a man is about to put his arm around her, she quickly gets up and pats his cheek before moving out of range.

Two men get up from the table and go outside. Ten minutes later they come back: one of them is bleeding from his lip, the other has a swollen eyebrow. Someone fills their glasses with schnapps and passes each of them a beer.

My aunt comes up from the kitchen and walks in my direction. I take a few steps back into the dark passage and wait for her. Before she reaches the bathroom, I block her path.

She tries to get around me, so I move again. A small dance, back and forth, she giggles. The men in the kitchen have started singing; it sounds ugly and violent.

"Why did he want forgiveness?" I ask. "My grandfather asked for my forgiveness. For what?"

"Move," she says.

I grab her arm and drag her through one of the doors in the passage. I find the light switch; the room is narrow, there's an old sewing machine under the window.

"What did he do to my dad?" I ask, and close the door behind us.

"The men are looking for a fight. If I scream, they'll come running."

"Sit down," I say.

She remains standing, fists clenched, looking at me. Then she sinks down on the couch by the wall.

"I don't know," she says. "I honestly don't know."

I stand in front of the door, not budging. My aunt sits there for a little while. When she starts talking the island's dialect is more noticeable than before.

"I remember the summer when it started. Your dad couldn't have been more than six, seven years old. He'd done something . . . I think he might have broken a window, so he was called to Dad's study."

She cries silently.

"There were days when I didn't even see your grandfather. I'd be in the kitchen, he'd be in the drawing room or in his study."

She looks into the wall, looks far away.

"I don't know what he did to your dad. But it wasn't . . . it wasn't anything good . . ."

She wipes her eyes on her sleeve, like a child wiping its nose. It leaves a smear of makeup that reaches her hair.

"I know what you're thinking," she says. "That he abused your dad. But I don't know what he did. For many years I didn't even consider that possibility. I didn't know that something like that could happen. These days that's all people talk about. As if that's the only way you can abuse a child."

She sits for a while, sniffs, and stares into the distance.

"When your dad ran off, taking you with him . . . I knew that had to be the reason. That's why he became ill."

She stays where she is until the tears stop flowing, then she gets up and walks up the stairs to her room.

A MAN STICKS a glass in my hand and fills it with alcohol. I sit on the steps leading down to the kitchen. The men raise their glasses and toast me. I'm reminded of nature programs I used to watch on TV with my sister, where a diver in a steel cage was lowered into the sea while sharks attacked the bars.

I watch the men drink, shout, and sing.

I draw them in my mind. I draw a man slumped over the table, trying to steer the flow from the bottle into his glass; his back is arched. I draw a man raising a bottle to his lips; the glass and the face merge into one single image.

I LIE IN bed. The last guests left less than an hour ago. I listened to their singing grow more and more slurred until it sounded as if everyone was shouting at the top of their lungs. Slowly, the house emptied.

It's early in the morning and still dark outside. I get dressed and put the rucksack over my shoulder. I walk downstairs as quietly as I can. The house smells of smoke and something darker. I find my grandfather's study, open the desk drawer, and take out the cigar box with the money. There are fewer notes than there were a couple of days ago; the funeral has been paid for. I empty the contents into my pocket. I don't know how much money there is, possibly 10,000 kroner, possibly more. I also take the photographs of my dad as a little boy and put them in my rucksack. I'm walking down the passage when I hear something behind me. The light comes on. In her dark blue nightdress my grandmother isn't much taller than a child.

"I'm going now," I tell her.

She makes no reply.

"I've taken your money," I say.

"Why?"

"You owe me. You owe me so much more."

"You can't do that."

"Call the police. I'm happy to repeat everything my grandfather told me before he died."

I saw no great reaction in her face when they lowered her husband into the ground. Now her mouth contracts and her eyes narrow.

I close the door behind me, the morning air is cold. I walk to the ferry.

AS I TRAVEL across Denmark, I sleep soundly and I don't dream. My eyes are still half closed when I show my ticket.

When I reach Hovedbanegården, I walk to the platform for local trains. My train leaves in twelve minutes.

I sit on a bench; I tighten my jacket around me.

When the train arrives, I've made up my mind. Perhaps I knew all along what I was going to do. I'd thought I'd taken the money as revenge, but this option was at the back of my mind the whole time. I head for the footbridge and walk away from the station. I go out into the city.

· 1999 ·

FIRST THERE'S A screech of metal against metal, then a loud buzzing noise. The conveyor belt sets in motion. The first crate of letters comes rolling towards me. I pick it up and carry it over to my workstation.

Behind me, Kasper's lips perform a drum solo to the music from his headphones. We work two men to each booth. In this hall we hand-sort all the letters that don't fit into the machines. Parcels are sorted in one of the halls above us.

The first hour is always the hardest. After that my eyes find the postal code on the letter and my hands pass it on, instinctively putting it in the right pigeonhole. The pigeonholes are made from blue metal. The conveyor belt keeps moving; the crates are made from yellow plastic.

OI, TURK," I hear.

I turn around. Kasper points to his bare arm where his wristwatch should be. I take off my headphones.

"Break time, Turk."

For a couple of years now my name has been Mehmet Faruk. It's the name on my passport and on my health insurance card. The name on my employment contract when I got the job here in the sorting office. Most people call me Mehmet, others Faruk. Kasper only ever calls me Turk. He says, What's the difference between a Turk and a hedgehog that has been run over? Then he laughs.

I follow Kasper along the conveyor belt. His clothes are crumpled; he has stubble and greasy hair. He looks like a homeless guy and has since my first shift here. We walk up the iron steps and down the corridor to the break room, which is only big enough to accommodate a single shift. The small room is already thick with smoke. By the wall are two coffeemakers which are switched on all night.

"She has to learn," Kasper says, nodding in the direction of the new girl Erik has pressed up in the corner between the coffeemakers and the fire exit.

Erik wears thick glasses; he's short and wide and is among those who have been here the longest. His breath smells of filthy carpets. When he talks about the sorting machines, his arm movements always get wild. Japanese machines, he says. They'll take over soon and make us redundant. When he isn't ranting about the sorting machines, he talks about being fired from the council office where he used to work.

Everyone in the break room has a reason for being here. Sitting at a small table along the wall is Michael, whose band is this close to a record deal. He's talking to

Flemming, who used to be a long-distance lorry driver, but kept falling asleep at the wheel. Dorthe, over by the coffeemakers, had a job in a cheese shop before she developed an allergy to milk.

THE HAND ON the clock reaches twelve, break time is over. We've managed one and a half cigarettes. I follow Kasper down the iron staircase. We put on the white cotton gloves that always makes me think we're about to perform a mime act on the concrete floor.

The hours pass, the letters keep on coming.

EARLY IN THE morning we line up at the exit. One hundred and fifty people with their shoulders slumped, their eyes reduced to tiny cracks. The guard sits in his booth behind the glass window; he looks at us, then he nods and presses the button. The lock buzzes.

I EMERGE OUTSIDE in the cold, windy February morning. I walk down the street with my collar turned up.

The wind always feels icier when my body is tired; it forces itself under my jacket and clings to my bones.

I walk past Hovedbanegården where the hookers stand outside the entrance, drinking coffee out of paper cups and getting ready for a long day's work.

I'M WEARING HEADPHONES when I wake up. The sun is setting behind the rooftops and casting a reddish light through the small skylight in the roof. The room I'm renting is an attic room in a luxury duplex apartment.

Two slices of toast are still sitting in the toaster, slightly burned on one side. Once again I fell asleep before I got around to eating them.

I get dressed. I splash water on my face and walk downstairs. Elsebeth has left her shopping list on the kitchen table. I find money in the metal tin next to the coffeemaker.

The supermarket is packed with people with tired faces and children tugging at coats and refusing to sit still in shopping carts.

Elsebeth would never ask me to do her shopping for her, but she's old and needs very little. Her change has its own special pocket in my jacket.

I always start with her groceries; I find crispbread and some caraway cheese that I know she likes. I get buttermilk and lemon marmalade. Then ham and cheese for me, food that can fit between two slices of bread.

No matter how short or long the line is, I always choose till number three. From there I can watch Petra, who works in the kiosk. She has the whitest hands I've ever seen. I know her name is Petra because it says so on her name tag.

When I've paid for the shopping, I go over to buy cigarettes from her. Other days I buy a newspaper or some sweets for my night shift at the sorting office.

A couple of times I've bought football pools coupons, even though I don't know how to fill them in.

She asks if there's anything else.

I shake my head and find the money.

I LET MYSELF in. I can hear classical music through the door to Elsebeth's drawing room. First I put her groceries away, then I take my own up the stairs and put them on the windowsill, up against the glass where they will keep cold.

The radio lies under the bed; I balance it on my stomach, a small short-wave radio with a long antenna. It was the first thing I bought myself when I got the job at the sorting office.

I put on my headphones. I lie there listening to the news from German, English, and French radio stations. Little snippets. Yesterday there was flooding in a town in Brittany. No one died, but the emergency services rescued a man sitting on the roof of his car. He was clutching a small, black-and-white spotted pig. He said he always drove around with it in the backseat. It had been a struggle to get it up on the roof and its trotters had scratched the paintwork.

I HEAR THE bell ring and I turn off the radio. Elsebeth is standing at the foot of the stairs, waiting for me. Her legs can't manage the steps these days so she rings a bell instead. Today we're having meatballs in a sweet curry sauce.

"Cooking for two is no more hassle," she says, "and much more fun. They can keep their ready meals with instant mash and meatballs still frozen in the middle."

After dinner we drink coffee and Elsebeth talks about her two husbands, both of whom she survived. The first one walked in his sleep and always managed to find his walking stick, no matter where she hid it. One night he walked out in front of a car. Her second husband was scared of cats; he said they had evil eyes and stole your dreams while you were sleeping. I've heard the stories before, laughed at them before.

Elsebeth takes out a bottle of cognac.

"You should never save these things," she says.

The bottle is older than I am.

Elsebeth always concludes by talking about life before the two world wars. About being a little girl in a big apartment filled with people. When they played hide-and-seek, the game could last hours. When our glasses are empty, I ask if it's all right if I leave.

She laughs, tells me I'm young and that I quite naturally have better things to do with my time.

I RETURN TO my bed and put on my headphones. More news, more snippets.

In Stuttgart a man has built a car out of bottle caps. He's still trying to get permission to fit it with an engine.

I keep an eye on the clock. When it's past midnight, I put on my coat and walk down the stairs. I can hear Elsebeth's snoring through the door. I don't think she'd be able to shout as loudly as she snores, even if she tried.

I walk on wet cobblestones, skirting around puddles.

I pick my bar depending on the weather. I choose from among four or five. If the bartender's smile is a little too familiar, I give it a couple of weeks before I return. Today the weather is drizzling and I go inside Påfuglen.

I watch the other guests in the bar. I watch them drink, I watch them talk, I watch the way they hold their glasses and smoke their cigarettes; I draw them in my mind.

I'm not the only person drinking alone. I draw the lonely people, those who sit at the bar or in a corner with a beer and a newspaper in front of them, pretending they're enjoying their own company. They stay put until they've picked someone in the room they want to mix with. Then they move closer, find a chair at the neighboring table. They take their newspaper with them, but leave it unopened.

I draw them in my mind as they slowly turn their chairs. One centimeter at a time. They wait for the right word. The one that lets them join in on the conversation.

I never seek out company and still it finds me quite often.

I'm on my second beer when she sits down on the barstool next to me.

She's blonde and very tanned. She looks like she's in her late twenties but is probably older.

She places a cigarette between her lips. Finds a lighter in her bag and puts it down on the bar. She looks at it as if she has forgotten how to use it.

Then she turns to me and asks me to please help. Says she always scratches her thumbnail on it and that she has just had her nails done. She holds up her hands so that I can see them. The nails are long and bright red and quite clearly not her own. She bites hers, she says, and laughs.

She offers to buy me another beer, pulls a banknote from a wad.

Tells me she's a model.

She buys drinks with umbrellas for us and tells me she makes porn movies.

When she gets home at night, she has seen so many dicks that she dreams about elephants trumpeting all night.

"OI, TURK, I'M going for a piss. Leave my sweets alone, do you hear?" Kasper laughs. "You Turks are worse than the bloody gypsies."

A couple of times a week Kasper leaves his place at the booth, but he never walks towards the washrooms. If the supervisor comes by, I tell him Kasper has a stomach bug and the supervisor says that it's probably the lousy coffee they serve here. We both laugh and the supervisor walks on.

Kasper comes back ten minutes later, a little flustered. We carry on working, back to back.

WE'RE HALFWAY THROUGH the shift when the conveyor belt grinds to a halt.

"Not again," I hear.

"For God's sake."

"Overtime, there's definitely going to be overtime," says someone a couple of pigeonholes further away.

People start emerging from their booths.

"False alarm," someone calls out from the far end of the hall.

The conveyor belts start moving again, people breathe a sigh of relief, no need to wait for an engineer.

Kasper and I swap cassette tapes before we continue sorting letters.

WHEN THERE'S ONLY one hour of the shift left to go, I feel Kasper's hand on my arm. I take off my headphones.

"Oi, Turk," he says. "Would you do me a favor?"

I nod.

Kasper glances around before pulling out a buff A4 envelope from under his sweater.

"Take this with you when you leave."

I tuck the envelope under my sweater.

"Don't you want to know why?"

I shake my head.

WE LINE UP in front of the exit. The guard sits behind his glass window as usual; he has yet to press the button that lets us out.

"What the hell are we waiting for?" says someone at the back of the line.

"Wake up, man."

Then we see two guards in dark blue sweaters with radios on their belts. They walk along the long line of postal workers.

"What the hell's going on now?"

They stop in front of Kasper, tell him it's just a spot check, and ask him to please follow them.

"Are you sure you wouldn't rather have the Turk?" Kasper nods in my direction, but they don't smile.

Kasper goes with them; shortly afterwards, the lock buzzes.

I WALK DOWN the street; I try not to walk too quickly.

Kasper's letter is starting to fill up my whole sweater; the corners of the envelope are pointy and making their way through the stitches in the fabric.

I go inside Bjørnen. The bar's real name is Bjørn's Bodega, but I've never heard anyone call it anything other than Bjørnen. Postal workers get a discount at Bjørnen. A schnapps and a beer will take away the dryness in my throat, the smell of paper glue, and help me sleep in a couple of hours.

It's the end of the month and the bar is almost empty. One of the regulars is sitting in a corner, leaning over half a bread roll and a shot of Gammel Dansk bitters. He used to be a postal worker.

I buy a beer and flick through a tabloid newspaper. Roy Orbison is turned down to a low crackling on the speakers. Beer number two is lined up in front of me when Kasper walks through the door.

"You should've seen their faces," he says. "You wouldn't believe how disappointed they were." Kasper laughs and orders beer and schnapps for us. "You should've seen their faces." He raises the shot glass to his lips; his hand is shaking.

I take out the letter from under my sweater.

"Open it," he says.

There's no sender on the manila envelope. Inside it are four photocopied sheets. The paper is mottled, as though it has been water damaged; the text is smudged. I read the first couple of lines.

"Richard the Third," I say.

"I didn't know you Turks could read."

He takes a sip of his beer, lights a cigarette.

"You probably shouldn't touch those sheets for too long," he says. "They've been dipped in LSD."

Kasper puts them back in the envelope.

"You have them sent here from Amsterdam," I say. "No sender, and to an address that doesn't exist. And so they go back to the post office. To the box for dead letters."

"You've already worked that out," he says. "Yes, the dead letter box, where I pick them up. Only this time something appears to have gone wrong."

Kasper orders more drinks. While the bartender pours them, Kasper puts money in the jukebox.

"Stop by my place tomorrow," he says, and drains his shot glass. "I have something for you."

He writes down his address on a coaster.

WHEN I WAKE up, I can still feel the schnapps at the back of my head.

I drink a glass of water and eat an apple. Then I do Elsebeth's shopping.

Petra is standing in the kiosk. When she sees me she turns around and takes a packet of the brand of cigarettes I always buy. She asks if there's anything else.

I stand there a little too long. Then I shake my head and put the money on the counter.

I'M HOLDING THE coaster with Kasper's address in my hand. It's early afternoon. He's waiting for me in front of a redbrick building. I follow him around the block and into the courtyard.

"I've seen you doodling at work," he says. We walk down the steps to the basement, he finds some keys. "Every time we're on a break or when you're waiting for the next crate, you get your pen out."

The basement passage is damp and dark. We walk past peeling wooden doors with numbers daubed on in white paint and end up in front of a door with a big padlock. Again Kasper fumbles with some keys.

"This isn't really my own storage space. Mine's a lot smaller, but I have an arrangement with the caretaker."

When he opens the door, all I can see are cardboard boxes piled from floor to ceiling. There are so many of them that I can't get a sense of the size of the room.

"If you get lost, hoot like an owl and I'll try to find you."

I follow him through a narrow path with walls of brown cardboard on both sides.

"One of my friends used to work in the parcel section. What he didn't sort, he nicked."

At the center of the room Kasper has cleared some space and furnished the place with a worn Afghan rug and an old brown leather armchair.

He picks up a ceramic ashtray from the floor, tips joint butts into a black garbage bag, then switches on an electric heater and a couple of wonky-looking standard lamps.

"I don't live here," he says, a little too quickly. "I just prefer it to my apartment."

He removes a box from the cardboard wall and disappears through the gap.

"It became a bit of an obsession for my friend." Kasper's voice is labored, as though he's crawling through several more gaps. "He just had to nick parcels. He no longer cared about opening them. At first he filled up his own apartment. Then he asked if he could put a few of them in the basement. I'm afraid I said yes and then they caught him."

The first thing to emerge from the hole is a long, rectangular parcel. It's followed by several smaller ones. Finally Kasper himself appears. He has cobwebs in his hair and he's licking a fresh scratch on his hand.

"Come on, open it."

I tear off the paper and find a box of small tubes and five brushes wrapped in cellophane.

"It's supposed to be the best paint you can get. Top quality."

I tickle my palm with one of the brushes; I can feel the fine animal hairs against my skin.

"I don't paint," I say.

"Of course you do."

Kasper rips the paper off the big parcel and an easel appears. He puts it up on the floor. The next parcel he opens contains rolled-up canvasses. He attaches one to a wooden board with a nail gun and places it on the easel.

Then he disappears back through the gap. When he reappears, he has a piece of chipboard in his hand.

"Your palette," he says, and makes himself comfortable in the armchair. "Start painting."

He reaches down one side of the armchair and produces a large plastic bag of pot. I'm still standing with the brush in my hand while he rolls a joint.

"If you can't think of anything, you can always paint a mournful landscape from the Andalusian plain of your homeland."

"Anatolian."

"That's right, the one down in Turkey, with the goats and feta cheese."

"What do you have against Turks?"

"Nothing."

"No?"

"I just don't believe that you're Turkish. Now get painting."

I open the first tube, breaking the small metal seal with the end of the brush. Vermilion red from China. Red like the inside of your mouth and highly toxic.

I squeeze out a little blob on the board, then I open the next tube.

Ebony black, made from bird and animal bones. So black that each line looks like a hole in the canvass. Then a little ultramarine, a smudge of Naples yellow.

Kasper passes me the joint, I hesitate, I haven't smoked for years. Then I fill my lungs, I exhale the smoke slowly. I get red paint on the thin paper. I take another drag.

PETRA BRUSHES THE hair away from her face with her very white hands.

"Anything else?"

My packet of cigarettes lies on the counter. A small line is starting to form behind me.

"Can I buy you a cup of coffee?" I ask, and at first I'm not sure if I've said it out loud.

She looks at me. The line behind me is growing.

She says yes as though I've asked if they sell football pools coupons.

I WAIT OUTSIDE the supermarket. When she comes out, she has changed from the supermarket's golf shirt to a black turtleneck sweater. She hides her hands in her sleeves so only the tips of her fingers stick out.

We walk beside each other.

I've been to every bar in the neighborhood, but none of the cafés.

I pick one at random and we enter. People speak in loud voices, they laugh and eat sandwiches and flick through newspapers. The espresso machine makes as much noise as a small spaceship about to take off.

Petra looks out at the street. I take the menu from the table; it says they have caffè latte, macchiato, mocha.

Lemon coffee from Bali. Indian hemp coffee.

I ask Petra what she'd like. At first I don't think she's heard me.

"Coffee," she finally replies, without taking her eyes off the cars outside the window.

PETRA SIPS HER coffee delicately, taking care not to spill. She leaves no brown coffee stains on the cup.

Beside her cup lies a small hard biscuit which she nibbles.

"Have you worked at the supermarket for long?" I ask, even though I already know the answer; I remember the week she started. In the winter she always looks cold, in the summer she never tans.

Petra nods and removes biscuit crumbs from the saucer with her index finger.

"Do you like it there?"

Again she looks out at the cars.

"It's a job," she shrugs.

I push my biscuit across the table to her.

"Thank you," she says. "It's nice to sit here."

When she speaks she sounds as if she has learned the words phonetically and doesn't quite understand what they mean.

We walk across the bridge from the city center to Christianshavn; we walk along the canal. She takes out her keys.

"I like my apartment," she says, letting us in.

The kitchen floor is covered with checkered linoleum. A cat is sitting on one of the white squares. It follows us with its eyes without otherwise moving.

"Its name is Kot," she says. "It means 'cat' in Polish."

The cat is skinny; its fur is gray with a bald spot at the back of its head.

"It's a very sad cat, I don't know why."

She opens a tin of cat food, tips the contents into a bowl. The cat sniffs the food and takes a single bite before losing interest.

"I give it the most expensive cat food money can buy. But its fur won't shine. And it refuses to smile."

"Do cats smile?"

"You know when they don't smile."

We smoke cigarettes in the kitchen while the cat looks at us. We stub them out in the sink and I follow her into the bedroom.

She undresses as if she were at the doctor's; her movements are stiff and practical. She folds her clothes and puts them on a chair.

Her body is almost as white as her hands, with visible blue veins right under her skin.

I can feel her heels on my back. Her skin flares up and she gets red blotches on her chest and inner thighs like an allergic reaction.

Her cat watches us from the doorway. She's right, it doesn't smile.

"PODOBASZ MI SIĘ," Petra says, when we're both lying on our backs in the bed. The words and her accent sound Slavic.

"My dad's Polish," she says, in answer to the question I haven't asked. She lights two cigarettes and hands me one of them.

"When I was a child I only spoke Polish." She tries to make a smoke ring, but fails.

"Last year I met some Polish students. They asked me to show them Copenhagen. Every time I opened my mouth, they laughed and said I spoke like someone in an old movie." She scratches one breast, the nipple is small and pink. "I miss someone I can speak Polish with."

"I can learn Polish," I say, but I only succeed in making her smile.

"*Podobasz mi się,*" she repeats. "I like you."

I tie my shoelaces. She asks for my telephone number.

I tell her that I live with an old lady. It sounds like a lie.

"I won't see you again, will I?" she says, when I'm standing in the doorway.

"I'll always need cigarettes."

She smiles as if her question was merely a joke.

The cat sits on the same square in the kitchen; it follows me with its eyes as I leave.

Now when I shop for Elsebeth, I have to walk for another ten minutes, past the supermarket where Petra works. I walk on the opposite side of the street to the next supermarket, where the choice is worse and the prices higher. When I've done the shopping, I put an extra ten kroner in the pocket where I keep Elsebeth's change.

KASPER IS WAITING for me in the street. I follow him down to the basement. There's a fresh white canvass on the easel. When I was here a couple of days ago, the black paint was nearly used up; the tube was the size of a thumbnail. Now a new tube is ready and waiting for me. Kasper doesn't look up from his bag of pot when I ask about it. He just shakes his head. We're not going to talk about it. It's not important.

Kasper rolls joints, I paint.

When I look up from the canvass, he's asleep in the armchair, his mouth slightly open. I find the white paint and paint his outline.

He starts to wake up, looks at me with one eye. "I hope you're not painting me?"

I shake my head.

"I've a friend you should meet," he mumbles, and goes back to sleep.

WE'RE SOMEWHERE IN Vesterbro, possibly Frederiksberg. Kasper is leading the way.

"His real name isn't Karlsson, obviously," he says, referring to a character from an Astrid Lindgren children's book, "but he does live on a roof like him."

We stop at a corner store; it's best if I bring something. I buy cherry brandy and a pouch of tobacco, things Kasper says Karlsson likes.

We enter a stairwell with no entry system and walk up the stairs to the top landing. There's only one door and it doesn't have a nameplate.

Kasper presses his shoulder against it and wiggles the handle until we hear a click and the door opens. We walk past attic rooms on both sides over to a short metal ladder that leads to a hatch in the ceiling.

Kasper climbs the ladder. He pushes open the hatch; light appears in the crack.

"This is never very easy," he says out of the corner of his mouth. He's holding a small key between his lips.

"Can I do anything?"

He shakes his head, sticks his hand out through the gap, and grabs hold of a strong chain with a padlock.

We've reached the roof, which overlooks Copenhagen. There's a small shed and a deck chair a little ways away from us.

I'm about to go over there when Kasper grabs my arm.

"I'm not sure what he might do if we knock on his door without warning."

Kasper picks up a handful of small white shingles. He throws them in a soft arc onto the roof of the shed.

"Doesn't he know we're coming?"

"Yeah, of course . . . But he's not very good with dates or times."

A few more pebbles and a door opens. The man who comes out wears an anorak over two sweaters. He has a full beard and his cap is pulled over his ears. He must be in his mid-twenties, but his skin is weather-beaten and ruddy. He gives Kasper a big hug and shakes my hand.

"We brought you presents," Kasper says.

I hold out the bag. The man looks inside it and nods happily. Then he shows us around the roof, pointing out the Chinese Tower in the zoo and the Round Tower. On a clear day you can see all the way to the Barsebäck nuclear power plant on the Swedish coast.

He shows us the gutter that he fixed himself. He tells us that he did it late one night with a flashlight. He nearly fell off the roof, but the gutter kept leaking and eventually someone would've come up here to repair it.

He also mended the deck chair himself with a needle and thread—that was all it took. He says that he sits in it in the summer and puts cucumber slices on his eyelids. In winter he wraps up warm and sits outside while he reads and drinks coffee from a Thermos.

WE ENTER THE shed.

"My humble abode," he says, showing me the sleeping bag and mat in the corner, the Primus stove, and the kitchen utensils hanging from hooks on the wall.

We sit down at a small folding table. Kasper and I get the two chairs, Karlsson takes a beer crate for himself.

He opens the cherry brandy and pours it into three chipped mugs.

"I was training to be an insurance agent," he says, by way of explanation. "I had a girlfriend, I thought my life was quite good. Once I'd qualified, there'd be no reason not to start a family."

Kasper has started to roll the first joint; he looks as if he has heard this story many times before.

"One day when I came home, she'd packed up all my things. She said I made her sad. She said it was her apartment. I'd forgotten that."

He wipes cherry brandy off his lips.

"I walked the streets. It was winter. I'd left my wallet behind in the apartment and I didn't want to go back for it. It was then that I remembered my afternoons up on the roof as a child. My uncle was the caretaker and used to bring me up here. We drank hot chocolate and played Old Maid. I found a screwdriver in a bike shed. All the padlock needed was a small twist."

Darkness falls. Karlsson lights his two petroleum lamps. He fries sausages and potatoes for us on the Primus stove.

"The first few weeks I lived on stale bread from bakeries. But I started to get dizzy. I needed to eat some meat."

Karlsson shares out the food between us.

"I used my last few crumbs to catch a pigeon. Just like in the cartoons: the pigeon follows the trail of crumbs under a box and then you pull the string."

Kasper takes a couple of bites of sausage before pushing the potatoes around with his fork. When we've finished, Karlsson gathers up the leftovers and puts them out on the roof where they'll keep cold.

He sits down on the beer crate again, pours more cherry brandy, and rolls a cigarette with the tobacco I gave him.

"I ate a gull." Karlsson's voice is soft. "I was starving. At first I tried to scare it off. But it refused to go away. It just stood there under the box, stuffing its face. You don't ever want to eat a gull."

I nod, I believe him.

"I stood here on the roof licking its bones, thinking about jumping. But I didn't want to do it on an empty stomach. First I wanted to have a hot dog with all the toppings and then run off without paying. I met Kasper at the hot dog stand."

"We went to school together." Kasper lights yet another joint.

"He lent me some money. I don't need very much; I just don't want to eat gulls."

"That was before I started the acid business."

"I sell it," Karlsson says. "Old hippies don't care what I look like. And they can afford to pay for quality."

"Most of the pills you get from Germany are crap. Largely chalk and codeine. Sometimes even rat poison," Kasper says.

"We sell good acid. Real acid, like the stuff the Mamas and the Papas drove around with in a big jam jar."

When we've emptied the third bottle of cherry brandy, I need to pee. I've held it in for some time because Karlsson hasn't stopped talking.

"There's a bucket outside," he says. "Don't pee over the roof. I know it's tempting, but don't do it."

WE'RE ONE AND a half hours into the shift when the supervisor comes over to me.

I distribute the letters in my hands before I take off my headphones.

"The boss wants to talk to you."

"Now?"

"He's waiting. It sounded important."

Kasper grins. "What's Turk been up to this time?"

The supervisor produces a strained smile, isn't sure whether it's appropriate to join in.

"The Turks are always trouble . . ." Kasper shakes his head.

I walk past stations where the same actions are repeated over and over. I walk as slowly as I can. The boss only works the night shift a couple of times a month. Or if something important is happening. Perhaps he wants to talk to me about Kasper's acid import, but I don't think so. They wouldn't have picked me up while I was standing next to him if that was it.

I know what the boss is going to say to me. I'm only wondering how they found out.

At first I tried to get work without any papers. But my dad had failed to prepare me for the new era of bar codes and computers. A world where the black market is only for black people, as a builder said to me. Unless, of course, you've finished your apprenticeship, he said and then laughed.

I started frequenting small shops on Nørrebro. My room filled up with pens, bags of nuts, and pomegranates that rotted over time. I had stacks of videos that I couldn't play and a pyramid of cigarette packets. I wanted to be known as a regular customer; I wanted them to feel safe with me before I asked for papers. Most of them said they could get me some; but every time, I ended up being offered only stolen toasters and VCRs.

Late one night I was in a pizzeria. I hadn't been there before and I had only gone inside because I was hungry. I'd almost given up so I just asked for papers straight out. At first I didn't think the guy behind the counter had understood me. He smoked a cigarette while the pizza was in the oven. I read a three-day-old newspaper and I could feel his eyes on me.

I had the pizza box in my hand and was heading out the door when he said, "Don't forget your receipt."

On a small piece of paper he'd written an address, a greengrocer in outer Østerbro. He told me to say hi from Öztürk.

The papers were expensive but genuine. I was now twenty-one years old and my name was Mehmet

Faruk. I got a birth certificate and a health insurance card and was assured that Mehmet Faruk was no longer around. He might have gotten the wrong girl pregnant and left the country or maybe he was lying in a ditch somewhere.

I got a passport. I opened a bank account. I went to job interviews and started working as a postman. Later I moved to the sorting office.

After my first shift I went for a beer with the other postal workers at Bjørnen. They told me I didn't look very Turkish. I said I was only half Turkish, that my mother was Danish. The redhead gene that wouldn't roll over and die. After a couple of beers they said yes, perhaps, if you look closely.

I'M STANDING WITH my hand on the door handle to the boss's office; I take a deep breath before I open it.

He's alone. I can smell tobacco. There's a calendar with building cranes on the wall.

"My son works with one of the really big ones," he says, and gestures with his hand for me to sit down.

The boss used to be a builder. He had his own business until his back went. Then he had to retrain.

"I might be wrong." The boss touches a pile of papers in front of him. "But I've gone through these. Several times. And . . ."

He looks at me; perhaps he's hoping I'll say something. Break down and confess. I force all explanations and apologies to stay behind my teeth.

"Can it really be true that you haven't taken any holidays since you started working here? None at all?"

I gulp, then I nod.

"I could turn a blind eye, but then we'll have the union on our backs. They always think we're trying to work you to death." He grins. Then he raises his eyebrows, big bushy eyebrows. "Listen, you have to take your holidays."

He pushes a holiday request form across the table. The first line has already been filled in: Mehmet Faruk, it says.

I'm about to get up.

"And another thing, as you're here. You work with Kasper Rasmussen, don't you?"

"Yes."

"The shop steward will probably have a fit because I'm asking you. But, even so, does . . . does he do his job?"

"Yes."

"What I mean is . . ." He searches for the right words; he has to tread more carefully here than he did when he was on a building site. "You haven't noticed if he does things which could be regarded as . . . a little different? Odd, possibly?"

"No. Or . . ."

"Yes?"

"No, it's probably nothing."

"It'll be between us, of course."

"During break time . . ."

"Yes?"

The boss looks at me. His eyebrows hang in the air like the wings of a gull.

"When he has taken the last cup of coffee, he doesn't always put on a fresh pot."

"Er . . . Yes?"

"And the sign says . . ."

"Oh, right . . . Well, thanks for letting me know."

I walk past the stations down to my booth.

Kasper grins at me. "They're not sending you back to Turkey, are they?"

During the next break I fill in the holiday request form and hand it to the supervisor.

I PUT ON my coat. I finish my cup of instant coffee. It's coming up on eleven o'clock. I've just walked past Hovedbanegården and I can see the sorting office when I realize that my holiday starts today.

The first hour I drink on my own, then a man sits down on the barstool next to me.

His skin is glowing; his clothes are clean and freshly ironed even though it's after midnight.

First we drink alone. Then we clink bottles. He tells me he's a photographer.

He has spent the whole evening looking for the right subject. He buys a round, looks down at himself.

"I'm not gay," he says, as though he could understand why I might think so. "I take pictures of sleeping girls."

I'm about to ask him when he nods.

"I take their picture while they're asleep. The tricky bit, of course, is to make them come home with you. You have to look presentable."

The bartender turns the light on and off; it's time for last call.

"I go running," the man says, and straightens his shirt collar. "I'm a member of two book clubs. Girls like books."

We empty our glasses and stand up.

"I've got something to show you," he says, as we step outside.

I follow him.

"I used Rohypnol once," he says. "Slipped a couple of pills in the girl's drink and she was out like a light. I had time to rig the lighting and put the camera on a tripod. Pose her. She slept like they only sleep in the movies."

We cross the road diagonally.

"But when I developed the pictures, I could tell that I'd cheated. So it didn't count. I tore up the pictures and destroyed the negatives." The man points to an apartment building further down the road. "It's right up there."

"I'm sorry," I say.

I turn around and walk down the street, away from him. He says something to me, but I don't hear it.

I WALK THROUGH the city. The streets are wet from the rain. I step around vomit and broken bottles. I'm not far from my room in Elsebeth's apartment, but I carry on walking. I cross the bridge, I walk along the canal.

I press the buzzer, keep pressing the button. At last I hear crackling, then the lock clicks open. Petra stands in the doorway; she's wearing an oversized T-shirt with Winnie the Pooh on it and white cotton underwear. Her eyes are tiny. She blinks a couple of times before she goes back to bed.

I undress and lie close to her back. She presses herself against me.

THE SUN IS rising when she turns to face me. I can feel her hand between my legs. I find her mouth. She pulls off her panties and guides me inside her.

Afterwards we lie soaked in sweat, still with sleep in our eyes. It's not until then I notice the red lines on her arms.

"It's Kot," she says. "It won't groom itself. So I take it into the bathroom and hold it under the shower. It whines and then it scratches me."

I CARRY PETRA'S cat down the stairs. Its skin is loose like an overcoat that's too big. Halfway down the steps it widens its eyes and sinks its claws into my arm. I don't let go. Petra opens the door.

When we're out in the courtyard, I put it down.

The cat is shaking from cold or agitation. It stands there a moment before it takes a few tentative steps. Then it starts to run and disappears into the nearest bin shed.

Petra is scared that it might run away, possibly out in front of a car. Perhaps on purpose.

"It can't get out, the courtyard is enclosed."

"Cats can always get out."

We sit down on a bench. We drink coffee from a Thermos. We can hear Kot move about. We watch it dart from one bin shed to another, to the bike shed and back. Then it disappears completely.

Petra is about to get up; I put my arm around her and make her sit down again. She takes a sip of coffee, but doesn't take her eyes off the shed where we last saw Kot.

Fifteen minutes later the cat returns. It's bleeding from a scratch under its eye, its tail has got a kink, and it's missing some fur. Between its teeth it holds a dead rat. The cat stops in front of us and lets its prey fall to the ground. I'm pretty sure it's smiling.

WE LIE IN Petra's bed. She tells me I don't look very Turkish.

"I'm only half Turkish."

She rests on her elbow, watches me with her very pale eyes which are blue today and not green. Then she shakes her head. She still can't see it.

"Tell me about your family," she says.

"There's not much to say." I fumble for the cigarette packet on the bedside table.

"Or not much you want to tell me . . ." I can still feel her eyes on me as I light the cigarette.

"I grew up with my dad."

"Who is Turkish."

I make no reply.

"Tell me about your dad."

"Later, perhaps."

"Then I won't tell you anything about my family. Nothing at all."

"I know your dad is Polish."

"And that's all you're going to get." She turns over and grabs the duvet.

I hear a sound from her, a soft sniffle which might be laughter. I stub out the cigarette and I hold her until we fall asleep.

PETRA WAKES ME up. She's in tears. She's scared that her cat is dying. I find it in the kitchen, lifeless with milky eyes.

We wrap it in a blanket and carry it downstairs. The vet isn't far away. We wait in reception; Petra rocks the cat in her arms. I can see a paw with exposed claws sticking out of the blanket.

The vet carries the cat to a steel table in his surgery. Unwraps it, squeezes its paws, examines its injuries, and looks into its eyes.

He can give it an injection; put it out of its misery, that's all he can offer. Petra's crying so hard she can't speak. She keeps shaking her head.

The secretary calls us a taxi.

We take it to an animal hospital. Petra runs inside with the cat while I pay the driver.

They give the cat an injection, open up its cuts and clean them. Petra squeezes my hand until I can no longer feel it. Five hours later we're told we can take the cat home with us.

I SPEND THE rest of my holiday looking after the cat while Petra goes to work. I apply ointment to its cuts and force the syringe with antibiotics into its mouth. Soon my hands are just as scratched as Petra's.

IT'S EASY AND fairly safe. It's almost legal." Kasper puts groceries into the shopping cart. "The best time is late in the day and early in the month when the shops are busy."

His voice is louder than usual.

"Visibility is part of the trick," he says, taking a box of cornflakes from the shelf. He throws it up in the air; it floats under the ceiling before it lands in the trolley. "No one expects you to talk about shoplifting in a supermarket. Just as no one expects you to try to shoplift something this big."

When we reach the till, Kasper takes a single bottle of beer and puts it on the belt. The girl has sleepy eyes after a long day at work. She rings up the beer. Kasper doesn't say anything about the crate of beers under our trolley. We carry it out of the supermarket between us.

"If you're caught, you can always act dumb," Kasper says, without lowering his voice. "I didn't check the till receipt, did I? Or you say you did tell the checkout assistant. At this time in the day their memory is like a goldfish's. How much is that? Three, four seconds?"

We're only a few steps down the road when Kasper sets down the crate and calmly lights a cigarette.

"The beauty of the beer-crate trick is that you get money back when you return the empty bottles and the crate. The supermarket pays you to drink beer."

We haul the crate up the stairs and pass the bottles through the hatch, one by one.

Whenever we sit on Karlsson's roof, he does most of the talking. Kasper says he saves up his words.

Today he talks about the school he and Kasper went to. About morning assembly. The suburb they come from was well-heeled. It's taken real effort to sink as low as they have.

"Or rather high, to sink as high," Karlsson says and flings out his arms, taking in the rooftops around us, the sun which is going down and glows gold and orange on the windows.

When the city lies in darkness and the dew has fallen, we go inside the shed.

Karlsson lowers his voice. Even here on top of the city, alone on the roof, he fears that someone might be listening in. He's no longer talking about himself or the art of catching a pigeon. He's talking about bombs. How easy it is to make a bomb from items you find under your kitchen sink. He says that a bomb is only worth its target. A bomb is a sentence that doesn't get a full stop until the next day's newspapers.

I glance at Kasper. He just smiles, rolls joints, and looks as though he's heard it all before.

Karlsson wants to bomb a lot of places: the National Bank, the stock exchange, Christiansborg Parliament, Lego.

Especially Lego.

"It's all about symbols," he says.

LATE AT NIGHT we fly kites.

I hold on to the string. Kasper stands a few meters from the edge of the roof with the kite above his head. He holds the string tight until the kite tears itself loose and takes off over the rooftops.

PETRA SCRUBS MY nails with a coarse sponge; colored flakes disappear down the drain.

"You can paint me," she says. "Naked, if you like. I promise to sit very still."

I've tried to explain to her that I don't paint specific things like people, animals, or teapots. I just like holding a paintbrush in my hand.

She keeps scrubbing my nails, somewhat harder now.

Perhaps she saw the sketches I'd left lying around, the ones I made of Kot while it was ill.

WE WALK ALONG the canal.

"Where are we going?" I ask.

"It's a surprise," Petra says.

She promised me a surprise late last night, but refused to give anything away.

We continue fifty meters down the street, then she opens the door to a gallery. It's small with white walls and it's in what was once a bicycle shop. A lady in her sixties walks around making notes on a pad. A young man sits with a laptop. His hair is artfully messy, he has a small leather string around his neck, and the sleeves of his T-shirt have been cut off so you can see his tattoos. If we have any questions, please don't hesitate to ask, then his attention goes back to the screen.

Petra takes a catalog for each of us.

There are three rooms in the gallery, all with speakers playing soft electronic music.

We walk from picture to picture. Petra decides when we move on. She tilts her head, asks me if I think they're good; she says she likes the colors.

The catalog is a two-page leaflet with text in Danish and English. The artist is only a few years older than the age I tell people I am. And yet he has already exhibited in London, Vienna, and Tokyo. Even though he went to a famous art college, his style is described as wild, free, and unschooled.

He's brave, it says. Broad brush strokes without fear of the consequences.

The artist says he likes exhibiting in a small gallery where you can get so close to the paintings you can smell the paint. He compares it to playing in small clubs. In brackets it says that the artist also plays guitar in a rock band.

"Is something wrong?" Petra says when we leave the gallery.

I shake my head.

"Sure?"

"Yes."

She takes my hand. "Was it a bad idea to go to the exhibition?"

We get coffee in one of the cafés overlooking the canal. It's still cold out, but the sun is shining. We sit outside with our jackets zipped right up, warming our hands on the coffee cups.

"I've another surprise for you," Petra says. "A small present, if you like."

She pushes a key across the table. It's silver and it looks new.

"It's just a key," she says quickly. "So you don't have to wake me up when you come over late at night."

AFTER WORK I walk across the bridge and lie down in Petra's still-warm bed. I sleep until she gets back from work. She brings bread from the supermarket's bakery. It's stale, but she gets it for free. She holds up two croissants to her forehead and pretends to be a bull. Bull is *byk* in Polish.

We go to a bar, but the smoke makes her eyes water.

We walk back across the bridge; she catches me watching her. The whiteness of her hands and body. She practically glows in the dark.

"I'm not an albino," she says.

"No."

"Albinos have red eyes."

"Just like vampires."

"No," she says. "Not like vampires. But possibly werewolves."

I'M CLOSE TO falling asleep when I hear it again; the strange sound in the room. I fumble my way to the power cord, follow it to the switch, and turn on the lamp. Petra sits on the edge of the bed with her face buried in her hands. She's whimpering. The tears run down her arms and collect under her elbows.

She looks at me before hiding her face in her hands again.

"You're going to leave me," she says.

I put my arm around her shoulders. She has retreated into herself.

"No," I say to her.

"Maybe not right now, but soon."

I sink back into sleep.

KASPER MEETS ME in the street. He has an old radio under his arm.

"Keep going," he says. "We've got something to celebrate."

Kasper lets us into his building; I follow him up the stairs.

"What are we celebrating?"

"Me, for Christ's sake. It's my birthday today."

It's the first time I've been inside his apartment.

"I'm not here very often, I just come here to sleep . . . I sleep here sometimes."

There are open cardboard boxes with clothes hanging over the sides from the hallway to the living room and into the bedroom.

Kasper's bed is a mattress on the floor with a sleeping bag. There are stacks of books along the walls. He starts rummaging through one of the boxes, throwing clothes on the floor in the process.

"Please, would you get the schnapps from the kitchen?"

At first I check the shelves, then I look inside the fridge. It's practically empty. All I find is some liver pâté and half a cucumber.

When I open the freezer compartment, four peas roll out and land on the floor. The bottle of schnapps lies next to the open bag.

"Get some glasses as well, will you?" Kasper shouts from the bedroom. "Karlsson's are gross, I think he licks them clean like a cat."

I look in the drawers. I find economy-sized packs of paper plates and plastic cutlery. In the last cupboard I find six small shot glasses still wrapped in clear plastic.

I wait for Kasper in the hallway. More clothes and several books end up on the floor while he searches through another cardboard box. Then he appears with a bottle in his hand.

"I nicked this from my dad the last time I visited my parents. I've had it for a couple of years now and I've been waiting for the right occasion. Today's the day."

The liquid in the bottle is brown.

"Whisky?"

"Not just any old whisky."

He points to the label; it says 1976.

"Single malt. Not that you Turks would understand."

WE WALK PAST a bakery and buy a cake with whipped cream and strawberries. In the kiosk next door we buy batteries for the radio.

Karlsson welcomes us; he wears a checked shirt and a wide tie with a brown pattern.

"The birthday boy," he says, holding up his tie. "Windsor knot."

Karlsson has put the folding table out on the roof, cut up a black garbage bag, and made it into a tablecloth.

First we put out the alcohol. Two bottles of cherry brandy that Karlsson has bought. Half a crate of beer from when we last performed the beer-crate trick. Whisky and schnapps. We put the cake in the shade.

"You should always start with the good stuff," Kasper says, twisting the top off the whisky bottle. He takes the shot glasses out of the wrapping and fills them up. "A toast to me. A toast to us. I hope my dad has discovered that the bottle is missing. I hope he has been crying his heart out. Cheers."

The whisky tastes of seaweed and smoke. Kasper drinks his in two gulps. I try to keep up; tears well up in my eyes.

"How old are you?" I ask, when I regain the power of speech.

"That's not important." And again he fills up my glass to the brim.

Karlsson sips his; after a couple of nips he says he prefers cherry brandy.

We eat the cake off paper plates, shoveling it into our mouths and laughing and getting whipped cream on our noses and chins and in our laps.

The sun goes down and we move inside. Karlsson lights some candles.

"Come on," Kasper says. "It's my birthday, drink up."

He opens a bottle of schnapps, fills my glass. I drink small sips of beer to quell the fire in my throat.

"Music, I almost forgot the music."

Kasper uses his teeth to rip open the package of batteries and he inserts them into the radio. He twists the metal knob until he finds an acceptable channel. A local radio station playing old blues like Howlin' Wolf and Memphis Slim from scratchy LPs.

"You look thirsty," he says, and fills my glass to the brim again.

The wind pulls and shakes the little wooden shed; Kasper keeps filling up my glass. I've nearly fallen asleep when I feel a pair of hands grab me by the collar. Kasper pulls me to my feet. We walk across the roof. Karlsson waves to us. I try to walk in a straight line; the whole time I'm only one meter from the edge. We walk down the stairs, several times I nearly fall.

Kasper hails a cab in the street.

"I'm quite drunk," I tell him.

We sit in the back. I lean against the door for support.

"Of course you are."

"Am I going home now?"

"No."

"Where are we going?"

"That's for the birthday boy to decide."

I'm woken up by the sound of a car horn. I don't know how long I've been out. We drive across Rådhuspladsen, across one of the bridges. The taxi pulls over. I look out the window and see a bar. Kasper props me up as we walk through the door. He helps me sit on a barstool and orders for both of us. On the wall behind the bar is a mirror with a picture of the Eiffel Tower. Kasper talks to me; I can only make out the odd word.

The bartender puts a beer and a bitters in front of each of us.

I didn't think I could drink any more, but the alcohol wakes me up.

A man comes over to us. I recognize him from somewhere.

"There you are," he says to Kasper.

They hug each other.

"Christ, it's been a long time. Are you still working at the post office?"

Kasper nods and they toast. I try to join in, but their glasses are too far away. And that's when I recognize the man in front of us. His messy hair, the leather string around his neck. I know that I'm very drunk, but I'm absolutely sure he's the man from the gallery.

THE LIGHT FALLS through the window. I've slept in yesterday's clothes. I've got the taste of vomit in my mouth and small splashes of it on my shoes.

The pain continues beyond my hairline and dyes the room orange. It takes me several attempts to stand up. On the small table under the window I find a packet of tablets and a note.

Take two, it says. *No more than two or you might die.* The pills are from Holland, prescribed to someone whose name I don't recognize.

I go to the bathroom and swallow three tablets with water from the tap. I lie back down on the bed and close my eyes. I wish I could go to sleep, but I can't. Slowly the pills begin to take effect; they take away the pain, but also my ability to feel my legs.

While I lie on my back reminding myself to keep breathing, it grows darker outside.

I get dressed. I put my feet on the sidewalk with great care; the distance from my head to my legs is great.

I find my place at the pigeonholes without having spoken to anyone. Kasper stands behind me, singing along softly to the music in his headphones. I lean against the cold metal of the pigeonholes for support, scared that I might pass out on the concrete floor.

The first crate rolls down the conveyor belt. I pick it up and stagger back to the pigeonholes with it.

"You got me drunk yesterday," I say.

At first I don't think Kasper has heard me, then he takes off his headphones.

"Of course I did."

"But thanks for the pills."

"Don't mention it." He holds out the headphones, ready to put them over my ears. "Ramones?"

I groan and return to the pigeonholes, hoping that my hands and eyes will soon take over, do the work for me, and take away the pounding in my head.

ON MY WAY up the metal staircase I nearly trip over. I feel Kasper's hand on my back.

"I didn't know you got so angry when you were drunk," he says, pouring coffee for me. "Everyone in the bar stopped talking when you went off. You screamed something about a scared little boy who was frightened of the middle of the canvass."

I start to remember fragments from the night. I remember spilling beer down myself, I remember shouting, *Brave, he's not fucking brave*. I think I was referring to the painter exhibiting at the gallery.

"And you jabbed your finger," Kasper says. "You did a lot of jabbing."

I take a sip of coffee, I blow on it and drink some more. I empty the cup before the break is over.

We're back in front of the pigeonholes, the letters keep coming.

"Why didn't they throw me out?"

"They did, eventually. But I think they liked you."

"Liked me?"

"You were entertaining. The crazy, ranting artist. It got to be too much in the end, of course. But you got a lot off your chest."

I put on the headphones and turn up the music.

A couple hundred letters later I go to the washroom. I try to be sick, but I fail. I drink water from the tap and go back to my booth.

The supervisor walks by. "You feeling all right?" he asks.

Kasper mimes raising a bottle to his lips. The supervisor laughs and walks on.

"It wasn't your birthday yesterday, was it?" I say to Kasper.

"Yesterday? No, of course it wasn't my birthday yesterday."

"You bastard."

"If I'd told you I wanted you to meet a guy I went to school with, a guy who runs a gallery, what would you have said? Would you have said yes?"

"No, I wouldn't have."

"You're mumbling. We're not speaking Turkish now, you know."

I put on the headphones. I don't want to talk any more. Yellow crates. Letters. The buzzing of the conveyor belt.

"You haven't forgotten what you promised him, have you?"

I make no reply. I continue to stare at the letters in front of me.

"You promised him. No, more than that, you shouted that you would bring a couple of your paintings to the gallery."

"I don't remember that."

"Seeing that you're so much fucking better than everybody else."

"You got me drunk."

"If you don't, I'll give him a couple of your paintings from the basement."

I keep focusing on the letters, Frederiksberg 2000, Helsingør 3000, København NV 2400.

"So what do you say?"

Brønshøj 2700, Odense 5000.

"What do you say?"

Even with my back to him I can see that he's smiling.

THE PAINTINGS ARE leaning up against the cardboard boxes in the basement. There are many more than I would have believed. Kasper must have hidden them somewhere behind the boxes.

"This isn't bad," he says, holding one up. "We should take them outside where there's more light so we can see them better."

"Just pick two." I don't remember painting most of them, but I can see that something that started as a hand has turned into a back.

"What do you think?" Kasper asks me. "I like these two, but it's for you to decide, obviously."

I just nod. He wraps the paintings in brown paper. Tapes them carefully.

"Now don't screw with me," he says.

"I'll take them to the gallery tomorrow," I say, avoiding his gaze.

"I don't believe you."

Kasper follows me up to the street and flags down a cab. He carefully places the parcel with the paintings on the backseat, then he gives the driver the address and money for the fare. Tells him not to stop, not even for a red light if possible.

THE OWNER IS sitting on a deck chair outside the gallery; his sunglasses cover most of his face.

He holds open the door for me.

"I enjoyed meeting you. I still have bruises on my chest."

I'm not entirely sure what he means.

"You were ranting, but you also kept jabbing me in the chest with your finger. Stab, stab, stab."

"I'm really . . ."

"Don't worry about it. Or at least not much."

When I put down the pictures, he shakes my hand.

"I'm Michael, you probably don't remember that. Shall we take a look at them?"

He rips off the brown paper, fiddles with the leather string around his neck while he studies them, offers me a French cigarette.

"To be honest, I'm not really an expert on this type of thing. Most of the stuff I exhibit is conceptual. This is very . . ." He shakes his head slightly and takes a drag of his cigarette. "It's not really contemporary . . . but it's not bad, either."

The telephone rings, he answers it and speaks English down the handset. Preparations for a party or an exhibition. He asks who is coming and says he hopes they'll bring better wine this time.

When he has hung up, he returns to my paintings.

"I'll keep them until the exhibition opens. I hope that's all right."

It sounds like a question, but I can tell from his voice that he has spoken to Kasper.

HE CARRIES THE paintings out into a small room at the back, leans them up against an economy-sized pack of toilet paper and a photocopier, and takes a fresh pile of catalogs with him.

"The whole point is that all the artists are unknown. Some are just a little more unknown than others." He grins. "But your pictures will obviously be up on the wall. Say hi to Kasper, won't you?"

He closes the door behind me. Through the window I see him pick up the telephone.

I SIT BEHIND the bar; the clock on the wall is plastic. Black hands against a white clock face. It's early afternoon. The bar is practically empty.

"A bunch of the regulars were in for the breakfast special," says the middle-aged barmaid behind the counter. "They're at home sleeping it off now. They'll be back soon for happy hour."

I follow her gaze down the dark room. A man is slumped in front of one of the tables; a half of stout is standing in front of him.

"That's Leif. I'm not even going to . . ." She puts a shot glass and a premium beer in front of me. "The breakfast special is long over, but what the hell, I'll throw in the schnapps for free."

PETRA WAKES ME up. She says I reek of booze. When she was a child and her dad brushed her teeth, his hands would smell of tobacco and his breath of vodka. She likes the smell. Then she falls silent, having caught herself talking about her family. Which she's promised herself never to do. As a punishment because I never tell her anything about mine. I wait a couple of moments before I tell her about the gallery and the exhibition.

She leaps out of bed.

"Fantastic!" she shouts.

She sits down and gets straight up again.

"What do you wear to something like that?" she asks.

I lie down; I hide my head under the pillow.

"I'll get something, obviously. I'll get a new outfit for the opening. Your girlfriend has to look smart."

The small bedroom falls silent. Kot stares at us from the doorway.

"Am I your girlfriend?" Petra lingers slightly over the word. As you do over the most precious thing you have.

"Of course."

The answer comes more easily than I'd have imagined.

Kot stretches lazily and strolls out into the kitchen.

"I'll get myself a new dress. Will you be wearing a tie?"

I'M STANDING IN the break room pouring coffee from the pot when Erik comes in. He walks right up to me, delighted to have news to deliver. There's no talk about robots taking over our jobs tonight. I've had a few days off. Erik tells me what happened while I was away, in small snippets spread across the ten minutes that make up the coffee break. He tells me how uniformed officers came for Kasper, that they must've had something on him. That they didn't handcuff him, but escorted him out with an officer on each side. They must've been watching him for some time, Erik says. God knows what he's been up to. Erik looks expectantly at me, hoping I'll suggest something. I drink coffee until he starts talking again. He tells me they summoned our shift to the break room, but said nothing except that they were investigating certain irregularities.

When the break is over, I walk back to the pigeonholes and I don't put on the headphones. For the rest of the shift I listen for the sound of footsteps coming down the aisles, expecting to see officers who would like a word with me. Or the supervisor pulling me aside. But it's a night like any other, only without Kasper standing behind me.

I LEAVE WORK early in the morning. I've only just gone through the archway when my hands start to shake.

I sit down on a bench outside Hovedbanegården, drinking apple juice from a carton. I feel like a beer and a schnapps, like getting a little too drunk and waking up in Petra's bed with her sitting on the edge trying to blow smoke rings.

Then I remember the paintings in the basement. I don't know why, but suddenly they seem very important. Like entries in a diary I don't want anyone else to read.

I take a taxi to Kasper's apartment. I wait until the courtyard gate opens as a woman with a bicycle lets herself out. In the courtyard I find a brick. I walk down to the basement door. The wood is old and crumbling and quickly gives way. I walk down the passage; I squat in front of the door to Kasper's basement room. There's not much light, but I feel my way along the wooden wall with my fingertips until I discover the crack where Kasper keeps the key. I unlock the padlock and open the door. No one has been here yet. The room is still crammed with boxes, but it can't be long before the police talk to the caretaker. I carry the paintings upstairs and leave them on the sidewalk, leaning them up against a wall.

It's the first time I see them in daylight. The colors are much brighter than they appeared at night when I painted them.

I order a cargo van from a telephone booth; I can barely see the pictures while I speak.

It starts to rain while I wait for the van. I could take off my jacket, drape it across the canvasses, but there are too many of them. I'd have to take off all my clothes.

THE DRIVER HELPS me lug the pictures into the van; he promises me he'll drive carefully.

I tell him it doesn't matter. He thinks I'm joking and slows down even more.

When I've got the last pictures inside my room, I can barely open the door and I have to hurl myself onto the bed.

I move them around. I put some of them outside in the hallway. Elsebeth hasn't been up here for a long time, so I don't think she'll mind. I clear a small space in front of the bed so I can swing my legs out in the morning, and I clear a path to the desk so I can put down my keys.

I fall asleep with the radio in my ears.

I dream I help Kasper escape from prison. He's wearing stripey clothes and his cheeks are sunken. As soon as he comes out into the daylight, he turns to dust and is blown away. No, Petra says, not like a werewolf, but possibly a vampire.

KARLSSON SITS IN his deck chair with his eyes closed. I've opened the hatch slightly, the chain is on. I had to shout a couple of times, drown out the noise of the city, before he heard me. He comes over and unlocks it, then he walks back to his chair with his shoulders slumped. He already knows. Or he guessed as much when Kasper failed to show.

"Perhaps they don't have anything on him, we might see him again in a couple of days. He's always been careful," Karlsson says, but doesn't sound as if he believes it.

I take the cherry brandy out of the bag. We share it. He's too despondent to roll his own so we smoke my cigarettes.

Karlsson talks about building a bomb. One big enough to blast a hole in the prison wall. We just have to find out which cell he's in. It's doable.

When the cigarette package is empty and there's no cherry brandy left, I get up.

"You're always welcome to visit me," Karlsson says. "Even if Kasper isn't here."

I walk across the roof; I know I'm not going to see him again.

PETRA HAS HIGHLIGHTED her eyes with thick black eyeliner. She has changed her outfit three times. Even Kot seems agitated. It marches from the kitchen and into the bedroom and back, sits down on the kitchen table, licks its paw and jumps down restlessly again.

"Aren't you going to wear something more festive?" Petra asks, looking at my T-shirt and jeans.

Her high heels click against the sidewalk, the sun shines in her eyes.

Outside the gallery people are smoking and holding glasses of white wine.

It's a struggle to get through the door; the gallery is packed. Everyone is well dressed in a casual way. Suit jackets over oil-stained trousers. T-shirts with holes so big you can see half a nipple. They talk in loud voices, they laugh, they hide their cigarettes in the palms of their hands so they don't set fire to each other. Petra asks if I see my paintings. I look around, shake my head. She drags me along past the DJ playing electronic music, the same small drum being hit again and again, mixed with monotonous Indian chanting.

We reach the second small room.

"Maybe we should come back a bit later," I say over the din. "In an hour or six months."

"Are they in here?"

I stand on tiptoe. I look around and shake my head.

"Maybe we should . . ."

Petra drags me past more people, into the last room. I can't see my pictures here, either. I'm bigger than her and when I start pulling her all she can do is follow. She nearly topples over in her high heels. Then I spot them: my pictures hang on either side of the door, slightly too close to the door frame.

"That's them, isn't it?" Petra asks.

I leave her in front of the paintings while I push my way back to the table with the white wine. I take two glasses, one for each of us. I want to give one to her, but she hasn't finished looking at the paintings so I'm left standing with the glasses.

Then she presses herself against me, kisses my cheek. The wine sloshes over and runs down my hands.

"Now we can go," she says.

Once again we have to work our way slowly between people who are sweating, smoking, and drinking. The door is in sight when I feel a hand on my shoulder.

"I'm glad you came," Michael says. "We need to take some photos."

I briefly consider saying no, but I don't get the chance. We're pushed out in the street, lined up in front of the gallery.

A girl with dyed black hair and piercings is placed in the middle. On one side of her they put a tall guy with clothes that are too short. He keeps adjusting his glasses. On the other side they put a young man with dark skin and a ponytail. He's wearing a poncho of a thin material, silk possibly.

I stand to the far left, a part of the composition.

Some of the guests have drifted outside with us. They stand behind the photographers, out in the street. I hear cars sound their horns, but no one moves. The cars will either have to wait or drive up on the sidewalk to get past.

We're told to smile. We're told not to smile. Could you move forward a little? Turn to the side. Pull your hood over your head. It's all right if you smoke. At the end the photographers take a lot of pictures with Michael squatting in front of us or standing between us.

"Remember to include the background. Get the gallery's sign in the picture, for Christ's sake." Then he laughs. "I'm being serious."

Michael asks everyone to come back inside; he wants to say a few words.

People move out against the walls of the gallery; Michael stands in the middle of the floor holding a glass of white wine. He promises to be brief and adjusts the tie he isn't wearing.

"Being able to showcase brand-new talent is fantastic, as is being able to say that I was the first to exhibit them." He grins at the girl with piercings on her face and the tall, skinny guy. "Even if it isn't strictly true. Surely it's okay to exaggerate a little."

Then he turns to the man with the ponytail and the poncho.

"Alonso, I'm delighted you were able to come to Denmark, we don't see you often enough." They raise their glasses, they smile at each other.

"And Mehmet Faruk." He looks for me in the crowd, but gives up before he finds me. "His paintings hang in the last room; make sure you don't miss them."

Petra squeezes my hand.

I follow her outside. She got up early to work in the kiosk; she's tired, but insists that I stay.

That I have a good time.

She wants to sleep for a couple of hours and then wait for me. She'll wait even if I come back late. She doesn't mind late.

I promise her I'll have a good time. I promise her I'll get drunk. She refuses to see me again unless I stink of alcohol.

I kiss her good-bye and watch her walk down the street and disappear around the corner.

I go back to the table with the wine. I take two glasses and stand holding one in each hand as though I'm waiting for someone. I drink from both of them, I catch snippets of conversation, the guests discuss other exhibitions, other galleries.

"He's from Chile," I hear someone say; they're talking about the man in the poncho. "His father was tortured in prison. He uses it when he paints. It can be hard to see, obviously."

When I've emptied the glasses, I go back to the last room. I want to say good-bye to my paintings before I find a bar where I can get drunk. A man is looking at them. He's wearing a brown tweed suit and he wipes sweat from his forehead with his sleeve, but he doesn't take his eyes off the paintings.

"Do you like them?" I ask him.

He looks at me, then apologizes in English with a German accent. I'm already regretting the question, but I repeat it in German.

He takes a step back so he can look from one picture to the other.

"Did you paint them?" he asks, in German this time.

When I confirm this, he asks me more questions, simple as well as technical: what kind of paints I use, how long each painting takes me. I try to answer him. He tells me my German is good, then he asks if I'd like to have a beer with him somewhere other than here.

WE STEP INSIDE the cool twilight of the bar. I order each of us a large draft beer.

"I wish I could pay," the German says. "I should be paying. You shouldn't be buying your own drinks, not tonight. But I've lost my wallet. Perhaps it's back at my hotel room. I don't really know."

I take out some money and put it on the counter; we sit down in a booth.

The man swigs a big mouthful of beer, holds out his hand and shakes mine.

"Ulrich," he says. "And I know your name."

He takes off his jacket and folds it. His shirt has circles of sweat under the armpits.

"I don't know if I ever answered your question. But I think your paintings are really good."

He cleans his glasses with his shirt.

"Of course, that's just my opinion. I'm a lawyer. Or rather, I was. But I've wanted to work with art for a long time."

The more beers I order, the better my paintings get.

When I start ordering schnapps with the beers, my paintings are the best he has seen for years.

It's past midnight when Ulrich slams the palm of his hand so hard against the table that the people near us turn around.

"I want to see some more," he roars. "You must have some more paintings."

I get up; I suddenly realize how much we've drunk. Ulrich bumps into parked cars along the street and triggers a couple of car alarms. We pass the street where Petra lives. I know she's waiting for me; I consider making up an excuse so I can go up to her. Then I hear a loud metallic sound: Ulrich has accidentally torn the side mirror off a car. He picks it up, he tries to put it back again, all the time on the verge of falling over. I support him while we cross the bridge.

I let him in and ask him to be quiet. He lifts a finger to his lips, putting his feet on each step with exaggerated caution like someone miming that they're tiptoeing.

I turn on the light. Ulrich remains in the doorway, looking at the paintings that fill my room. He says a German swear word I don't know and now seems much more clear-headed.

"We need some light," he says.

I hold the bedside table lamp for him, aim it at the pictures while he moves around, squats down in front of them.

"Didn't we pass some pictures in the hall?"

He drags them in, leans them up against the bed, holds the lamp up to them.

WE SIT ON the bed, he has seen all the pictures, we share the last of my cigarettes.

"You're good," he says, smoothing his tie across his knee. "I can't remember where my hotel is. Would it be all right if I slept here?"

He doesn't wait for an answer. He lies down on the floor next to my bed, folds his jacket, and uses it as his pillow. He falls asleep in seconds; I can hear one of his nostrils giving out a faint squeak.

I wake up alone in the room and swallow a couple of Kasper's Dutch headache pills.

I had some banknotes and coins lying on the table under the window. Now they're gone. On the back of a train ticket the man from last night has written that he's very sorry, but that he'll get the money back to me somehow.

THE CAFÉS ARE quick to set out chairs on the sidewalks. Those who live in the apartments next to them have to squeeze their way past people drinking lattes. A few weeks later, the chairs have spread out across the whole street.

The waiters risk getting hit by cars as they run back and forth with empty glasses and overflowing ashtrays. The chairs are centimeters from falling into the canal.

Even so, many people come in vain; they hover around hoping that some of us will drink up quickly or die under the hot sun.

Petra is wearing a broad-brimmed straw hat. She dangles a sandal over the water.

She says that she loves the sun, but it's not so keen on her.

EVERY MORNING I ring the sorting office and ask if they can manage without me. They usually can. Not many large letters are sent in the summer months.

Mostly postcards, lots of postcards. They're sorted by machines.

Petra doesn't have to work so much either; during the holidays students offer themselves as cheap labor.

We don't scrimp, but neither of us has ever learned how to spend a lot of money. We buy coffee and food you can fit between two slices of bread.

Petra stretches out in the café chair. The legs scrape across the cobblestones, edging a little closer to the water.

"We'll move the table," she says. "You can paint in the kitchen. We'll move the litter tray, Kot won't mind. It doesn't matter if you spill paint."

I raise my hand to shield my eyes from the sun.

"And I'm not going to scrub paint off your fingers any more."

She takes my hands in hers: they're clean. I haven't painted since Kasper was arrested.

"I'll nag you," Petra laughs. "'You always get paint on your fingers,' I'll say loudly. I'll keep repeating it until someone asks me about it and I'll have to tell them that my boyfriend is an exhibited artist."

I'm almost certain that Petra has been past the gallery since the private view. She hasn't said anything about it, but there are days when she has come back late, smiling, as though she's keeping a secret.

She showed me a cutting from a newspaper she read at work. A couple of lines in the arts section about a gallery that's concentrating on new art. With a picture of

Michael squatting in front of us. I'm standing near the edge, only a grainy shadow.

I WALK ACROSS the street for more coffee, our third cup. Petra asks if she can please have a cognac with it.

I try not to spill when I cross the street again; a cyclist has to swerve to avoid me, I don't hear what he shouts. Petra sips the cognac tentatively, looks up, and smiles.

"My dad organized my communion," she says. "He's a Catholic, but he doesn't believe in God so we went to Tivoli Gardens instead. We had to have a cognac with our coffee, now that I was practically a grown-up."

Petra licks the inside of the glass.

"I think I talked constantly when we left. I prattled in a loud, silly voice and my dad was so ashamed he'd got me drunk."

Petra giggles before she remembers again that she's promised herself she wouldn't tell me about her family.

On our way back to Petra's apartment, I take her hand and we go into an off-license. I buy a bottle of cognac. When the cat has been fed and the condom is in the trash, we drink cognac from water glasses. I look at Petra; after a couple of mouthfuls, she gets a red circle on each cheek that looks like it's been drawn with lipstick.

"I look like a clown, don't I?"

I nod, she lashes out at me but misses.

IT TURNS INTO a long, hot summer where every little vacant shop is rented out and sells ice cream; Italian ice cream, homemade ice cream. The bakeries put out signs advertising home-baked waffle cones. Everyone competes to sell the biggest: the biggest waffle cone, the most marshmallows. The number of scoops reaches double digits.

Petra buys a leash for Kot. We try to take it for a walk, but the cat keeps turning around and biting at the leather. Petra nudges it with her foot; the cat walks ten meters then turns around again and bites.

Eventually it refuses to walk any further. I pick it up and carry it around town.

In Nyhavn I buy Petra an ice cream. I buy her the biggest one they sell. I hold Kot's leash while she tries to eat it; she has to hold the cone with both hands.

IN BED THAT night Petra grabs a skin fold on her tummy. She says I've made her fat by feeding her ice cream. In the soft light her eyes are dark blue like police uniforms.

"I don't think I can stick to our agreement any longer," she says.

WE'VE TAKEN TWO buses and almost left the city. now we're standing outside a community hall. There's a poster on the door: the name of the band is the Blue Cat. *Polska jazz,* it says below. The photo of the musicians looks as though it was taken in the eighties.

"My dad plays the trumpet," Petra says.

The man in the picture has a wreath of black curly hair around his head. He has a bushy mustache and wears an embroidered waistcoat that looks like part of a folk dancer's costume.

We enter, walk past a notice board with flyers about senior gymnastics and opening hours for the ceramic workshop in the basement. Folding chairs have been set out in the hall; we sit down in the middle. Around us the seats fill up with elderly people; several of them speak Polish to each other.

Petra leans towards me. "My dad was well known in Poland, but he couldn't keep his mouth shut. My mum would shout *zamknij się,* shut your mouth. He had too many opinions."

Some of the old people kiss Petra on the cheek. When they've greeted each other and everyone has sat down, the musicians enter.

I recognize Petra's dad from the poster. His hair's now reduced to two dark tufts on either side of his head. He's wearing the same waistcoat as when the photograph was taken, but his stomach has grown and he'd never be able to button it now.

They get ready on stage and exchange a few words with each other.

Petra's dad attaches the mouthpiece to the trumpet, then he nods to the man behind the electric organ, who strikes the first chords. He's quickly followed by the bass player.

Petra's dad blows her a kiss and puts the trumpet to his lips.

The orchestra plays Polish folk songs with jazz harmonies. Petra tells me what the songs are called.

"'*Ułani, ułani,*'" she whispers in my ear. "It's about handsome soldiers on horseback with long lances. The children wave good-bye to them, their faces are painted. All the girls are in love with them."

The last song before the interval is slow and lingering. Petra's dad keeps the jazz phrasing to a minimum.

"'*Czerwone maki na Monte Cassino,*'" Petra says. "My dad hates playing this one."

Around us I see old men and women with tears in their eyes; I see tissues come out of handbags.

"This one is also about soldiers. Dead soldiers."

IN THE INTERVAL they sell coffee in plastic cups and bottles of beer from a crate.

A woman puts a basket of cakes on the table. Petra says they're called *babkas* and suggests that I try one.

The second set is pure jazz, but even in "Birdland" and "Moose the Mooche" I can still hear the harmonies from the folk songs.

Petra's dad is about to put the trumpet back in its box when they're asked to play the song about the dead soldiers at Monte Cassino again. They play a longer version where the chorus is repeated over and over. Afterwards people get up, they clap and clap, again with tears in their eyes. They shake hands with Petra's dad. Some give banknotes to the musicians, others coins. Petra's dad thanks them and smiles. An elderly man gives him a bottle wrapped in newspaper.

WE FOLLOW PETRA'S dad down the street. The tips have been shared out and Petra's dad has put the waistcoat in his rucksack. He swings the trumpet box back and forth; he smiles a lot, kisses me on the cheek when we're introduced.

"I made *bigos* yesterday," he says.

"You made *bigos* for yourself?" Petra asks, looking as though she finds that very hard to believe.

"It always tastes better the day after. I was hoping you might stop by for a bite to eat."

"I think Mehmet might be working tonight?"

Petra looks at me.

"They let me off," I say.

She flashes me a grateful smile.

"Then of course we'll stay for dinner, *tata*."

THE APARTMENT IS small, with yellowing jazz posters on the walls. Petra shows me her old room. It's filled with stuffed toys and porcelain dolls. Across her bed lies a large crochet bedspread. Her dad has touched nothing since she moved out.

"Sometimes I sit in here and play the trumpet," he says.

The dining table is set for three. *Bigos* turns out to be a sausage casserole with cabbage; we drink beer with it. Petra's dad puts an LP on the turntable, a recording from the seventies on which he's playing. Modern jazz with no hint of folk songs.

When Petra has put the plates in the kitchen, her dad takes out the bottle he got after the concert. Close up, I can see that the newspaper in which it's wrapped is Polish. He tears off the paper, smiles happily.

"Proper vodka," he says. "You need to taste this."

We drink a couple of glasses. Petra drinks tea; she says the last bus will leave soon.

"Stay here," her dad says. "Your room is ready, you can have *bigos* for breakfast."

His laughter turns into a long cough. Petra looks at me, I nod.

"We'll stay over," she says.

Her dad smiles and goes to the bathroom to carry on coughing.

Petra tells me she's tired and wants to go to bed; she hopes I'll join her shortly. She says she's never had sex in her old bedroom. Her dad is a heavy sleeper and she promises to turn away the porcelain dolls so they won't stare at us.

"My old *tata*," Petra says, when her dad returns to the table. She kisses his cheek. "Don't stay up too late."

From the doorway she sends me a look that can't be misinterpreted and closes the door behind her.

Petra's dad lights a cigarette and fills my glass.

"You make my daughter happy," he says, coughing into his hand a couple of times before taking another drag of the cigarette. "You're Turkish?"

"Not very much."

"I was Polish once. Now I'm Danish and I speak the language badly. No, you don't have to say that my Danish is good. My German is better."

"We can speak German if you like."

"Danish is my language now. I speak it badly, but I speak it."

We drink and we smoke. For the first half hour I look for an excuse or simply the right time to leave the table and join Petra.

But her dad carries on talking. First about jazz. Then about escaping to the West. It had become necessary because he'd spoken up too much about Poland. About the Soviet Union. Eventually they got fed up with him. He wasn't allowed to play at anything other than weddings and holiday resorts out of season. He tells me how the family sold everything they owned and made a deal with a coach driver who often just got waved through when he crossed the border late at night with his coach full of sleeping pensioners returning from a spa holiday.

Petra's dad was due to perform at a seaside hotel. When the last set was finished, they'd board the coach, sit at the back, and cross their fingers. Her dad played, Petra clapped her hands and joined in the chorus, her mum was supposed to ring their family to say good-bye and buy bread and cheese for the trip.

Petra's dad finds another bottle of vodka from the freezer. He fills our glasses and tells me that they waited for Petra's mum for twenty-two minutes. Then the coach driver said they'd either have to get on or stay behind.

They left without her. Perhaps she would join them later, in a taxi, before the border. Perhaps she would find another way across. It was the hardest decision he'd ever had to make. But if his wife had been taken by the police, returning to the apartment in Kraków was a bad idea—sitting there waiting for the police to take him, too, and orphan his daughter.

Petra's dad has given up translating all the words into Danish; he says them in Polish and carries on talking.

I understand that they never saw the mother again.

Many years later they learned that she had a new family. That she'd married a doctor. That it wasn't them who had abandoned the mother, but the mother who had abandoned them.

We've almost finished the second bottle when I lie down next to Petra. She's sleeping heavily; I brush the hair away from her face.

THE SUMMER TURNS into early autumn and the city grows restless.

Street corners and benches are filled with bare-chested men, parks with half-naked girls on picnic blankets. Everyone wants to catch the last rays of sunshine.

I follow the canal down to the gallery.

There's a sign in the window: *Closed for the summer,* it says, with a date for the next exhibition. I can see Michael through the window. He's talking on the telephone. He smiles at me and opens the door.

Most of the pictures have been taken down; the few still hanging have small labels saying *Sold* and give the address of the buyer.

My two paintings are leaning against the wall in the last room of the gallery.

When Michael has hung up, he gets out some corrugated cardboard and a big roll of packing tape.

Then the telephone rings and he disappears again.

It takes me only a couple of minutes to wrap up my paintings. I've tucked them under my arm and I'm heading out the door when Michael calls me over, putting down the handset.

"This isn't a post office, you know," he says, smiling, and hands me a letter.

I follow the canal past the cafés to the end of the harbor where there are fewer people. I sit down with my feet dangling over the water.

The letter lies on my lap. For a long time I just sit there staring at it.

Then I tear open the envelope. Inside is a single handwritten sheet of A4.

He uses my new name even in the letter itself. He respects that I have the right to choose my own name.

The letter is short.

He wants me to visit him. It's very important that I visit him. The address is written more clearly than the rest, as though he has traced the pen many times over every single letter.

The letter is signed *Your dad*.

I stay sitting with the letter in my lap; I look at the sailboats leaving the canal for the open sea. I see motorboats and tourists on canal round trips; they wave at me.

I get up. I find a dumpster and toss the paintings into it.

A couple of streets from Petra's apartment, I stop at the bank to take out some cash.

Petra kisses me. She asks me if anything is wrong. I shake my head, I try to smile. She cooks dinner for us, Polish food today. She serves potatoes, cheap beer, and vodka. Big sausages swimming in fat. I drink more than I eat.

I take the cash from my pocket and tell her that my paintings were sold. That the money is for her.

She counts it.

"I'd have thought you'd get more for your paintings. I mean, if they've hung in a proper gallery."

"Won't it cover the rest of Kot's medical bill?"

She nods. For the last couple of months she has been paying off the visit to the animal hospital.

I put a bite of sausage into my mouth. I chew and force myself to swallow it.

"It's really great that you sold the paintings," she says, pouring more beer into my glass.

IT TURNS AUTUMN while I sit on the train. The leaves lose their color as I leave the city behind.

At the bus station the wind tears at my clothes. I ask the bus driver to tell me when my stop is. When I mention the name of the road, he stares at me a little too long.

I walk up a gravel path with grass on either side. The building is single-story, so I can see only the front from here. It's difficult to get an idea of how big it really is.

The gravel path leads up to two glass doors. When I get nearer, tiny scratches to the surface reveal that they're not made from glass but thick, transparent plastic.

Ring the bell, says a small cardboard sign taped to the inside of the window. I press the bell. I think I can see movement inside. The lock buzzes.

I WALK UP to the woman behind the counter and state my dad's name. She looks up. I tell her I'd like to visit my dad. She freezes, her hands on the computer's keyboard. I give her my real name, a name I haven't used for years. She carries on staring at me.

"I'll need to see some ID," she says eventually.

I fumble in my pocket; I find my old health insurance card, the one I used when I still lived with Karin and Michael.

"Visiting hours are almost over, but I think we can make an exception."

She opens a visitor's log and shows me where to sign in. Then she presses the intercom and asks a carer to come up to escort me.

She prepares a visitor's card for me.

"Don't take it off. Or we might decide to keep you."

She smiles a tired smile at the little joke she has probably used many times before. Then her face darkens.

"I don't know when you last saw him."

"A long time ago."

"People who are admitted here are very sick."

I WAIT ON the sofa and read an old newspaper. A carer throws open the door. He's in his mid-forties and weighs fifteen kilos too much. He announces that visiting hours are over and is about to add something when the woman behind the counter tells him who it is I've come to see. Then he goes quiet. Only for a moment, like a single clap of the hands. He nods for me to follow him.

The carer has a bald patch at the back of his head, a third eye that watches me while we walk down the long, white corridors. He holds the doors open for me until

I've only just gotten through; he's already on his way to the next one. His rubber-soled clogs make a slurping sound against the linoleum. I think he hates me.

"You're his son?" he says, and it sounds like an accusation.

"Yes."

"I haven't seen you before."

"I haven't been here before."

We walk through several locks where one door has to be closed before the next will open. It could be a prison except that everything is painted white and there are brightly colored posters on the walls.

We pass a couple of carers and they nod to each other.

"Most of them haven't been here as long as I have," says the man in front of me when we're alone again. "They don't remember what your dad was like when he'd just been admitted to this ward."

We stop in front of a numbered door.

The carer finds a key.

"You mustn't give him anything. No lighters, no pens, no containers or glass bottles. No alcohol and no illegal substances," he intones. Then he turns the key in the lock and pushes open the door.

The only light in the room is coming from the window under the ceiling. A tall, thin man sits on the bed; his hair is close-cropped. He's leaning slightly forwards. An undernourished soldier sleeping at his post.

"You have five minutes," the carer says. "And the door must remain open."

I hear his footsteps: they stop right outside the door.

The man on the bed looks up. His eyes shine in the dim light. They haven't grown bigger, but his face has grown smaller. He looks neither stunned nor surprised.

Then he gets up and pulls me into an embrace. I can feel his lips against my arm, sense the hospital smell in his clothing and skin.

"I knew you'd come," he says in a croaky voice.

I pull the chair over and sit down opposite him.

"I've been waiting a long time. I knew I'd find you eventually."

"You saw the picture in the newspaper?"

"I'd recognize my own son anywhere. Even if he has chosen a new name for himself." He scratches the short stubble on his scalp. "I'm sorry I couldn't stop by the gallery and see your paintings. But circumstances prevented it."

He smiles a pale smile out into the room.

It might be the shadows in his eye sockets, but I think his eyes are moist.

"I'd like to have seen you grow up," he says. "Seen you grow. Now I'm no longer sure that anything mattered more."

I hear three knocks on the door. The carer waits for me in the doorway.

As I get up, my dad grips my wrists, a swift movement I didn't see coming. I can feel every joint in his fingers.

"Promise me you'll come back," he says.

I nod.

My dad swings his long legs up on the bed and lies down.

I WATCH MY own reflection in the window of the train.

I'm good at lying. I know I can do it and my voice won't even tremble.

But my face can't lie.

I was glad that I'd made plans to see Petra. I'd held on to that thought in the train to the hospital. I knew she'd be waiting for me with half a bottle of cognac. With arms and breasts and a depressed cat in the kitchen. But my face can't lie and she'll keep asking until I tell her.

I GET OFF at Hovedbanegården. I walk past the bars, past cars and buses and people. The light changes to green. There are potholes in the pavement under my feet and I decide to focus on that.

I press my ear against the door to Elsebeth's apartment, I listen to the silence to be sure that she isn't in the hallway or in the kitchen before I let myself in.

I lie on the bed, my hand under my head.

I wish I could sleep. A deep, dreamless slumber. I force my eyes shut. I open them again and stare at the ceiling.

I GET DRESSED and go outside. I walk and I keep on walking.

I walk until my calves ache, until my feet are flat and too big for my shoes. I walk in circles within the Ramparts. I buy a hot dog from a stand. I take a few bites before I throw it in the trash.

Just before eleven o'clock I stand in front of the sorting office. I walk in with the others; I find the supervisor and ask him if he needs me. He looks surprised and tells me that my shift isn't on tonight.

I ask him if they can use me on one of the other teams.

The supervisor looks as though it's the strangest question he has ever heard.

That night I work a shift where I know no one and nobody knows whether I always look like I do now.

One hour later my hands and eyes take over and I no longer have to think.

My new station buddy peers furtively at me when I pull yet another crate with letters off the conveyor belt. I must be three or four crates ahead of him.

PETRA AND I are standing in the corner store. I put my arm around her shoulder; she turns around and looks at me.

The words I'd rehearsed, the ones I'd voiced in my head while I tried to go to sleep last night, are now impossible to utter.

"Kot doesn't like salmon," I say.

"You're right."

She puts the can back on the shelf.

JUST OVER A week later, I'm back on the train.

Several times I almost get off. I'm tempted to rush out onto the platform, a little too quickly as though I hadn't paid for my ticket. Hasty footsteps on squashed chewing gum; buy some cigarettes and a newspaper at the newsstand and then head back to the city.

But I stay on the train. I wait for the bus, I get on, and I follow the bus stops with my eyes. This time I don't have to ask the bus driver for help.

The same carer as last time meets me at the counter.

We walk down corridors; I try to make a map in my head, try to remember when we turn right and when we turn left. Form an impression of how big this place is. It's big, I know that now.

The carer inserts the key into the lock.

"You mustn't give him anything. No lighters, no pens. No containers or glass bottles . . ."

He opens the door, is still reeling off his list, but stops. We're staring into an empty room. The carer takes a few steps across to the wardrobe and throws open the doors. It contains nothing but jeans and faded T-shirts. He rushes out into the corridor, looking to both sides, then he rips the radio from his belt. The clip makes a small snap.

"Resident 314 isn't in his room, should I sound the alarm?"

He speaks as loudly as he can without shouting. Then he listens to the voice down the other end, his facial expression going from controlled panic to irritation.

"I should've been told. No, just telling Poulsen isn't enough."

He returns the radio to his belt and locks the door to my dad's room. He gestures for me to follow him.

He walks quickly, angrily, down several corridors, through several locks.

"Most staff haven't been here as long as I have," he tells me again, slowing down so that I can come up beside him. "They weren't here when your dad was admitted. They can read his file, of course, but few of them bother."

We carry on walking; the carer watches me out of the corner of his eye.

"I came over from Neurology; I'd just started here. Your dad had locked himself in the bathroom. We had a key, of course, but he'd managed to destroy the lock so we had to force the door. He'd smashed all the lightbulbs in the ceiling so it was completely dark. He'd taken off his clothes and smeared soap all over himself. There was nothing to hold on to. We were four carers and yet he eluded us several times."

We're on our way down a glass corridor when the carer stops, pulls down his sweater so I can see the scar. It starts right above his collarbone and stops somewhere under the sweater.

"He'd managed to rip a soap dish out of the wall. He used it as a weapon."

We've reached two doors made from reinforced plastic. *Library,* says the sign. The carer holds open the door for me.

"Henrik still can't see properly out of one eye."

Behind me the door slams shut. I follow the bookcases. It looks like a school library.

At a desk a man with a badge is putting lending slips back into some books. He looks at me until he notices my visitor's badge and carries on working.

I find my dad at a table in the small reading room. He has today's newspapers spread out in front of him.

"I'm not allowed to cut them," he says, smiling at me. "So I hide the clippings in here." He taps his temple.

A man behind my dad is busy taking books from the shelves. He studies them briefly before returning them to a new place.

"People can adapt to almost anything," my dad says. "But that's not the same as saying they have to. Some things you should never adapt to. I miss beer. So very, very much. I miss the taste."

The carer who was inserting the lending slips comes over to our table. In his hand he has a newspaper which he puts in front of my dad.

"It had fallen down behind—" Then he notices the man by the shelves. "Damn you, Holger."

He rushes over to the man and snatches the book from his hand.

"But they're better this way."

"Damn you, Holger."

"The alphabet isn't—"

"Who the hell let you in here in the first place?"

Holger is escorted out of the library; we hear him knock books off the shelves along the way.

"It's hard to tell from looking at them." My dad takes my hands in his. "They're getting much better at disguise. You'd think they didn't even recognize themselves."

I can hear Holger fighting the two carers. I hear the thud of his body hitting the floor while they put him in a straitjacket.

"Like here at the hospital," my dad says. "For most people this is just a job. They turn up in the morning, they earn their money, and then they go home. But a few of them are really the White Men. It's so hard to spot them. You have to study them a long time. You have to watch them when they think they're alone."

The carer returns. He stops in front of the shelves where Holger had been standing and looks at them in despair.

"I don't know if this helps, but Holger spent hours doing that," my dad says.

The carer starts pulling books out and putting them back in the right place while muttering curses under his breath.

PETRA PUTS PEAS on my plate.

"No one's forcing you to be my boyfriend," she says.

"I'm not sleeping too well."

"Maybe you should start painting again?"

I fill my mouth with potato, avoiding her eyes.

When the plates have been cleared and put in the sink, I borrow Petra's telephone. I call the sorting office and speak to an answering machine. I say that I thought I'd be feeling better. I really did. But I've got a stomach bug and I can't go to work.

If you're going to call in sick, you have to do it before noon so they have time to find a replacement. Perhaps I'll get a warning, but I don't care.

Today we leave Kot in the kitchen and close the door behind us.

I get a red rash around my mouth from Petra's pubic hair. She apologizes for not having shaved.

I throw the condom on the floor. She turns over on her side. I tell her this wasn't a one-act play. That the curtain might have come down, but only so the scenery can be changed for the next act.

We drink cognac from the bottle. I hold her, I hold her so tight I can see marks from my fingers on her skin.

PETRA SLEEPS WITH her hand under her head. I look at her naked shoulders. I grab her arm, shaking her lightly.

She mumbles in her sleep, turns towards me, rubs her eyes.

"There's something I have to tell you."

She blinks a couple of times, looks at me quizzically. When I don't say anything else, she turns over, grunting a little.

Kot looks at me from the doorway. Its eyes reflect the streetlight.

THE WOMAN IN front of me has small mother-of-pearl studs in her ears. There's a row of holes for many more earrings in her left ear.

"Any questions, just ask," she says.

We're sitting in her office with stacks of medical books on the desk between us. Her name and title, Consultant, is displayed on a small sign next to the telephone. "I'll try to explain if there's anything you don't understand."

"What are the chances that my dad will ever be discharged?"

She looks at me long and hard, summing me up. Then she pushes a strand of blonde hair behind her ear.

"I can tell you that he's improving. But I don't want to give you false hope. He's better now than he was three years ago. Much better than he was five years ago . . ."

"Will he ever be discharged?"

She blinks a couple of times.

"I need a cigarette," she says.

I follow her into one of the common rooms. She unlocks a glass door and we step out into a small courtyard with brick walls on all sides.

She takes a long menthol cigarette from a packet; I hand her my lighter. She takes a couple of drags.

"There's no way he'll ever be discharged. I'm not supposed to tell you that. We should always hold out hope to patients and their next of kin. It's part of the treatment. Hope can be just as important as medicine." She burns a round hole in the leaf of a birch in a big pot. "I could recommend it. But there would be no point. His file would land on the desk of someone higher up. Alarm bells would ring." She taps the ash into the pot.

"I'd like to take him outside, go for a walk with him."

"You could always bring him out here."

"Then I prefer the library."

She nods.

I COMPLETE SEVERAL copies of the forms. I agree by my signature to take responsibility for my dad.

We get stale bread for the birds from the hospital kitchen.

A carer unlocks the door for us. My dad takes his first tentative steps outside; the gravel crunches under his feet.

He looks over his shoulder, up at the dark windows.

"Do you think they're watching us?" I ask.

"Of course they are."

We walk across the lawn. We're not allowed to step onto the sidewalk because then we're no longer on hospital property.

We sit down on a bench along one of the gravel paths. We watch the cars drive past on the road.

I hand him the cola bottle. At the bus stop I filled it up with beer, trying not to spill a single drop.

He looks over his shoulder again before raising the bottle to his lips. He drinks the first gulp greedily. The second he holds in his mouth for a long time before he swallows it. The third he spits out.

"I know exactly what they give me." He rolls the bottle between his hands. "Whenever I get new medication, I look it up in the library. If I drink more than this, my head will swell up, my eyes will get dry and hurt."

I open the bread bag and hand my dad a stale poppyseed loaf.

"There is a way to escape the White Men," he says, breaking off a chunk of bread. "A door in the wall. A door you can only see if you want to see it. If there are no other ways out, that door is always there."

Tentatively he tastes the bread before he throws it to the birds that have started gathering around us.

"The body isn't worth a whole lot; it's a box, a rabbit cage."

My dad grins and points to a gull struggling with a piece of bread that's far too big for it.

Then he falls silent again, scratches the top of his head; a crumb from the bread gets stuck in his short stubble. I remove it.

"Their walls, their locked doors, and their strait-jackets trap you so you can't escape. That way they've always got you right where they want you. Ward R, Corridor 7, Room 314.

"And while you lie there, strapped down, the medicine dulls your brain. You can see your hands and the wall, and that's all."

We empty the last bread out of the bag. Our twelve minutes are up.

"I've tried," he says, as we walk across the lawn and back to the hospital. "God knows I've tried. But I don't have the strength anymore."

We wait to be let back in. We can see the carer like a shadow through the glass doors. My dad's voice is so soft that I struggle to hear it over the wind.

"You have to help me find the door in the wall," he says.

Then the carer lets us in.

ELSEBETH RINGS HER bell. She's standing at the foot of the stairs waiting; she says there's a telephone call for me. She looks a little confused, I've never received any calls at her place, I haven't given out her number to anyone.

"I think he's German," she says, as I follow her to the telephone in the kitchen.

The man on the line starts by apologizing for last time: he was very drunk though that's no excuse, of course. It's Ulrich, he then says.

Elsebeth continues to stand there looking nervously at the receiver. I smile and nod to her. She goes back to the drawing room where the radio is still playing classical music.

Ulrich says he has sent me a letter. He asks if I got it. Then he laughs nervously, of course I haven't. He only posted it today. He just wants me to know that he meant what he said. Even if he was very drunk. He drank on an empty stomach and everyone knows that gets you very drunk.

He really liked my paintings and wants to exhibit them. A special exhibition, only my work. He just called to tell me that; everything else is in the letter.

I sit down on the chair by the table, still holding the telephone after he has hung up. I listen to the dial tone.

PETRA HAS STOPPED asking what's wrong. I wake up at night when I hear the sound of her crying, but I no longer turn on the light. Somewhere above the foot of the bed I see my dad's eyes. They float over the metal pigeonholes at the sorting office until my hands take over.

I'M BUSY PUTTING away Elsebeth's shopping when I see the letter on the kitchen table.

It's addressed to the artist Mehmet Faruk.

Inside is a photo of Ulrich; he's standing in front of a former butcher's. He's smiling, flinging out his arms, proudly showing the empty display windows. He writes that he has finally found the perfect place. He's going to call his gallery "*Fleisch*." My paintings will open it.

There are some Deutschmarks in the envelope. He's repaying his loan, he writes. There's a little extra which he hopes will cover my train fare.

I PLACE THE items on the counter.

Tubes of paint. An easel. Brushes of different sizes.

The shop assistant asks if I need help. I shake my head and keep finding more things. I've stopped looking at the price tags.

I buy as many canvasses as I can carry. I move all the old paintings out into the hallway and stack them on top of each other.

I put up the easel in the middle of the floor and mount a canvass. I open the first tube of paint. I paint until sunset; then I turn on the light, light some candles, and carry on painting.

I don't go to bed until the early morning. My hand has yet to unclench from gripping the paintbrush. I close my eyes, I can smell the pigments in the paint so strongly that I can see colors on the insides of my eyelids.

The sun wakes me up and I carry on painting.

After another hour I drink a glass of water and smoke a cigarette.

I switch on the travel kettle and make myself a cup of instant coffee, which I drink, cold, a couple hours later.

I use the paintings from the basement for reference, finding details, a hand, a gaze. Then I carry the old painting down to the courtyard, rip it out of the frame, and throw it in one of the big garbage cans. I keep the frame and stretch out a fresh canvass.

IT'S AFTERNOON AND I'm squeezing ocher paint onto the palette. When I look at the clock again it's five minutes before I need to be standing in front of the pigeonholes with the postal codes. I run down the street, I can feel paint dry through my T-shirt.

A couple of days later I call the sorting office. It's midday and I speak to a woman from Admin. I say a family member is ill. Terminally. I'm feeling terrible, really terrible. But I'd still like to go to work. The woman on the telephone sounds sympathetic. She must have typed in my name and seen from my records that I've taken only one sick day in the last two years. She tells me to call back when things are a bit better. Then she corrects herself and tells me to call again when I feel ready to come to back to work. And that sometimes you need to give things a little time. I promise to do that. At an ATM I check the balance of Mehmet Faruk's account. For several years I've worked Sundays and holidays to earn overtime and there's enough money to last the year out.

I'VE A CARTON of cigarettes under my arm when I meet Elsebeth in the hallway.

She opens and closes her mouth. She stares at me as though she's just seen one of her late husbands.

"You've lost weight," she says. "You must eat."

"I'm painting."

"Yes," she says, smiling. "I can see that."

It's not until then that I realize I've got paint on my cheek and under my fingernails.

"I'm careful," I say. "I don't get paint on anything, I watch what I'm doing."

"Doesn't matter. If you're painting, you're painting. But you have to eat something."

She grabs hold of my sleeve and pulls me into the kitchen, she sits me down.

"I'd prefer it if I was the first of us to die," Elsebeth says, lighting the gas burner. "It's hard to find a good tenant."

She makes scrambled eggs and bacon. The bacon sizzles in the pan.

"A girl came by asking for you," she says, without taking her eyes off the food. "Very pale-skinned. I said you were out. It's none of my business."

It's been only a couple of days since I last saw Petra, but I've been thinking about it for a while. Thinking that tomorrow I'll go over to see her. Or in a few days. Soon, anyway.

Elsebeth puts the plate in front of me, she pours milk into a tall glass and watches me to make sure that I eat.

The first couple of mouthfuls swell up in my mouth. My stomach groans in protest. I get a stitch as though I've been running too fast.

I need a cigarette, I ran out last night. A cigarette and a cup of coffee.

Elsebeth keeps her eyes on me until my stomach wakes up and hunger takes over. I clear my plate and eat four slices of rye bread as well.

EVERY DAY FROM then on I discover plates of food in the kitchen with small notes. *Eat!* says the plate of meatloaf in the fridge. *Drink!* says a glass that looks like milk, but tastes like cream.

I find apples and hard-boiled eggs. Fried sausages that I eat cold while I paint.

I PAINT AS the storm blasts the country. The windows rattle while I dip the brush in paint. The next day I see uprooted trees and cars whose windows have been smashed by roof tiles. It's not until then that I realize that the storm really did happen, that it wasn't just inside my head and in my room. Winter is coming; I know this because I now have fewer hours of daylight in front of the easel.

My dreams come in muted shades of green and blue. Other nights they're fiery red like blood, mailboxes, and the insides of mouths.

I PAINT UNTIL noon and then I pack my rucksack. The digital watch I've bought is waterproof. I change into my swimming trunks and walk past the main pool to the cold water pool, a small, round basin where the water is just above freezing.

I usually have the place to myself; on the few occasions I see other people they're old with leathery skin. They smile strained smiles as they exercise by the edge of the pool.

I look at the digital watch, I see the seconds mount up. By the hundred. I have to last one minute longer than yesterday. My body hurts; my hands turn white.

One of the lifeguards asks me if I'm okay. He says I've been in there quite a long time. The muscles in my neck are stiff and stand out at the back of my head like the number eleven. I keep my mouth closed to stop my teeth from chattering. I give him a nod. He moves on.

I do the finger exercise: When you can no longer press each fingertip against your thumb, you've been in the cold water for too long. I stole a book about it from the library; I cut off the magnetic strip with a razor blade and slipped the book into my bag. The clinical term is hypothermia.

A range of symptoms is used to diagnose degrees of hypothermia.

I look at the digital watch again. I've managed to add another minute. I lift myself out of the cold water and bang my foot against the metal ladder. It won't start to hurt until later.

I walk alongside the pools on stiff legs. I walk past people swimming, children splashing. I check my body for symptoms; severe shaking is one of them.

The body trying to heat itself.

Another symptom is speaking incoherently. You start to mumble.

I recite nursery rhymes to myself. On my way back to the changing room, I say: *Tinker, tailor, soldier, sailor, rich man, poor man, beggar man, thief.*

But I don't know if you can hear yourself mumble. If your thoughts are messed up and frozen, surely your words will be, too.

I sit in the sauna until I can feel my hands and feet again. I massage the muscles in my right forearm, the ones I'll be using when I'm back in front of the canvass.

I'M SITTING ON a bench opposite the playground. I'm wearing several layers of clothing. Two pairs of socks in my winter boots.

I've my sketchbook with me. I've unscrewed the top of the Thermos and I drink from it. It's December and my coffee is steaming.

At first I draw the school building: loose lines with a charcoal pencil. Then I fill in the details. I could be a student from the art college. Or the school of architecture. On an academic assignment. Architecture from the early seventies. If anyone were to look over my shoulder, they'd see the approximate measurements I've noted down, the height of the building, the width of each glass section.

The bell rings, it's break time. I go to the wire fence and look into the playground. The double doors are thrown open so hard they jump on their hinges. The playground quickly fills with children.

A teacher on playground duty comes over to me. Even though I'm not wearing a raincoat and have no sweets in my pockets, I know I've been standing there too long.

Before he opens his mouth, I ask him if he knows when the school was built. I turn over a fresh page in my sketchbook, ready to write down his reply. The sentence he'd prepared doesn't cross his lips. He scratches his head and guesses sometime in the early seventies.

I'm welcome to come with him to the office, where they'll definitely know for sure. I smile. I've been sitting in front of the school during five breaks over two days.

THIS PRIVATE SCHOOL is the last on my list, a small school with fewer pupils. It can't be more than ten years old. The jungle gym in the playground isn't rusty, the paint isn't flaking off.

I sit outside the school from the first break until cars with parents start pulling up to collect their children.

At night I dream about a charcoal pencil so small I can only hold it with my fingertips.

I have to draw the whole world, otherwise it'll fall apart.

THE NEXT MORNING I'm back in front of the school. The Christmas holidays start in two days.

The bell rings for the lunch break. For the first ten minutes the playground is empty while the children eat their packed lunches in their classrooms. Then they come outside in small groups. I stand in front of the fence. I see a little blonde girl walking with her friends.

I think I recognize a movement, the way she holds her head. I walk through the gate and into the playground.

She looks straight at me, but has already moved on. All she saw was a grown-up, someone she doesn't know, not a proper person. She runs a little before turning around again. Our eyes meet, she blinks once. Then she throws her arms around my neck. I think I can detect makeup on her face.

My sister has grown; I can already begin to see what she'll look like as an adult.

"Do Mum and Dad know you're here?" she asks, when she finally lets go of my neck.

"No. It's probably best if you don't tell them."

"That might be difficult . . ." She bites her bottom lip like she used to do when she was unsure of something or wanted to pester her dad for new toys.

"In return I promise not to tell them you're wearing makeup," I say, and she laughs. "I'm going to go away for a while."

"You've already been away. Mum and Dad went crazy . . ."

"Far away. I'm going far away. All gone. I don't know when I'll be coming back."

She looks at me. Her eyes are big and blue, even bluer than I remembered them.

She's about to say something when I pick her up and press my face into her collar to dry my eyes.

"Will I see you again?" she asks.

"Of course. But I don't know when."

"Do I have to grow up first?"

"Yes, you have to grow up first."

She nods. A girl calls out to her. She kisses my cheek, then she runs back to her friends.

I'M STANDING IN the street in front of Elsebeth's apartment, taking small steps on the spot to keep warm. The wind smokes my cigarettes, raindrops threaten to put them out. I'm about to go back inside the stairwell when the van comes around the corner. A box van with German plates; at first it drives past me, then it reverses.

The van has a big scratch on its side that reveals several layers of paint. Once it was yellow; it has also been brown and blue.

On the side in big letters it says *Ergüls Frucht und Gemüse*.

The driver gets out. He's a big man in a hand-knit sweater whose stitches are stretched to bursting. He opens the back doors and I can smell rotten vegetables.

He helps me carry my paintings down from the bedroom. He can manage three at a time; he holds them in outstretched arms, resting them on his stomach. He puts them into the back of the van, moving them around so they won't fall over. Before he gets back in the driver's seat, he shakes my hand; his fingerless gloves scratch my palm. I watch the van drive down the street and disappear around the corner.

THE CAR'S HEADLIGHTS pass in a few seconds; they're followed by the sound of tires against wet tarmac.

I walk up the gravel path to the reinforced plastic door. I ring the bell, the lock buzzes, and I enter.

The woman behind the counter has sleepy eyes after a long shift or a Christmas party the day before.

"I have an appointment," I say.

She enters my dad's name on the computer. Then she shakes her head.

"Are you sure it's for today?"

"It wouldn't be the first time they've forgotten to log it."

She presses another couple of keys.

"Can't you ring someone? Try the consultant."

"We can only do that if it's an emergency . . ."

"It's Christmas Eve. I just want to see my dad, I promised him."

She looks at me, hoping that I'll give up. Go away and disappear and leave her with the crime novel she's pushed under the counter so all I can see is one blood-red corner with a bullet hole.

"I'm afraid there's nothing I can do," she says.

I stay where I am.

If only I'd start shouting. If only I'd throw papers and pens on the floor; then she could press the silent alarm which sits somewhere under the counter, the one her index finger has been resting on for a couple of minutes now.

But I speak calmly; I look into her eyes without staring.

"I just want to see my dad."

I don't move a millimeter.

She's about to say something else, then she shrugs.

Her finger leaves the alarm and she presses the intercom.

"Mikkel, would you come up here, please?"

I WAIT ON the sofa, I flick through three newspapers before a young man with a nametag and a ponytail appears.

I follow him through the wards I'm starting to recognize. From Ward E all the way down to Ward Q. Past R and V. The corridors have been decorated with wonky Christmas cards and paper chains cut with blunt scissors by shaking hands.

A man in a dressing gown is sitting in front of a piano in one of the common rooms.

"So how about it? How about a Christmas carol?"

The patient turns his head slightly, not enough to see us. A long thread of saliva hangs from his lower lip and nearly touches one of the black keys.

"Or what about *'Für Elise'*? Everyone knows that one."

The man hits the keys at random. The piano needs tuning.

The carer slaps him on the shoulder. "I'll be back in a minute, then we'll get you back to your room."

We walk on.

"You have to keep a sense of humor in this job. Otherwise you don't last."

The lighting is subdued; we see no patients or other carers in the corridors.

"You're visiting your dad, right?"

"Yes."

"He's probably heavily medicated. I'm just telling you now so that you don't come back in ten minutes asking what the hell's wrong with him."

He finds the key card, opens the door to yet another lock.

"This place is always badly understaffed around the holidays, so they drug the patients to the eyeballs. Normally I don't work this ward, but a boy with a stick could look after them right now, frankly. The night shift will have to change a lot of soiled underwear, but that's not a problem when they don't resist."

He unlocks the door. My dad is sitting on the bed, leaning against the wall.

I get him dressed. I stick his naked feet into his trainers, tie his laces for him. I tell the carer that we're going outside, going for a little walk. He lets us out a side entrance so we don't have to walk all the way back to reception.

MY DAD'S MOVEMENTS are slow. He stumbles his way across the lawn, he puts his foot in a mole-hill and sinks to his knees. I help him back up, we walk on, he mumbles, speaks in half-sentences, lips so soft I'm afraid he'll chew them to pieces.

After a couple of minutes the cold air starts to wake him up.

"Where are we going?" he asks.

"To the forest, Dad."

"Yes," he says. "Yes, so we are."

A few meters from the sidewalk I ask him if anyone's watching us.

"No," he replies, without turning his head. "Not today."

We wait for the bus. No one comes running after us.

I buy two tickets, I have exact change. The bus is almost empty. I follow my dad to the backseat, I lean him up against the window.

The bus ride takes just over twenty minutes.

When I see the first trees, I know that we're getting off at the next stop.

I'm about to press the button when I feel my dad's hand on my arm.

"May I?" he asks.

He manages it at his third attempt.

"It's been a long time," he says.

The bus stop is at the edge of the forest. For a couple of minutes we walk along the road; headlights blind us temporarily, but the car is soon far away from us.

We walk across a parking lot, past an old car with smashed-in windows and no license plate.

We pass a board with a map of paths through the forest, scenic places you should pay attention to, advice on how to avoid ticks. Dogs must be kept on a leash. We walk for ten minutes. We take a smaller path to the left, it's almost overgrown, you have to know it's there, I hold the branches aside.

My dad's feet get tangled up in the dense undergrowth; I bend down to free him.

We cross a small clearing and pass wet, charred logs surrounded by empty beer cans, the remains of a campfire.

Finally we reach the shore. The lake in front of us is dark.

"We don't need a frog. Today we don't need a frog, Dad. We'll get to the other side, don't you worry."

I take his hand. He follows me.

The cold water seeps through my shoes.

I SINK INTO the seat and cover myself with my jacket. The train sets in motion with a couple of grunts and a metallic squeal. It's just past six o'clock in the morning, it's Christmas Day. I walked around the town all last night, forcing myself not to run every time I heard a siren. I drank coffee in bars and walked on while I waited for the first train.

The train speeds past apartment buildings, terraced houses, and bungalows; their windows are dark, a few lit up by Christmas lights. The train stops at empty stations, then it pulls away again.

In a couple of days Elsebeth will start to wonder where I am. It'll take her a long time to climb the stairs. She'll knock on my door, which is ajar, then she'll find the note. The letters are big and clear so she won't have to strain her eyes to read them. An apology, but no explanation. Next to the note is an extra month's rent. In a couple of days down at the sorting office they'll realize that I'm not coming back to work. I won't be the first to quit by staying away.

THE TRAIN DRIVES through Denmark. The sun rises and families with gift-wrapped presents get on board.

A little girl in a pale blue parka sits down in the seat opposite me. She has fallen out with her mother, who's sitting further ahead in the carriage.

The girl is busy playing with her shoelaces when the cramping starts. My muscles spasm from my neck to my toes. My body remembering the cold water. I grip the armrests and dig my nails into the synthetic material. When I've regained control of my body, I look at the girl; her eyes are wide. I try to smile but taste blood in my mouth. I must have bitten my tongue. The girl starts to cry.

I DON'T NOTICE us crossing the border. The signs at the railway stations now have German place names.

I change to a modern train with a racing stripe along the side. When I've found my seat and put down my rucksack, I walk to the dining car. A middle-aged German woman sells me a cup of coffee, a sausage with mustard, and a small bread roll. I gobble down the food. I've drunk half my coffee when I can no longer keep my eyes open.

My sleep is restless; it's green and dark blue.

I DON'T KNOW how long I've been asleep before the dreams come.

I'm too tired and too shattered to shake myself awake.

In my dream I'm standing on the shore watching two figures in the lake. A boy and a man. The boy is bent over the man, holding him down. The man is resisting. The body struggling to surface, gasping for air. Then acceptance. Even here, from the shore, I can see my dad's eyes. The man in the water looks up at the boy. Through the green water I can see the serenity in his face and a faint smile.

At last the boy lets go of the man. His body remains submerged; it floats away, out into the middle of the lake. The boy wades back to the shore; green plants cling to his clothes, refusing to let go until they're ripped apart. The boy finds his rucksack on the forest floor, covered by branches. His movements are stiff and mechanical. He starts to undress; he's wearing several layers of soaked clothing. His skin lights up in the twilight. The boy takes out dry clothes from the rucksack and gets dressed. He puts the wet clothes into a plastic bag. Then he starts to walk.